CW01390829

Of Course He Pushed Him
& Other Sherlock Holmes Stories

The Complete Collection

By

Chris Chan

Edited by

David Marcum, Derrick Belanger and Ray Riethmeier.

First edition published in 2022
© Copyright 2022
Chris Chan

The right of Chris Chan to be identified as the author of this work has been asserted by him in accordance with the Copyright, Designs and Patents Act 1998.

All rights reserved. No reproduction, copy or transmission of this publication may be made without express prior written permission. No paragraph of this publication may be reproduced, copied or transmitted except with express prior written permission or in accordance with the provisions of the Copyright Act 1956 (as amended). Any person who commits any unauthorised act in relation to this publication may be liable to criminal prosecution and civil claims for damage.

All characters appearing in this work are fictitious. Any resemblance to real persons, living or dead, is purely coincidental. The opinions expressed herein are those of the author and not of MX Publishing.

Hardcover ISBN 978-1-80424-056-4

Published by MX Publishing
335 Princess Park Manor, Royal Drive,
London, N11 3GX
www.mxpublishing.co.uk

Cover design by Brian Belanger

List of Original Publication Dates and Venues

"The Adventure of the Specious Spouse," published in *Sherlock Holmes: Stranger Than Truth*, edited by Ray Riethmeier, Belanger Books (April 2021).

"The Adventure of the Villainous Victim," published in *Sherlock Holmes and Dr. Watson: The Early Adventures Volume I*, edited by David Marcum, Belanger Books (November 2019).

"The Bitter Gravestones," published in *The MX Book of New Sherlock Holmes Stories, Part XXX: More Christmas Adventures (1897-1928)*, edited by David Marcum, MX Publishing (November 2021).

"The Chapel of the Holy Blood," published in *Sherlock Holmes and the Great Detectives*, edited by Derrick Belanger, Belanger Books (July 2020).

"The Diogenes Club Poltergeist," published in *The MX Book of New Sherlock Holmes Stories, Vol. XVII: Stranger than Fiction*, edited by David Marcum , MX Publishing (October 2019).

"The Heinous Half-Crowns," published in *Beyond the Adventures of Sherlock Holmes, Volume Three*, edited by Brian and Derrick Belanger, Belanger Books (December 2020).

"Intruders at Baker Street," published in *The MX Book of New Sherlock Holmes Stories, Part XXII: Some More Untold Cases 1877-1887*, edited by David Marcum, MX Publishing (November 2020).

"The Man in the Maroon Suit," published in *The MX Book of New Sherlock Holmes Stories, Part XIX: 2020 Annual (1882-1890)*, edited by David Marcum, Belanger Books (May 2020).

"Merridew of Abominable Memory," published in *The MX Book of New Sherlock Holmes Stories, Part XXII: Some More Untold Cases*

1877-1887, edited by David Marcum, MX Publishing (November 2020).

"Of Course He Pushed Him," published in *Mystery Weekly* (October 2019).

"The Outline of Mystery," published in *Sherlock Holmes: Further Adventures in the Realms of H.G. Wells, Volume One*, edited by Derrick Belanger and C. Edward Davis, Belanger Books (October 2021).

"The Switched String," published in *The MX Book of New Sherlock Holmes Stories, Part XXV: 2021 Annual (1881-1888)*, edited by David Marcum, MX Publishing (May 2021).

"The Search for Mycroft's Successor," published in *After the East Wind Blows: WWI and Roaring Twenties Adventures of Sherlock Holmes, Vol. II: Aftermath (1919-1920)*, edited by David Marcum, Belanger Books (September 2021).

Once more, to my parents, Drs. Carlyle and Patricia Chan

And to my USM escape room friends, who did so much to keep my spirits up during the pandemic:

Anjail Floyd-Pruitt

James Grossman

Bill Lent

Blake Wanger

Contents

Introduction

Part One: Traditional Sherlock Holmes Pastiches

Part Two: Crossovers and Alternative Histories

Introduction

Part One: Traditional Sherlock Holmes Pastiches

Sherlock Holmes has been a part of my life ever since I was a child. I have always loved the movie and television adaptations, the radio plays, and especially, the original stories. However, ever since I was about ten years old, I have been very disappointed in Sir Arthur Conan Doyle, due to the fact that he got his work so incredibly wrong. By reading a book introduction, I learned that Conan Doyle believed that the Sherlock Holmes stories were beneath him, and he had grown to loathe his detective. I didn't know what had happened to lead such a talented man so horribly astray, but even at the age of ten, I knew that Conan Doyle was horribly, inexplicably misguided. How could a seemingly intelligent fellow come to believe that these wonderful stories weren't worth writing? How could he dislike such a brilliant character as Holmes? To this day, I still don't have a convincing answer to those questions.

A few years ago, I saw an advertisement from Belanger Books asking for submissions to one of their anthologies. They were looking for new Sherlock Holmes stories, and I, having a bit of extra time, decided to try my hand at one. After my first tale was accepted, MX Publishing asked me to submit to another anthology, so I did, and I kept on writing.

Many of these stories were written under a theme. "The Diogenes Club Poltergeist" was for an edition of *The MX Book of New Sherlock Holmes Stories* with the theme "Stranger Than Fiction," a collection of mysteries featuring a crime that at first glance seemed to be connected to the paranormal, but actually weren't. I've always been fascinated by Sherlock's brother Mycroft, as well as his coterie of totally unsociable associates, so I decided to set my story amongst them.

"The Man in the Maroon Suit" wasn't for a themed anthology, but it was inspired in part by seeing some graffiti on a piece of public art. I wondered who would deface something lovely. It gave me an idea, which mutated several times before becoming that story.

"Merridew of Abominable Memory" and "Intruders at Baker Street" (originally titled "The Darlington Substitution") were for an MX anthology with the theme *Some More Untold Cases*, based on references in the original stories to cases that never made their way in full into the canon. I tried to give Mr. Merridew a different spin. Most readers think he was such a horrid man that the memory of him was abominable to all. I decided that maybe he just had a terrible memory. But why was his brain so impaired? As for "Intruders at Baker Street," I remembered thinking after learning that Holmes left 221B to study bees in Sussex, that no one else could really feel like they belonged there. So what might happen if some interlopers were living at 221B when they shouldn't have been?

"The Heinous Half-Crowns" was for a Belanger Books anthology of sequels to the original stories. The bad guys, who were counterfeiters, get away at the end of "The Engineer's Thumb." My story wraps up that dangling thread.

"The Switched String" was for an unthemed MX anthology. I wanted to start with something amiss at 221B. What would happen if someone replaced one of the strings on Holmes' violin? Why would they do such a thing? Therein lies the mystery.

Finally, "The Bitter Gravestones" was for a Christmas-themed MX anthology. My inspiration was a present-day story about some people who had never forgiven their mother for abandoning them when they were children. They wrote and published an obituary outlining her many transgressions that went viral, and finished by saying "She will not be missed." What might happen if somebody had similarly angry comments carved onto headstones? And so, Holmes and Watson investigated some nasty epitaphs at Christmastime.

I hope that all of these stories are as fun to read as they were to write.

Part Two: Crossovers and Alternative Histories

The Sherlock Holmes universe is iconic. There are few rooms in all of literature more well-known and detailed in the public imagination than 221B Baker Street. The major and minor characters in the world of Sherlock Holmes are so well-drawn that even characters that only appear in one story or have just a handful of lines of dialogue in the entire canon are now legendary. The Sherlock Holmes Universe is so memorable that thanks to fandom, it branches out into other universes. For years, writers have introduced Holmes to classic fictional characters and famous figures from history. Others have changed the Sherlock Holmes universe a bit. A few years ago, I decided to get in on the fun.

When I was a senior in college, working on writing a novel for my senior project, I reread the entire Sherlock Holmes Canon from start to finish. Along the way, a friend of mine was the victim of a very cruel and totally false rumor campaign that nearly crushed her, though thanks to the support of those close to her, she overcame the lies and graduated on time. As the situation passed, an idea suddenly popped into my head. Readers only had Watson's word for what happened at Reichenbach Falls in "The Final Problem." What if some villain, possibly one of Moriarty's henchmen, decided to spread a baseless rumor that Watson had actually pushed Holmes off the cliff? Nothing came of this idea for about a decade and a half, until I finally revisited the plot and turned it into a short story: "Of Course He

Pushed Him." I submitted it to a few venues, all of which rejected it, until after several months, the periodical then known as *Mystery Weekly* (now *Mystery Magazine*) accepted the tale and published it in their annual Sherlock Holmes issue.

"The Adventure of the Villainous Victim" is from a Belanger Books anthology covering the earliest years of Holmes and Watson's partnership, which are largely ignored in the Canon. I did a little research, and discovered a fascinating real-life case from that era featuring a train, a brutal murder, and an investigator named George Holmes. Could the newspapers have gotten Sherlock's name wrong? I decided to insert Holmes and Watson into this actual case.

"The Chapel of the Holy Blood" was written for a Belanger Books collection where Holmes solved cases alongside famous fictional detectives in the public domain. In my story, Holmes pairs up with one of my favorite sleuths, G.K. Chesterton's Father Brown, to solve a particularly sanguinary crime that may or may not have a link to the supernatural.

The real-life crusading lawyer Mary Grace Quackenbos Humiston (1869-1948) was a remarkable figure. At a time when few women received law degrees, she defended many poor and downtrodden people, getting a woman who had killed in self-defense off of death row, solving a missing persons case that turned out to be a murder, and exposing a human trafficking and exploitation ring in the American South, among many other adventures. For her successes, she was nicknamed "Mrs. Sherlock Holmes." What, I wondered, would happen if her path crossed with the real Sherlock Holmes, and people thought they were really married? And so, for a Belanger Books anthology where Holmes worked with actual figures from history, I wrote "She Is NOT My Wife!" which was retitled "The Adventure of the Specious Spouse."

Sherlock Holmes' brother Mycroft is said to be so influential, that at times, "he IS the British government." In a Belanger Books collection set after the Great War, I wondered, what would happen to the government if Mycroft was no longer around? Could anybody replace him? And so, Holmes and Watson began "The Search for Mycroft's Successor."

Finally, for a Belanger Books collection featuring crossovers between Holmes and the world of H.G. Wells, I wrote "The Outline of Mystery." Wells gained much wealth and fame for writing "The Outline of History," a massive tome that claimed to cover the entire history of humanity. It was a controversial book, especially when a Canadian woman named Florence Deeks sued Wells, claiming he'd plagiarized her unpublished manuscript. This led to a lengthy legal battle that Deeks lost, though the allegations are still debated today. What if Deeks came to Holmes for help, and his investigation led to interactions with other famous figures connected to the controversy?

These are the first six stories that I wrote featuring Holmes in alternative universes and meeting classic fictional characters and figures from history. They won't be the last.

–*Chris Chan*

Part One: Traditional Sherlock Holmes Pastiches

The Diogenes Club Poltergeist

Readers who follow the exploits of Sherlock Holmes and myself will be familiar with the Diogenes Club, that remarkable gathering place for those antisocial men who wish to read quietly in a comfortable chair without having to deal with those most frustrating of creatures: their fellow human beings. Holmes' brother Mycroft is a fixture of that peculiar assemblage of the resolutely unclubbable. Members of the Diogenes Club are strictly forbidden from speaking, and an atmosphere of absolute silence is rigidly imposed within its walls, except in the Stranger's Room. While the majority of men, including myself, might find the values of this club to be utterly alien to their own tastes, the world is composed of every conceivable sort of person, and the members of the Diogenes Club continue to bother no one and insist that no one bother them.

The rigidly enforced peace of the Diogenes Club was shattered one overcast winter's day when Holmes received a telegram from Mycroft at breakfast. He read it, raised an eyebrow, and wordlessly handed it to me. It read:

SHERLOCK–

PAY NO ATTENTION TO THE LETTERS FROM MY FELLOW MEMBERS OF THE DIOGENES CLUB. BURN THEM UNREAD.

–MYCROFT

"Why on earth would Mycroft want you to destroy letters from his fellows at the Diogenes Club?" I wondered. "And how could you possibly know that the letters were from members of the Club without reading them first? Surely you don't know the names of every man who belongs to that bizarre organization?"

"As for your second question, the correspondence of men writing from the Diogenes Club is immediately distinguishable by the club's stationary, which is thicker than the standard envelopes and writing paper, and possesses a distinctive watermark. It's true that I only know a handful of the Diogenes Club's members' names, and at the moment I have no idea why Mycroft would be so anxious for me to avoid reading their correspondence. But if I may point out an important point, Watson, you are missing a much more important question."

"And that would be?"

"Why would members of the Diogenes Club be writing to me in the first place? One of Mycroft's fellows might conceivably choose to consult me about something, but more than one? Surely it is too much to believe that multiple members of that group would simultaneously feel compelled to write to me with different problems? Therefore, they must all be writing about the same issue. Now, there is no link between the club members other than the club itself. They come from all walks of life, and they mostly have no contact

3

whatsoever outside the walls of the Diogenes Club. It follows, then, that there is some problem threatening the sanctity of the Diogenes Club. The members are not in the habit of consulting each other, so multiple members are sending letters of their own initiative, rather than one letter representing the entire group. We can further deduce that the problem is one that involves some crime or mysterious circumstance. If it were some simple matter such as an overly talkative member, they could simply take the normal steps to remove the offender. But if there is a problem that would require my involvement, why would Mycroft request that I stay out of the matter? Normally, Mycroft would jump at the chance at letting me handle such a situation, because his deep-seated indolence would make him resent any call for him to investigate himself. I can only assume that Mycroft considers the problem at hand to be a situation that is unworthy of my modest powers, and that he feels so strongly about the matter that he decided to send me a telegram that would reach me before the morning post."

Holmes' theories were verified less than an hour later, when he received no fewer than nine envelopes which bore the watermark of the Diogenes Club stationery. After rifling through the sealed stack, he declared, "Clearly, Watson, the members of the Diogenes Club are under a great deal of distress."

I knew he was expecting me to respond with an incredulous "How could you possibly know that, Holmes?" Perhaps it was a sudden impulse of recalcitrance, but I refused to provide him with the prompting question he obviously desired. After a few silent moments, Holmes looked up at me with an expression that was both slightly chiding and a gentle plea, and my resolve shattered. Reluctantly, I asked the question I had refrained from posing mere moments earlier.

"Quite simple, my dear fellow. Smell the sealed adhesive on these six envelopes."

I did so. "Brandy. Whiskey. Whiskey again. Beer. More whiskey. Gin."

"Precisely, Watson. The men who composed these letters have been drinking profusely. But the members of the Diogenes Club never drink to excess, at least inside the walls of the building. Overconsumption of alcohol leads to loosened tongues, which leads to conversation, which is exactly what members come to the Diogenes Club to avoid. If six members required several strong drinks to write a letter to me, then something particularly upsetting happened there, something disturbing enough to make previously restrained men succumb to the comforts of the bottle. And I notice some important points on these two that do not smell of alcohol. The penmanship on both envelopes clearly shows the untidiness of a distraught mind. The stamps are askew. The ink has splattered a bit on both of these envelopes, clearly the pens were being held by people in a state of nervous agitation. Of course, the similar ink blots on the other six envelopes further prove that the men who wrote these letters drank to excess."

"Yes, but what is the cause of their distress?"

"That I cannot tell without opening the letters, Watson. And as curious as I am to figure out what is going on, my dear brother has specifically requested that I burn these envelopes unopened, and I would not dream of jeopardizing my relationship with my sibling over something so trifling as curiosity over the contents of some envelopes."

At that moment there was a knock at the door, and Mrs. Hudson entered with a telegram. Holmes tore it open, laughed, and tossed it to me.

SHERLOCK–

ON SECOND THOUGHT, DON'T BURN THE LETTERS. BRING THEM TO ME AS SOON AS YOU GET THEM.

–MYCROFT

"Mycroft certainly enjoys giving you orders," I mused.

"He has no doubt realized what can be deduced from this morning's correspondence, but for once Mycroft is a step behind me. He cannot determine who is behind whatever event is shaking up the Diogenes Club without seeing these envelopes, so I must bring them to him. It should only take Mycroft a few seconds to make the same deduction I did about the identity of the party behind whatever is bothering the members of the club. Let us meet Mycroft at his rooms, Watson, and see what has caused this wave of unrest."

It was not until we were shaking hands with Mycroft in his sitting-room that I realized that Sherlock had failed to explain exactly what in the unopened correspondence he had received was so revelatory. I had no time to ask, however, since Mycroft took control of the conversation before I could speak.

"I heard from my sources that you led the police to make an arrest in the Gunton case," Mycroft told his brother.

"That's correct."

"Did you make the connection to the Barnett garroting from three years ago?"

"I wasn't aware of that case. Remember, I was pretending to be dead at that time. I was on the other end of the world and I was unable to follow the local crime news."

"Of course, of course. You need to have a word with your Scotland Yard friends. I suspect that Malvern may have been involved in both crimes. The signature is identical."

"I shall inform Lestrade to look into that immediately. But you didn't summon me here to talk about the Gunton case. What exactly is happening at the Diogenes Club, dear brother?"

Mycroft groaned and leaned back in his chair. "It's a terrible inconvenience. The calm and quiet of my sanctuary has been shattered. Many members of the club are convinced that there is… a poltergeist disrupting the building."

"Excuse me?" Holmes responded as if he hadn't understood a word Mycroft had said.

"A poltergeist or some such rot. The outlandish belief that some malevolent supernatural being is haunting the Diogenes Club, wreaking havoc and upsetting the members."

"Surely a collection of grown men could not possibly give any credence to such a ridiculous supposition," I scoffed.

Mycroft frowned at me. "You forget, doctor, that the membership of the Diogenes Club is not based upon being skeptical or level-headed. The sole criterions are to dislike unnecessary conversation and to be able to refrain from speaking. Many of the men who populate our membership may well be superstitious and possess a belief in ghoulies and ghosties and long-legged beasties and things that go bump in the night. I wouldn't know. I've never shared two words with the vast majority of our membership, so I have no idea what sort of men they are. Frankly, until now, I've never really cared about their personal thoughts or beliefs, and I hoped that they never extended any curiosity towards mine. Now, I am reluctantly forced to conclude that I am surrounded by hysterics."

Holmes pressed the tips of his fingers together and frowned. "Surely there must be some sort of reasons for this widespread delusion."

"Of course. It's nothing more than a series of practical jokes. Mean-spirited ones, but all easily explainable. Windowpanes, bottles, glasses, vases… anything that's fragile is shattering without apparent cause. The past week, members have been reading their newspapers, only have them catch fire while they were reading them. Members are being pelted with rotten food or splashed with icy cold water while they doze off in their chairs."

"There's absolutely nothing mysterious about that," Holmes scoffed. The broken glass and china? A simple catapult would explain that. The newspapers? A magnifying glass focusing the rays of a light sources. The rotten food? All that would take is an arm with good aim, or perhaps the catapult again."

"What about the ice water?" I asked.

"Any mechanic or engineer could design a simple device shaped like a pistol that sprays a stream of water when you pull the trigger. Or possibly a smaller version of a syringe used to spray pesticide on plants."

"Of course, Sherlock. As expected, your train of thought is following mine precisely. Nothing that occurred cannot be explained by pranks known by any mischievous schoolboy. The mysterious disembodied voices that have been plaguing several members of the club at inopportune times–"

"Ventriloquism."

"Obviously. But a number of club members– and some members of the staff– insist that they've actually seen the poltergeist."

"Really? What does it look like?"

"Eyewitness descriptions disagree, which is not surprising. They all agree that the supposed poltergeist can fly, and that an unearthly glow emanates from it. But after that point, the witnesses' testimony differs. Some people claim that it has a massive tail, others say three heads, others say enormous wings, or bright red eyes. No two descriptions match."

"How long has the poltergeist been active?"

"Just under a week. But the damage it has done to the club is incalculable."

I seized this opportunity to reenter the conversation. "You mean the physical harm caused by the destruction?"

"No, Watson! The noise! Because due to all of the disruption, all of the chaos, the unthinkable has happened. Members of the club are actually... *talking to each other*. The Stranger's Room is filled to bursting with club members chatting, sharing their experiences being pestered by the poltergeist and their personal theories about its origins and what it's trying to accomplish with its hijinks. And the members of the club of carrying on their conversations elsewhere! They are interacting with each other socially and even forming the beginnings of friendships!"

I attempted to keep my voice level. "And how does that pose a danger to the Diogenes Club?"

From the look on his face, Mycroft's evaluation of my mental powers had never been lower. "It means the end of all we stand for! If a majority of the members of the club petition to amend the rules so they can spend time together, they will destroy the spirit and purpose of the Diogenes Club. The Diogenes Club as we know it will cease to exist! It will become a place of socializing, just like any other club in London!"

I realized that it would not be a wise decision to voice the thoughts that were currently running through my mind, and I worried that my facial expression would produce a similar effect to the one that I sought to avoid, so I rose with a quiet "excuse me" and crossed over to the window. Mycroft's well-known aversion towards moving longer distances than necessary played a pivotal role in his selection of the building across the street from his personal rooms as the site of the Diogenes Club. As I looked through the window and stared at the building across the street, I mentally noted how undistinctive it was, noting that there was no sign identifying its purpose. Had I not known what was inside its walls, I would have walked past the building without a second thought, and had anybody asked me to take a guess as the structure's use, I would have been left at a complete loss.

I was brought out of my meditations by the sound of shattering glass, followed by the sight of a man falling out of a top-story window of the Diogenes Club. As he fell, I saw a small object with an eerie green glow flying out the window, zigzagging through the air, and zooming away out of my line of sight.

Immediate action was clearly necessary. "Holmes! Mycroft!" I rapidly explained the situation as I bolted out of Mycroft's flat and sprinted down the stairs. Holmes was right behind me. Though I couldn't see him, I knew that if he did choose to follow us, Mycroft would be proceeding at a much slower pace.

I had neither enough time nor enough breath to tell Holmes what I had seen. Within moments, I was examining the man who had just defenestrated from the club. Fortunately, the building was not particularly tall, and the man had struck a fairly leafy tree on the way down, which had destroyed several branches, but had also slowed his rate of falling enough so as to substantially reduce the risk of fatal damage. After a basic check of his limbs, it was clear that both of his legs and his right arm were broken, though mercifully there did not seem to be any damage to his head.

The poor man was clearly suffering from shock. I gently leaned over him until I could make direct eye contact with him. "Sir, if you can hear me, you have sustained some serious injuries, but at the moment I do not believe that they will be life-threatening, nor will they be permanently debilitating." The injured man did not reply, but his eyes latched onto my gaze, so I concluded that he could hear me. "Can you tell me what happened to you? Why did you fall out the window? Did you jump or were you pushed?" That was probably more questions than I ought to have asked, but I was rather shaken from what I had just seen, and my bedside manner probably needed a little refinement.

The injured man blinked a few times and then sighed very softly. I crouched over him for a little over half a minute, until finally he spoke.

"The... polt... er... geist..." After these two words, his voice trailed away and his eyes broke contact with mine.

"Will he be all right?" Holmes abruptly reminded me of his presence, causing me to start involuntarily.

"He's passed out, but he'll live and most likely recover after a lengthy period of convalescence."

"I have summoned an ambulance, but it will be some time before it arrives. How are you feeling? Will you need a drop of brandy in order to recover yourself?"

My first instinct was to happily accept, but I immediately remembered that I still had a patient that needed my attention, and when the ambulance arrived I wanted to explain the injured man's condition without liquor on my breath. After I politely declined, Holmes took a moment to direct the gathering crowd to stand back further. Having finished, he leaned over to me and asked, "As you were running out of Mycroft's rooms, you mumbled something about a green glow. Would you mind explaining what you meant, please?"

I nodded, and rapidly informed Holmes of the flying object with the unearthly aura that sailed out the window and into the street. "I've no idea what it was, Holmes. I'm quite certain that it wasn't really a poltergeist or any other paranormal creature, but for the life of me I couldn't possibly tell you what it really was."

I was grateful to observe that there was no incredulity or judgment in Holmes' face. He listened my eyewitness account, nodded, thanked me, and immediately left the scene, returning a little under five minutes later.

"Where did you go?" I asked.

"I summoned some much-needed assistance. Have you determined this injured man's identity?"

With a bit of self-reproach, I confessed that I hadn't checked his wallet or searched for any other form of identification.

"I can save you the trouble," Mycroft's voice boomed from behind me. "His name is Rufus Darbington, and he is one of the men who sent you a letter." Mycroft turned to Holmes. "Before this happened, you were about to show me the correspondence you received today. May I please see it now?"

Holmes swiftly withdrew the stack of envelopes from his pocket and passed it to his brother. Mycroft grunted something that I could only assume was an expression of thanks, and he rifled through the sealed correspondence, squinted at the writing on each one, and sniffed each envelope in turn.

"Darbington's is the one that smells of gin," Mycroft proclaimed. "He is very fond of some bizarre concoction known as a martini. He has been drinking a great many of them the last few days."

"Now that you have had a few seconds to examine the evidence, no doubt you have arrived at the same deductions that I have," Holmes commented.

"Of course. I suspected him from the beginning, of course, but his letter confirms it."

I felt the need to re-insert myself into this conversation. "Excuse me please, but what are you two talking about?"

"We will explain everything in a moment, Watson. The ambulance is arriving. As soon as this man is safely on the way to hospital, the three of us will– Mycroft, should we meet inside the Stranger's Room or your own flat?"

"My flat, I think. We can be assured of utter privacy and no ears to the keyholes there."

The moment the three of us were securely ensconced in Mycroft's comfortable chairs, Holmes began explaining everything to me.

"I realize that you did not get a chance to examine the letters I received this morning, but I believe that I described them sufficiently enough for you to figure out *which* was the notable one, even if you could not possibly know *who* is the person who is currently our most prominent person of interest."

"And you haven't even opened the letters yet!"

"True, and it's certainly possible that there may be useful information inside of them. But use your powers of memory, Watson. Describe what you know of the letters."

I cast my mind back. "Nine letters. Six of them smell of various kinds of alcohol. I believe that at least one smelled of whiskey—"

"For the moment, the types of alcohol consumed by those who licked the envelopes are irrelevant. What else?"

"Two more did not smell of alcohol, but the writing was sloppy and the stamps askew. The liquor-scented ones were messy as well."

"Precisely! Which leads to which important point?"

"Six plus two is eight. What of the ninth envelope?"

"Capital, dear fellow, capital! Of the nine envelopes sent to me today, only one was addressed in neat handwriting and did not smell of alcohol. I hasten to add that several of the envelopes that smelled of liquor also had messy handwriting on them. Clearly, the men who wrote the letters were distraught. It showed in their shaking hands in their excessive consumption of spirits. But one man sent me a letter that did not betray any signs of distress. What does that mean to you?"

I took a breath and pondered my answer for a moment. "It means that the person who wrote the ninth letter was not upset like his colleagues were. It might be concluded that he is simply a preternaturally calm and unflappable person, or at least does a better job of disguising his distress from the world. But it might also imply a more sinister motive. This man may not be visibly nervous because he knows for a fact that he has nothing to be worried about, which would only be the case if..." I realized that I was pausing for dramatic effect, and silently I chastised myself for doing so. "Maybe, he knows the true facts behind the appearance of this supposed poltergeist. Perhaps he's the hoaxer who has been playing the unexpected pranks. I do not know for certain, but I perhaps the whole reason for writing a letter was to deflect suspicion. This was a miscalculation, because you and your brother were wary immediately."

Holmes laughed and his eyes twinkled with delight. "Don't forget to include yourself along with Mycroft and myself. It fooled none of us."

"I do have one more question, Holmes."

"And that, no doubt, is "Whose name is on the suspicious envelope?"" With a smile, Holmes once again removed the stack of correspondence from his pocket and handed me the top envelope.

Reading aloud, I declared, "Ian Dynell."

"What do you know of him, Mycroft? I realize that the nature of the Diogenes Club makes it unlikely that you would ever have a lengthy conversation– or even a short one– with him, but surely you would have done some research regarding his background before admitting him to membership?"

"I know precious little of Mr. Dynell, other than the fact that he is a solicitor's clerk, he's married with four energetic children, that his wife is very fond of talking, and they live with his wife's extremely opinionated mother."

"That explains why he might seek out the solace of the Diogenes Club."

"Indeed. I was surprised that he could afford the membership fees, as the well-worn state of his suit made it clear that he was a man of limited income."

"How long has he been a member?"

"A little under a month. Only a few weeks, in fact. He's the most recently inducted member of the club."

I could not help myself from asking a question, even though I was certain that I already knew the answer. "Is there any sort of initiation ceremony for new members?"

Mycroft stared at me as if I'd asked him to knit a sweater for an elephant. "Of course not! In fact, one of the questions we ask prospective members is what they'd like us to serve at their welcoming banquet. If they fail to recoil in horror at the prospect of an evening of socializing, or if they don't ask if they can eat their banquet dinner alone or something like that, we know at once that they are not Diogenes Club material, and we deny their application for membership at once."

All I could manage was a very small nod.

"Perhaps we can speak to Mr. Dynell now," Holmes said. "Do you know where he would be right now?"

"There's a chance that he's at the Diogenes Club right now. He's been in the habit of eating an early lunch at the club most weekday afternoons, and then returning at some point in the evening."

"Then may I suggest that the three of cross the street to question him? Normally I would not wish to disturb you, dear brother, but your presence will assure our entry."

As we entered the club, I noticed that there was no sign of the police, and mentioned the fact.

"There's no reason why they should be here," Mycroft replied. "None of the members want the authorities tramping about our sanctuary and asking impertinent questions. Besides, the members are well trained in scrupulously ignoring their fellows. I wouldn't be surprised if everybody simply failed to notice Darbington falling out the window. Now, remember the rules of the club. No more talking from this point on, please. If you absolutely must communicate, use these pads of paper and pencils." Mycroft took those items from a pair of baskets on a nearby table and then handed them to us.

Holmes immediately began scribbling. "Shall we investigate the dining room?"

Mycroft did not bother writing a reply. He simply nodded and gestured towards a pair of large oak doors. As we passed through them, we saw a couple of elderly gentlemen sitting at a table and drinking. Both looked like they'd already imbibed well past the point of propriety, especially it being so early in the day. Mycroft wrinkled his nose, as if it was positively abhorrent to him to see two club members sitting in such close proximity to each other, even if they were not speaking a single word.

Holmes' pencil flew across his pad of paper and showed it to us. "These are Grove and Quarles, I presume?"

Mycroft nodded.

"How did you know their names?" I wrote.

Holmes replied by scrawling, "The men are clearly unnerved and using alcohol to steady their nerves. Clearly the type of men who would write to me to investigate a supposed poltergeist at their club. The ink stains on their right hands matching the ink on the letters further supports my conclusions. You will note that Grove is drinking brandy and Quarles is gulping down beer. I matched them to the names on the alcoholic odors on the envelopes. Simplicity itself."

Mycroft pointed a large finger at a table in the corner. No one was seated at it, but there was a glass of water and a large bowl of some lumpy beef soup upon it on it. The bowl was only half full, and a great deal of the muddy-looking brown broth had spilled over all the floor-length white tablecloth. Holmes crossed over, examined the aforementioned items, as well as the saltcellar, the napkin, fork, and spoon on the table, and frowned.

"What's missing, Watson?" he wrote.

"The man eating this food?" I scribbled back.

"True, but what else?"

After two more seconds, I had it. "Where's the knife?" I wrote.

Holmes nodded and looked thoughtfully at the table, and then lifted up the long white tablecloth that reached the floor. Underneath it was a very dead body with a table knife sticking in its throat. I took a moment to confirm that life was extinct, then got up to look at what Holmes was writing to Mycroft.

"Dynell?"

Mycroft nodded.

"We shall have to summon the police now." Holmes scribbled.

"Nonsense. It's clear who did this. You just need to find the proof, and the police should be satisfied. They won't ask the club members any impertinent questions then."

"I just need to find the proof?"

"Well you don't expect me to investigate, do you?"

I joined the silent conversation, writing, "How can you possibly know who did this?"

"Look at what's next to the body."

As soon as I read Holmes' note, I noticed a large, bloodstained white napkin lying on the ground beside the corpse.

"The sort of cloth worn by a waiter over his arm while serving. Dynell was stabbed by his own waiter while he ate, and the waiter used the cloth to protect himself from being spattered with blood."

"You can't be sure of that. There are a hundred–"

Holmes didn't let me finish writing. "A quick investigation will prove it."

Grove and Quarles were still drinking silently. "Shouldn't we question them? They could be witnesses?"

Mycroft dismissed my idea. "Useless. Diogenes Club members take no notice of each other, alive or dead. When Major Strausser had his fatal heart attack last fall in a library armchair, it was five days before the smell alerted his fellow clubmen to the fact."

I was finding not being able to use my voice to be increasingly frustrating. "Can I please start talking now? I'm running out of paper and the lead is wearing out on my pencil."

"Certainly not." Mycroft wrote that two-word note with such authority that I didn't have it in me to question it.

Holmes crossed the room and opened a door, causing the sound of kitchen noises and the odors of cooking to fill the air. He motioned to the two of us, and we followed him inside. A chef was calmly chopping vegetables.

Holmes scribbled another note and passed it to Mycroft, who nodded. Holmes then showed it to me, so I could see that it read, "Where are the waiters?" Holmes then showed the note to the chef.

The chef wiped his brow with the back of his hand and glared at Holmes. "Listen, gov. I know the rule about not talking in the club, but this is my kitchen and I set the rules. I can't write little notes when I'm filleting fish, can I? If you have a question for me, you can use your bloody voice."

"Very well," Holmes pocketed his notepad and pencil. "What is the name of your waiter, how long has he been working here, and where is he now?"

"His name's Canterville, he's been here for about a week because he's filling in for our regular waiter who's been ill, and he stepped out for a smoke."

"How long ago has it been since you've seen him?"

The chef's forehead creased. "Quite some time, come to think of it. At least ten minutes. Maybe fifteen."

"He won't be coming back." Holmes turned to Mycroft. "There's nothing for it now. I suggest that you bite the bullet and summon the police."

Mycroft made a sour face and took a spoonful of Lancashire hotpot from a casserole dish, presumably in order to comfort himself. "Very well. I shall not call for your friends Lestrade or Gregson, though. I happen to know an inspector who I can trust to be completely discreet and keep inconvenient questions to a minimum."

"It does not matter to me who you tell at Scotland Yard, Mycroft, only that you begin the search for this waiter. This supposed poltergeist is no simple prank. It is part of a far more dangerous and sinister plan."

I need not explain the events of the next hour. When the inspector Mycroft referred to earlier arrived, I was struck by the fact that I had never before met an officer of the law so disinclined to assert his authority. The man was completely obsequious to Mycroft, and accepted Mycroft's suggestions as to how to track the missing man down without question.

After the inspector left, the three of us settled in the Stranger's Room. I initiated the conversation by asking, "What do you intend to do to catch that waiter Canterville?"

"We have already done everything we ought to do, Watson. The official police are far more suited to a major manhunt than a private detective. They have the funds, the time, and the inclination to catch a killer who is almost certainly not named Canterville."

"What makes you so sure that it's an alias?" I asked.

"Perhaps you haven't read it, but there is a popular novella by Oscar Wilde titled *The Canterville Ghost*. I dare say that when our perpetrator applied for the job as a waiter, he consciously or unconsciously used a reference to a paranormal tale when planning a plot about a fake poltergeist."

"But what was the purpose of the whole charade? Simply to annoy the members of the Diogenes Club?"

"Oh, no, Watson, I'm convinced it was far more sinister than that. I must admit that I have only a fair guess at what the culprit's endgame was, though I can take some solace in the fact that brother

Mycroft clearly has a better idea of the motive, judging from his posture."

Mycroft grunted in reply, then gave a tiny nod.

"Think less about the action– creating a fake poltergeist– and focus more on the consequences of the action, Watson."

"Many members of the Diogenes Club were scared."

"True, but that was not the main desired consequence, Watson. The ultimate goal was more than merely spooking the gullible. Consider what happened."

I pondered for a moment. "The Diogenes Club ceased to be a sanctuary for men seeking peace and quiet."

"Precisely dear fellow! Exactly!" Holmes beamed. "So what does that mean?"

"That members would be less likely to visit the club."

"Magnificent! And the desired result of that would be?"

I hesitated. "Fewer members would lead to reduced payment of dues. That would lead to financial problems for the club, which could conceivably lead to the eventual closure of the club and the sale of the building. Could this whole charade have been driven by someone's desire to purchase the property?"

Holmes folded his fingers together. "An intriguing theory, Watson, but given the fact that the members pay annual dues, it would be months and months before the club would be short on funds."

"In any case, some of the club's members are sufficiently wealthy and dependent on the Diogenes Club as a refuge that they would gladly donate the necessary funds to keep it afloat in times of financial need," Mycroft added.

At that moment, the dour concierge of the club entered the room, placed a salver with a pile of glowing matter and a note on the table next to Holmes, and shuffled away. I thought that he was far too dedicated to the club's theme of silence. It was only later that I learned that he was a lifelong mute.

"Aha! My resourceful band of street urchins have managed to track down the object in question." Holmes held up the salver. "Behold the remains of the Diogenes Club poltergeist, Watson."

"What is that?"

"A form of rubber balloon, decorated with bits of glue and rubber to give it the appearance of a ghoul, and then painted with phosphorescent paint. The device the blown up, then released, causing it to fly around the room, making a shrieking noise as air escaped. A nervous person like Darbington could be startled by it to the point that he may have accidentally fallen from a window in a panicked desire to escape from it. Our culprit never expected that to happen. No, Darbington's injuries were not part of any plan. Neither was the balloon posing as a poltergeist planned to sail out of the broken window. Darbington's fall was a doubly tragic accident, because not only was the poor man injured, but Canterville, the mastermind of this plan, realized that his confederate Dynell was shaken up by the injury. I am quite sure that Canterville paid for Dynell's membership dues so that Dynell would serve as his assistant with the various pranks. Canterville himself took the role of a waiter so as to maintain an even lower profile. Perhaps his predecessor was paid off to feign sickness, perhaps he was mildly poisoned so as to give Canterville a chance to take over the job. Diogenes Club members make a point of ignoring each other. They even more studiously ignore waiters. Dynell was guilt-striken over Darbington's injuries, doubtless wished to confess, and Canterville silenced him."

Holmes coughed, then continued. "You wondered, Watson, why I suspected a waiter. I was not inclined to write down my suspicions at that time, but I noticed numerous minute traces of phosphorescent paint on dozens of items in the dining room, such as eating utensils, saltcellars, candleholders, and napkin rings. I already suspected the use of a glowing device to simulate a poltergeist, and logically, a quantity of that paint would stick to the culprit's fingers. Who else would touch all of those items but a waiter? That is how I knew who was behind these disruptions."

Turning to his brother, Holmes asked, "So, Mycroft, why exactly was our man Canterville trying to empty out the Diogenes Club of its members? Surely he was up to some skullduggery where it would be in his interests to have as few potential witnesses as possible. And nothing of note ever happens within these walls. I remembered a case where a man was drawn away from his place of business so a couple of scoundrels could dig in his basement to rob the bank next door. Could a similar principle be in play here? There is no bank next to the Diogenes Club. The only neighboring location of note is... your flat, dear brother."

"Precisely," Mycroft replied. "I'm in the middle of some tricky negotiations with a representative of a foreign government. In a few days, he is coming to my rooms for a secret meeting. I recently received some intelligence telling me that a trained assassin might be trying to strike my guest. I believe that Canterville is that assassin, and he planned to empty out the Diogenes Club so he could prepare for a strike. He wouldn't know the exact time of the meeting, but he could set up his rifle in the largely deserted building, and be prepared to take out the ambassador." Mycroft gave a little sniff that sounded suspiciously like a chuckle. "Little did he know that I have already taken precautions to protect my guest and myself. All of the windows and walls in my flat are bulletproof. This whole charade was laughably misguided from the beginning."

31

There is little more to tell. Darbington made a full recovery, aside from a slight limp in his left leg. Members of the club managed to take up a collection for Dynell's widow and children without saying a single word, and they easily raised enough to keep the Dynell family comfortable for several years. The man we knew as Canterville was captured and arrested the next morning, and Mycroft's meeting passed without incident.

Within a month, everything returned to normal at the Diogenes Club. Mycroft's fears that the members would begin forging amicable and talkative friendships proved unfounded. As the members who had been severely shaken by the antics of the "poltergeist" began to converse with each other, they overwhelmingly realized that they didn't really enjoy each other's company very much. The status quo of the Diogenes Club members ignoring each other was restored.

Holmes kept the "poltergeist" balloon, inflated it, and hung it in our rooms at Baker Street. "It is a reminder, Watson, that the unscrupulous can manipulate others with the possibility of the paranormal. We must remember not to dismiss the supernatural out of hand, but to thoroughly investigate such claims in order to determine if there is a more prosaic explanation."

=

The Man in the Maroon Suit

"That sounds delicious to me, Watson. I shall also order the mulligatawny soup and curried lamb at dinner tonight."

"Capital!" I said with a smile. Immediately, my muscles stiffened, as I realized that my friend had performed one of his trademark performances, where he had managed to read my mind without my speaking a word.

I resolved not to give him the satisfaction of asking him how he had managed to follow my thought processes this time. Holmes sat in his chair, staring at me with an amused smile on his lips, pressing his fingerprints together, until I finally broke my silence. I thought I had managed to hold out for at least ten minutes, but a glance at the clock told me I'd managed to stay quiet for only twenty seconds.

"How did you do it, Holmes?" Holmes and I said simultaneously.

My friend allowed himself a little chuckle, and replied, "Quite simple, Watson. I noticed you rubbing your stomach a minute ago, a sure sign that your gastric juices are informing you that your body needs sustenance sooner rather than later. We have, of course, already made reservations at Wilton's at seven-thirty tonight. You are a frequent patron of that establishment– I believe that you have eaten there no fewer than seven times in the past two months. Therefore, you ought to be familiar with their menu and have determined which dishes rank as your favorites."

Holmes paused, either to take a breath or for dramatic effect. I suppose he was only silent for a couple of seconds, but I am embarrassed to say that my impatience got the better of me, and I found myself asking rather louder than I had any right to, "But how did you know what I wished to order?"

"Quite simple, Watson. I notice you running your hand over the wound caused by the Jezail bullet. You were not wincing, as you do when your war injury causes you pain. Therefore, you were reminiscing, which causes you to unconsciously touch your scarred limb. You developed a fondness for curries and other southern Asian foods during your time in Afghanistan. I next saw you looking down on the right lapel of your suit and examining it between thumb and forefinger. Three weeks ago you permanently stained your tan suit when you dribbled mulligatawny– one of your favorite starters– on your right lapel. I therefore calculated that you were determined to partake of a beloved food, but this time you would take special care to protect your clothing from spills. As for the lamb curry, I suspected that you would continue to dine upon foods of southern Asian origin, and then I saw your gaze light upon the fleecy quilt that Mrs. Hudson crocheted for you last Christmas. Soft, white, and woolly, I daresay it made you think of a sheep. I tie the threads together, and I concluded that you had developed a craving for lamb curry. Simple, of course."

"Of course," I replied, not meaning to include sarcasm or asperity in my tone, but realizing that I might have inserted a touch of those unpleasant attributes into my voice inadvertently. Holmes, thankfully, displayed no offense over how I enunciated my words.

Later that evening, Holmes and I were enjoying our meals at Wilton's. I had carefully draped a large napkin over the front of my clothing in order to preserve my suit from being damaged by the mulligatawny. I had recently lost rather more money than I care to admit in a card game, and my budget for sartorial matters was completely wiped out for the foreseeable future. My current wardrobe would have to last me for some time, and I was grateful to Holmes for treating me to dinner that night.

I had just carefully and neatly deposited the final spoonful of mulligatawny into my mouth when a young man wearing a perfectly pressed suit and sporting a shock of dark curly hair that probably hadn't been combed in weeks rushed forward to our table, carrying a chair. He set down the chair with a heavy thud between Holmes and myself, and turned to us both with a desperate look on his face.

"Mr. Holmes, Dr. Watson. My name is Ernest Townshore. Please forgive me for interrupting your dinner like this, but I'm in a terrible state, and I didn't know what to do, and I was walking down the street trying to make heads or tails of my situation, and when I looked through the window and saw the two of you eating it was like kismet to me. I know that I should have made an appointment to see you both at your lodgings at Baker Street, but I think that if I have to wait to talk to you I might explode."

If I didn't know Holmes as well as I do, I would have sworn that the slight upward twitching of his lips was amusement rather than polite annoyance. "Very well, Mr. Townshore," Holmes said. "I would not like it on my conscience that my desire to have a pleasant, quiet meal with my friend inadvertently led to a case of spontaneous human combustion. Please tell me what's bothering you. And if I may make a suggestion, there is no need to include every single detail. A general sense of your predicament will be sufficient for my investigative needs at present. You will, of course, not mind if we continue to dine while you tell us your problem," Holmes added as the waiter cleared away our soup bowls and replaced them with our lamb curries.

"Yes, of course." Mr. Townshore gulped and tugged at his collar. "The problem, you see, is the man in the maroon suit."

"I beg your pardon?" I asked, my fork unconsciously suspended in the air. "A maroon suit? I don't believe that I've ever seen anybody wearing clothing of that color before."

"Nor have I, Doctor, but he's taken over the gallery."

"Do you know this man's name?" I queried.

"Well… no. You see, he's not a real person, as far as I know. He's a little man wearing a maroon suit and tie. And sometimes a maroon top hat. Not always. I forgot to mention that. I've never seen him before, but over the past three days he's been popping up in most of the pictures in the Sternhull Gallery."

"Popping up in pictures?" I was thoroughly confused. "Is he an actual human being?"

"Well, I don't know if he's a true-to-life representation of a real person, but I don't think I've ever seen him in the flesh myself. I've only seen the little pictures of him that have been added into the paintings."

A glint danced in Holmes' eyes, and I knew at once that he had developed an interest in our unexpected dinner guest's problem. "Some vandal is taking a brush and paint and adding a human figure to the artwork at the gallery?"

"Precisely!" Mr. Townshore produced a small brown paper parcel from under his coat. "Please, take a look!"

Holmes took another bite of curry, and then picked up the parcel gingerly, weighed it in his right hand for a couple of seconds, and then untied the string and neatly unwrapped the brown paper. He examined it for a few moments, and then set it down on the table.

"Not a particularly distinguished work," he finally pronounced. "It's a simple pastoral scene. The kind of art you see on chocolate boxes."

I leaned over and examined the painting. It was a depiction of a small brown cottage in a green field, with several trees along the sides. A little man wearing a maroon suit and hat was leaning against the wall of the cottage. It was rather skillfully done, and if I hadn't known that the figure was not supposed to be there, I would never have guessed that the maroon suit man wasn't supposed to be a part of the painting. Personally, I didn't see anything very wrong or for that matter very right about it, but I have never declared myself to be an art connoisseur. "Who painted this?" I asked.

Mr. Townshore gulped. "I did."

Holmes' face betrayed no embarrassment or contrition for his blunt assessment of Mr. Townshore's work. "I can understand your distress at seeing your work vandalized, Mr. Townshore. Do you have other pictures at the Sternhull Gallery?"

"Yes. Seven of them. And all of them have had that man in the maroon suit added to them."

"How many pictures does the Sternhull Gallery hold in all?"

"I haven't counted. At an estimate, I'd say around two hundred."

"Have all of those pictures been altered?"

"No. Only about sixty-five of them."

Holmes put down his fork and shot Mr. Townshore a piercing glare. "You didn't count them? Why didn't you take the time to acclimate yourself to the details of the situation before coming to me?"

Mr. Townshore squirmed and had the decency to look shamefaced. "I figured that you could take stock of the situation more effectively than I could."

Holmes' face demonstrated that he could see the justice in this remark, but despite his lingering annoyance, he was still clearly intrigued by this unusual problem. "Are all of the other pictures of the men in the maroon suit the same size?"

"Roughly, yes. Some are a bit bigger or smaller, so the figure's proportionately sized to fit into each picture. None are more than a few inches tall, and it's not always a complete man. In some cases, it's just the top half of him sticking out from behind a tree, or just his face and maroon top hat looking in the window. In one, he's swimming– fully clothed– in a pond, in another he's sitting on a rock or talking with people who were already in the painting."

"Do you recognize his face?" I asked.

"No. I've never seen the man before in my life."

Holmes resumed the questioning. "Have there been any threats to the gallery? Any attempts at vandalism?"

"None that I know of."

"Are the paintings permanently defaced?"

"Well, as far as I can tell all of the images of the maroon suit man are in oil-based paint. I suppose that it could be cleaned off by a skilled restorer, but it would take time and probably would cost quite a bit. As I said, the images are all quite small. It would probably be a lot easier for the artists who painted the pictures to simply paint over the man. That's what I plan to do."

"Hmm. Have you spoken to any of the other artists about their defaced work?"

"No. It's only by pure chance that I even found out about the damage. I visited the gallery an hour ago to meet with the owner, Mr. Bradnick. He had a check for me after one of my paintings sold a few days ago. The gallery was closed today, so no one had been there for almost twenty-four hours. Plenty of time for some miscreant to have painted those little men. Anyway, I met Mr. Bradnick at the door, he let me in, and we discovered the vandalism together. I rather lost my grip on things, and before I knew it I was here."

Holmes ran the tip of his finger gently over the painted man in the maroon suit. "How long do you think it would take for a skilled artist to paint one of these men?"

"It's a bit crude. Not very true to life. I suppose that if I were going for speed rather than detail, I could paint one in three or four minutes. No more than five. Less if I fell into the rhythm of reproducing the figure."

"Hmm." The calculations flashed across Holmes' eyes. "With about sixty-five paintings, at three to five minutes per figure, it would take between three and a quarter hours to just under five and a half hours to complete the project. And the gallery was empty was a full day. Plenty of time. And it would take several hours for the figures to dry. This one has no trace of dampness, so whoever painted it didn't do the job too recently." He paused. "How many people would know that the gallery would be empty today?"

"Everybody. It's always closed on Mondays."

"And nobody was supposed to be there at all?"

"Well, Mr. Bradnick sometimes stops by on a Monday for one reason or another. I made the appointment with him to pick up my check around lunchtime today. I've no idea who else might have known about it. I certainly didn't tell anybody."

"No security guard?"

"I don't believe so, no."

"No cleaning staff?"

"Oh…" Mr. Townshore closed his eyes and thought for a few moments. "There is a charwoman who comes by a few times a week to dust and mop the floors. I don't know her very well, but I am aware that Mr. Bradnick trusts her completely. He gave her a key to the gallery, and she comes by when she has a spare evening to do her work. Perhaps she does come in on Mondays. It would make sense. But you don't think that she would do something like this, do you?"

Holmes lifted his shoulders a fraction of an inch. "I haven't got nearly enough information to draw any conclusions at all. I do content that one would need to be a fairly proficient artist in order to paint so many figures so quickly."

"I wonder, Holmes, is it possible that the vandal sought to paint the man in every single picture, but he ran out of time?"

"That's one of many possibilities, Watson. I shall have a better idea of the vandal's motives when I examine the gallery."

Mr. Townshore looked elated. "Then you'll help me?"

"I shall. After I finish my meal, of course. My curry is getting cold. Mr. Townshore, if you wish to order some for yourself, I highly recommend it. I have no intention on rushing as I eat, and you look as if you could use some sustenance in order to regain your composure. Also, I have an eye on a bit of bread and butter pudding for afters."

Holmes firmly informed Mr. Townshore that any further talk of the man in the maroon suit could wait until we arrived at the gallery. Mr. Townshore took Holmes' advice and ordered some dinner, and over the next half-hour the conversation centered around Holmes' musings on the career and legacy of his great-uncle, the French artist Vernet.

Once we'd all finished our generous servings of bread and butter pudding, we started on our walk to the gallery. Holmes peppered Mr. Townshore with a handful of additional questions regarding the details of the damage, though our new acquaintance's memory was not nearly as helpful as Holmes wished. Eventually, we reached the gallery, where three men were standing in the entryway. Mr. Townshore identified the eldest, a stocky man with a large, gleaming forehead, as Mr. Bradnick. A wispy man with a trace of cropped rusty hair was introduced to us as the artist Auguste Pilston; and a tall, strongly built fellow with a light brown mane that fell past his shoulders was the successful painter Marcus Hallard.

It took mere seconds to make the proper introductions, and the moment after Holmes mentioned that he had been asked to investigate the vandalism, Bradnick burst into a rage that made me fear that he would fall into an apoplectic fit. My remonstrations to convince him to calm himself down met with no success whatsoever.

"Calm down! Like hell I'll calm down!" Bradnick's face was now approaching the color of a beet, and he began pounding his walking stick against the floor with such vehemence that I was sure that either the cane or the tiles would crack, but I wasn't sure which would be damaged first. "This is a deliberate attack on my life and legacy! I've devoted my entire career to finding the best and most beautiful works of art that London's painters have to offer, and now, and decades of building up a reputation, I'm going to be a laughingstock! No artist is going to want his pictures to be displayed in my gallery if there's a chance that they're going to be defaced. I just know the connoisseurs are going to amble into my gallery and crack snide remarks like "This portrait's nice, but do you have any with a man in a maroon suit on them?" My business is ruined! And now that I've finally got some top-drawer talent displaying their work here…"

"Thank you so much for your kind words," Hallard replied lazily. "And you needn't worry about my continued willingness to work with you. So far, I haven't suffered in any way. My work remains unharmed."

"I wish that I could say the same," Pilston sighed. "All five of my paintings have that ridiculous little fellow prancing about in the background. They're ruined!"

Hallard laughed, but there was an unpleasant undertone. "I don't know if "ruined" is the right word to use, my dear Auguste. That would imply your little efforts had any artistic value whatsoever. I rather think that the presence of the little man has made your work much more charming, if not actually any better, really."

Pilston turned scarlet, and jerked his arm back, closing his fingers into a fist.

"None of that," Holmes said sharply, as he placed his hand over Pilston's fist. "Now is not the time for violence. Right now, if you want to do some good, I suggest that you answer all of my questions about this vandalism."

"What are you doing here?" Pilston asked. That is actually a bowdlerized version of his question. The original query was marked by a couple of profane terms that would not be accepted by my readership, so I have taken the initiative to delete them here.

"As you heard just a few seconds ago, I am Sherlock Holmes, and I am a detective. If you would be so kind as to give me a tour of this gallery and point out the damage, it would be my pleasure to assist in finding the person responsible."

Pilston quivered and looked as if he was much too furious to provide any help to Holmes, but Bradnick leapt forward, pushed Pilston to one side with a red, beefy hand, and offered his other hand to Holmes. "Sir, it's a pleasure to finally meet you. I've been following your adventures for some time, and I'd be honored if you would please condescend to use your enormous talents on this little problem. I know it's not a murder or a bank robbery or an affair of state– I'm afraid you might see this as something of no more interest than a nasty little scribbling on a public lavatory wall– but to me, this gallery is hallowed ground to me. You must excuse my tantrum a moment ago. I have a notoriously short fuse. Always have, and probably always will. Your name didn't sink in for a while, but when I finally realized who you were right now, I thanked my lucky stars, because you're just the man I need to figure out who performed this little joke."

Holmes smiled. "Thank you, sir. I'm glad to see that you have calmed down and are approaching this matter in a much more constructive way."

Hallard laughed again. I did not like his laugh at all. It sounded as if it came from a man who treated the rest of humanity with contempt, and his eyes were cold and joyless. "I didn't want to point out that you were indulging in an awful tizzy of hyperbole a few minutes ago, but if you'd only take a moment to observe exactly which picture sere damaged, you'd realize that there's nothing very much to get upset over, is there? After all, it's only the cheap pictures that are damaged. The valuable art– the work by talented fellows like myself, that's all untouched. None of it is damaged in the slightest. But the dreck– the work by the artists you only give a place as a favor in order to give them a chance at finding an audience for their tawdry little attempts at creation, those are the pictures where the maroon man has made his appearances. Grissold's appalling landscapes. Frug's lifeless panormas. And Pilston's... Well, I'm not sure what word you'd apply to his wastes of perfectly good paint, other than "garbage.""

Pilston swore again and lunged at Hallard, who seemed highly amused by the attack. Hallard performed a little backwards shuffle and pivoted on his left heel, and Pilston couldn't correct his balance in time, so he fell forward in a painful-looking somersault. I stepped forward in an attempt to perform my duties as a medical professional, but before I could examine Pilston, he waved me away, raised himself up, whipped out his handkerchief, and began wiping away dust that was invisible to my eyes, muttering vulgarities under his breath all the while.

Holmes observed Pilston with a look that might have been a glare of contempt or a gaze of repressed amusement. I could not tell which. Once Pilston had dusted off his entire body, Holmes took a deep breath and asked Bradnick, "Sir, would you like me to investigate the damage to the pictures in your gallery?"

Bradnick was not the sort of man to limit himself to two words when he had the ability to use hundreds, and after a few minutes of ranting and politely yet loudly asking for Holmes' help, Holmes finally cut him off and announced his acceptance of the case. "I should like to interview each of you shortly, but for the moment I shall need to examine the entire gallery. I trust that you can all be reasonably quiet long enough for me to concentrate and make the necessary observations?"

Pilston pocketed his handkerchief in a failed attempt to appear dignified. "Mr. Holmes, I shall be delighted to help you, but I shall not stand around in silence, wasting my time. I believe that I shall go out and purchase an evening newspaper. I'll return shortly."

Hallard made a half-hearted attempt to suppress a yawn. "I am rather peckish. There'a baked-potato cart down the street. Would anybody else care for one?" As there were no takers, Hallard shrugged and ambled out the door.

Bradnick's face was still unnaturally mottled. "I'll be going to my office and pouring myself a very stiff drink." As he walked away, Holmes withdrew his powerful magnifying lens from his coat pocket and began a circuit of the gallery, examining each portrait in turn, whether or not it had a little man in a maroon suit in it, though he paid particularly close attention to each image of the unusually-dressed man. I followed Holmes around, and though I possessed no item to aid in my examination, I scrutinized each picture to the best of my ability. Luckily, Townshore's estimates were high, and there were only one hundred forty-two pictures in the gallery, and just fifty-one of them had the maroon-suited man added to them.

Our examination of the gallery lasted just under an hour, though none of the three men who had left had returned yet. Townshore had perched himself on a windowsill near the entryway, and had spent the entire time nibbling away at his fingernails. Holmes didn't seem to be in any hurry to speak to the other gentlemen. After looking over the last painting, which featured the maroon suit man performing what appeared to be an awkward soft shoe dance, Holmes leaned against the wall and started tapping his magnifying lens against his palm, as he stared up at the ceiling. I stood there quietly and watched the gears of his mind turn for a while. After several minutes, I regret to say that my impatience got the better of me, and I interrupted Holmes' reverie to prompt him to share his thoughts.

"I was thinking… about fairy tales."

His answer stupefied me. The thought of Holmes reflecting on Cinderella and Sleeping Beauty seemed painfully out of character. My friend noticed my amazement, and with no shortage of amusement in his face, elaborated on his comment.

"Are you familiar with the story of Ali Baba and the Forty Thieves from the Arabian Nights? Or Hans Christian Andersen's The Tinder Box?"

"I'm fairly sure that I read them as a child, but adulthood has wiped them from my memory."

"Both of them contain the same plot point. In Ali Baba and the Forty Thieves, a clever family servant notices that someone has marked the door of their house with a piece of chalk, so she takes some chalk and places an identical mark on every other front door on the street. In the Tinder Box, a dog with enormous eyes performs exactly the same trick to save his master."

"And what do clever servants and big-eyed dogs have to do with this defaced gallery, Holmes?"

"My dear fellow, consider this possibility. Only one of these little men in maroon serves a purpose. The others are merely decoys."

"I don't follow you."

"Have you noticed what all of the vandalized pictures have in common, Watson? Aside from the nature of the addition, what quality connects the paintings that had the maroon man added, and which were left undamaged?"

I reflected for a moment. "Only the oil paintings had the little maroon man added. None of the watercolors were altered."

"True. But there are only thirteen watercolors in the gallery. All the rest are oils, and there are many oil paintings that were not harmed."

I thought for a little while, trying to find a link in the subject matters. Eventually, I conceded defeat.

"You're focusing on the pictures themselves, Watson. Look at the little cards tacked to the side of each picture."

I took a quick walk around the gallery, and midway through my review, I realized something notable. "Only the cheapest pictures have been vandalized!"

Holmes chuckled. "Precisely, my dear fellow. All of the damaged pictures have been created by the same seven artists, and–" He lowered his voice so that Mr. Townshore couldn't hear him. "They are the least talented of the artists displayed at the gallery. None of their pictures are priced at more than twenty pounds, and most of them are worth even less. And none of these works are likely to rise in value, either. Of course, I do not profess to be an expert in art, but I feel fairly confident that the artistic merit of the damaged paintings is of fairly low quality. In contrast, the paintings that remained untouched are being valued at minimum, a hundred pounds apiece, and many of them are fetching a price of several times that. The creators of those paintings are, to my untrained eye, far more worthy of the higher price than their more amateurish peers. About a dozen of them are quite valuable. Those have real historical value, and are worth well over a thousand pounds.

"Do you think that the vandal was afraid he'd get caught, and didn't want to get billed for damaging the priciest works?"

"I think that the motive has a touch more nobility than that, Watson. Consider this. The vandal didn't want to damage a work of genuine art. He couldn't bear to deface something created by someone with genuine talent."

"You're being as clear as mulligatawny soup, Holmes."

"Let's take a look at some of Hallard's paintings. Whatever personality defects the fellow may have, even his harshest critics can concede that he can paint. There's genuine warmth in those portraits, they have a real glow that makes them seem almost lifelike. No hack can create that sort of effect. It takes true talent. The pictures are fetching prices from five to seven hundred pounds apiece, and though I would never pay that much myself, even if I had that kind of money to fritter away, I still concede that the gallery is justified in asking such a price."

"I'd disagree, but I don't want to start an argument."

"That's very generous of you, Watson. Now, take a good look at the pictures created by Pilston. What do you think of them?"

I leaned forward and examined the price. "This picture of a picnic is going for fifteen pounds. I wouldn't give five for it." I paused, then added, "I'm really not sure if that little man in maroon actually adds to the painting or damages it." The maroon man was sitting next to a lady in a blue dress, eating a sandwich.

"Indeed, Watson. Compare the man in the maroon suit to the others at the picnic. Does anything strike your eye?"

I pondered for a while, and then surrendered. "Sorry, Holmes. I'm coming up empty here."

My friend looked regretful. "We'll leave it there for a bit, then. Take a look at this other picture by Pilston. This one, with three deer in a field."

I shrugged. "Twenty pounds. Still overpriced, but I do like it much more than the picnic one." The maroon suit man was petting the largest of the deer.

"What is your critique of the artwork?"

"Nothing special, I'd say."

"I would be the first to note that much of the painting– the grass, the shrubs, the clouds in the sky… all of those are fairly pedestrian. Clumsy work, really. But observe the eyes of the deer, Watson. Don't you see the spark of life in them? And that little tree off to the right. Do you see the skill that went into that to give it a three-dimensional effect?"

After Holmes pointed it out, I could see it. "But what does that mean?"

"It means that Pilston's work is rather like that cartoon in *Punch* about the curate's egg– parts of it are excellent! Mr. Pilston does have a flair for painting, but for the lion's share of the picture, he is willing to content himself with producing flat and uninspired work."

"A bit harsh, Holmes."

"Not so, Watson, just stating a fact. Mr. Pilston has talent, yet he chooses to paint pictures as if he's a first-year student at a disreputable art school. These are pictures painted by a man who isn't putting very much effort into his compositions."

I thought for a few moments of my time as a schoolboy, and how one of the more brilliant fellows of my acquaintance consistently scored just enough points on his exams to pass, even though he could have earned a place at the top of the class if he had only tried. When I'd asked him about his marks not reflecting his potential, he'd laughingly explained that school was boring, as the eldest son of a prominent peer of the realm his future was assured even if he was illiterate. He proclaimed that his time would be far better spent exploring topics of real interest to him, although he never explained to me what he considered more intriguing than school. Upon further reflection, the comparison didn't appear to be a particularly apt one, since my classmate was a privileged young man, and Pilston was a man who was probably trying to make a living off his art, so it would be in his interest to create the best pictures possible.

I voiced my thoughts to Holmes, who smiled and replied, "Quite right, Watson. Now, how would you judge the images of the man in the maroon suit?"

"On an artistic level? Nothing very notable. A bit crude, rather more of a cartoon than a realistic representation of a person."

"True, the artwork is rough, but notice the form and style of the brushwork. Though unrefined, it shows a familiarity with human anatomy, not like the completely untrained, who reduce the form of the body to a compilation of shapeless blobs."

"The artist was probably in a rush."

"I concede your point, but the argument I am advancing is the fact that no matter how much a skilled artist tries to hide his talent, he can never truly produce work at the same level as a rank amateur. So now we have two collections of works that reflect suppressed talent. I cannot expect you to draw the same conclusions I did, due to the fact that you lacked a magnifying lens of your own, but after a careful examination of the brushstroke patterns used to create the maroon suit man and Pilston's paintings, I would wager my violin that they were created by the same man."

"Pilston is the vandal? But why would he damage his own paintings?"

"From the lack of effort he put into them, it's obvious that he doesn't care about them very much."

"But Holmes, what would be the purpose of this entire charade?"

"The answer comes from observing everything, old chap. You thought that I was only examining the pictures, didn't you? You really ought to have known better my friend. You know my methods. I examined the walls and floor as well and found..." Here Holmes crossed the room and pointed at a pair of small dark ovals on the wainscoting. "These."

I scrutinized them. "I can't be certain without that test of yours, but could they be blood?"

"I'm fairly certain of that. There are other, tinier droplets here–" he pointed. "And there. And there. Given the lighting, they're easy to miss."

"But what does this mean? Was someone injured?"

"One can only hope it was something so simple and comparatively harmless." Holmes's mouth twitched upward into a wry smile. "I dare say that if you choose to write an account of this adventure, the odds of your recording my covering myself in glory are far outweighed by the probability that in less than a minute, I shall humiliate myself so badly that I shall have no choice but to abandon detecting forever and take up bee-farming in the countryside."

"Heaven forbid, Holmes. But what are you thinking?"

"Watson, the droplets on the wall suggest that some unfortunate person was killed here. From the angle and shape of the blood, I would suspect a stabbing. It's my belief that after the murder, some blood spattered on one of the paintings, most likely this one here. Now, after the killer hid the body and wiped away as much of the blood as he could find, he came back and realized that he had to cover up the bloodstain on the picture. He couldn't wash it off the oil paint, so he came up with the idea to cover it with something– a man in a maroon suit. The problem was, the image would draw a great deal of attention, so the killer realized that the best way to disguise his vandalism would be to paint similar figures on as many other painting as he could."

"This "he" you refer to, are you referring to Pilston?"

"I am. If you observed, his jacket pocket contained a little case, the kind artists use to carry brushes and some tubes of oils, so we know he would have paint handy."

"But who did he kill? And why?"

"You'll notice that he only damaged the cheap, poorer quality paintings. When I scrutinized the pictures, I discovered that several paintings, the older ones costing over a thousand pounds, had brush strokes that matched some of Pilston's paintings."

"Forgery? Pilston replaced the valuable paintings with his own copies?"

"Precisely. And his victim walked in on him in the act, and the poor woman died simply because she was in the wrong place at the wrong time."

"Who is this woman?"

"The charwoman, of course. Pilston came in during the night to make his latest switch, she saw what she was doing, and he stabbed her with his pocketknife. You can tell that the gallery hasn't been cleaned in a few days. The rest of the coverup occurred as I said."

"What did he do with the body?"

"I can't say for certain before further examination. He must have found a hiding place nearby, hid the unfortunate lady, and I suspect he's spent most of the past hour trying to move the corpse. In any case, Townshore hasn't left that windowsill, I can hear Bradnick and the sound of clinking glass in his office, and you can see Hallard sitting on the wall out that window there, munching on a baked potato and reading a newspaper. As far as I can tell, Pilston is nowhere to be found–"

Holmes' voice faded away as a couple of police officers appeared in the window, with a handcuffed Pilston in tow. Holmes let them inside, greeted them, and asked, "I presume you caught Mr. Pilston attempting to dispose of a woman's body?"

One policeman's eyes widened. "Yes. How did you know?"

Holmes summarized his conclusions, and surprisingly, Pilston chimed in every few moments to confirm what Holmes had deduced. If being amazingly right based on scanty evidence was feeding his ego, he did a remarkable job of disguising his self-satisfaction. Pilston, for his part, was being a remarkably good sport about his capture, and he accepted his fate with more grace than I'd ever seen before or since.

"Just one more question," Holmes asked Pilston as the police led the criminal away. "Why on earth did you choose to paint that little man in a maroon suit?"

Pilston shrugged his shoulders. "I had a limited amount of paint with me, and not many colors. I just so happened to have a lot of maroon paint, so it seemed like a sensible idea at the time to make that the color of the man's suit.

Merridew of Abominable Memory

"My collection of M's is a fine one," said he. "Moriarty himself is enough to make any letter illustrious, and here is Morgan the poisoner, and Merridew of abominable memory, and Mathews, who knocked out my left canine in the waiting-room at Charing Cross, and, finally, here is our friend of to-night."

– "The Empty House"

"Thank heavens you're back, Doctor. I'm at my wits' end trying to figure out what to do next."

My landlady, Mrs. Hudson, was rarely flustered, but this evening, she seemed terribly shaken.

"What on earth is the matter?"

"Well, you've been gone for three days visiting your army friend, Doctor, and Mr. Holmes has been away for even longer, working on another of his cases. But the night after you left, this gentleman knocked on the door and insisted on coming inside. Well, I tried to tell him I didn't know when Mr. Holmes would be back. It might be a few minutes, or it might be a few days. He didn't care. He said he had no idea who this Mr. Holmes was, but I could show him in when he arrived. He was adamant on waiting in your rooms, even though I said that I didn't like leaving a stranger there with both of you away. But I couldn't stop him, Doctor, he just staggered up the stairs, sat down in a chair, and said that he needed rest and wouldn't listen to a word I said, and to the best of my knowledge, he hasn't stirred from that chair."

"Not for nearly three days?"

"Well, if he's gotten up to stretch his legs or answer a call of nature I haven't heard him. I've been checking in on him every hour, and he's starting to gather dust, he is. Mind you, I'm not in the habit of doling out free meals to strangers who show up at the doorstep, but I don't think he's eaten a crumb since he arrived. Do you know what he said when I asked him if he'd had his dinner?"

"What?"

"He said, "Dinner? What's that?" And then he turned his head to one side and started staring at the window. Only the curtains were drawn, Doctor. That's a very odd duck, if I do say so myself. I think you'd better see what he wants, hadn't you?"

"Absolutely! Did you give you his name or tell you why he came here?"

"I asked him, Doctor, and I tell you, his answer made the hairs on the back of my neck stand on end. Shall I tell you what he said?"

"Yes! Please don't keep me in suspense!"

"Very well. He told me, "I don't know. Don't ask me again." And then he closed his eyes and wouldn't say another word, not even when I spoke directly into his ear."

I was dumbstruck. "Are you saying he claims not to be able to recall his own *name*?"

"Exactly. I thought he was having a joke at my expense at first, but when I looked at him closely, I didn't see the faintest hint of a smile. It makes no sense to say this, but I think he meant it."

"But that's absurd."

"With all due respect, Doctor, you should be telling him that, not me."

I saw the justice in this comment, and I hurried up to my rooms and opened the door. I saw no one at first, until I approached the fireplace and discovered a small, elderly man sitting in one of the high-backed chairs.

He didn't appear to notice me at first, until I cleared my throat and his body quivered and he finally looked up to meet my chilly gaze. "Who are you and what do you want?" he demanded.

It took a bit of effort, but I managed to keep the asperity I was feeling out of my voice. "My name is Dr. John Watson and this is my home. May I ask who you are and what you are doing here?"

My guest did not seem upset or surprised by my reply. "Are you sure?"

"Of course I am. I know for certain who I am and where I live. Can you say the same?"

He clenched his jaw. "This is my home." He paused. "I think it is." His voice quavered and cracked. "I thought it was."

My annoyance vanished as I suddenly realized that this man might be suffering from some sort of stroke or dementia. "Sir, I am a medical doctor, and I think I should examine you to see if you are–"

"No!" His voice grew so loud and shrill that I felt my eardrums vibrate. "I won't be touched! You can't! You have no right! This is my house! Leave me alone!"

Involuntarily, I took a couple of steps back, but regained my composure when the suddenly enraged man shook and deflated like a punctured balloon, until he was just a frightened and lost-looking old fellow.

I approached him again. "Sir, what is your name?"

He looked agonized. "My name? Don't you know?"

"I do not, sir. I'm afraid we're strangers."

"How bizarre. I wonder what you're doing here, then."

"Sir, what is your name?"

"I... I think I know. I ought to know it. I just need time to think of it. Give me time. Give me time!" He clasped his head in his hands and rocked back in forth in the chair. I placed my hand on his shoulder in an attempt to steady him, but he slapped my arm away immediately. He was quite frail, so he caused me no pain by striking me, and my overarching emotions were of concern for him rather than annoyance.

The next two hours followed the same pattern. I would attempt to examine him, he would fight me off, I would ask his name, he would be unable to answer, then he would ask me my name and demand to know what I was doing in his home. When I would patiently re-introduce and re-re-introduce myself, he would become disoriented and confused. All attempts to come close to him were rebuffed, and I was starting to grow frustrated when the door swung open and Holmes made his welcome return.

After greeting him and quickly apprising him of the situation, the familiar interest glint entered Holmes' eye, and he strode over to the fireplace without even taking off his coat. "Good evening, sir. My name is Sherlock Holmes."

"Who?"

Holmes was compelled to repeat his name thrice, each time receiving the same response, until he finally asked for our guest's name, and received a response similar to the ones our guest gave me.

Looking thoughtful, Holmes rang for Mrs. Hudson. When she arrived, he asked for tea and scones. When they arrived, he filled a cup and handed it to our anonymous visitor. "Your tea, sir."

"My... tea?"

"That is correct. I suggest that you drink it while it is hot."

Obediently, our guest took the cup and sipped. When its contents were nearly emptied, he started sagging, and the cup tilted and began to slip from his fingers. Holmes snatched the cup from him before the dregs spilled, and chuckled as he sank his teeth into a scone.

"Holmes, what did you put into that tea?"

"A bit of sugar. It disguises the taste of the mild narcotic I slipped into the cup."

"But you can't just go about knocking out people with drugs!"

"This is a special circumstance, Watson. Our guest is clearly ill and will not allow us to examine him. This is the most efficient and humane way to subdue him." Scrutinizing our visitor as he slipped into unconsciousness, Holmes took a sip from a teacup that I presumed was devoid of narcotics. "I think he'll be more amenable to an examination now. I suggest that you start immediately. The dose I gave him was so tiny that I doubt that he'll need more than fifteen minutes or so before awakening."

Setting my last, lingering concerns about medical ethics aside, I started to look over our guest. He was not in the best health. The fact that he quite likely had not consumed any nutrients or water in the last few days aside from his recent cup of tea had left him weak and dehydrated. Yet it was clear that he had been in decline for some months previously, and from the pallor on his skin and a handful of other indicators, I suspected that he was in the advanced stages of some sort of cancer.

I voiced my initial diagnosis to Holmes, who was in the middle of his second scone. "Could his disorientation be due to a brain tumor?"

"Anything is possible. I need to examine him more closely. It's possible that a stroke or an aneurism, or simply senility, caused this."

"Or a blow to the head?"

"That's possible, yes." Our guest's head was largely bald, but as I examined the eggshell-colored fringe along the edges of his skull, I noticed a little brown patch the size of the nail on my littlest finger. "Holmes! Look at this!" I pointed to a small piece of metal that was sticking out of the back of his head. "What is that? Could it be a nail?"

"There's no head to it, and the edge is rough, like it was snapped off... An ice pick, perhaps?" Holmes picked up his magnifying glass, nodded in response to my warning not to touch the metal projection, studied the wound, and handed the magnifying glass to me. After examining it, I returned the magnifying glass to Holmes and informed him, "I would say that this man was stabbed in the head, most likely with an ice pick. The wound almost certainly caused lasting brain damage and probably permanently impaired his memory."

"Abominable. Is it possible to remove the weapon to study it?"

"At this point, I would strongly advise against it. To pull out the weapon might cause even more damage, and would possibly even kill the patient. Perhaps a skilled surgeon specializing in brain disorders might be able to operate, but to attempt to do anything with the wound here would be so foolhardy that any doctor who attempted to perform such a procedure might justifiably be expelled from the profession."

Holmes shook his head. "That is unfortunate on multiple levels. Yet now that you know the cause of this man's memory impairment, you can say with certainty that he requires proper medical attention?"

"Of course! Not only for his wound, but for his malnutrition, dehydration, and general illness as well."

With a nod, Holmes crossed the room and summoned our page-boy. When he arrived moments later, Holmes told him, "Go and fetch an ambulance at once. Inform them that we have a gravely ill and wounded man here, and he requires urgent medical attention. Quickly now."

As the lad sprinted away, I shook my head. "It's amazing that the man was able to walk and retain so many of his cognitive functions after suffering such a terrible wound, but such things do happen. Though in his condition, I'm not sure whether to dub him lucky or not."

"Where there's life, there's hope, Watson, and in any case, we have to make use of the precious time we have before the ambulance arrives and takes away our guest." Holmes immediately started searching the pockets of the unconscious man. I started to make some sort of objection, but Holmes waved a dismissive hand at me. "If we are to find out who attacked this man, we will need all the information we can obtain, and first on the list is the man's name."

After completing his preliminary search, Holmes sighed. "No wallet. The man was the victim of a pickpocket."

"Surely he could have simply misplaced his wallet or left it behind. We don't know how or where he received his injury."

"First of all, Watson, I will draw your attention to these greasy smears and coal-dust on the inside of this poor man's pocket where most men keep their wallets. This man's hands have not been washed recently, but they are not nearly at that level of uncleanliness and are well-manicured. Obviously, another hand, not his own, dipped into his pocket and extracted his wallet. No doubt some filthy denizen of the streets saw our visitor in his discombobulated state and thought he was a wealthy and easy mark, so he picked his pocket."

"He? There are female pickpockets you know, Holmes."

"If you were to look at the size of the dirty smears in that pocket, Watson, you would know it was unlikely that a woman's hand could have created that level of damage. We also know that he was attacked at night, inside a building where he felt comfortable and safe and where he was prepared to spend a substantial period of time, though not, most likely, his own home."

I was still smarting from Holmes' rebuttal to my female pickpocket remark, so I said nothing, and Holmes, looking disappointed at my missing my cue, continued. "You'll note that our guest is clad in evening wear, Watson. Quite expensive, well-tailored, surely, this fellow is a man of means. But he has no coat, no hat, and no scarf. That is because he removed those garments upon entering the domicile he visited when he was attacked. He was probably not in his own home because had he let himself in with his own key, which he would have then returned to his pocket, the key would have been at the top of the pocket's contents. Instead, this handkerchief rests on top of the key, suggesting that he has had need of it since he last used his key. His hands, though not dirty enough to cause the smears in his pockets, still have evident traces of street grime on them, but no corresponding marks are on his handkerchief, indicating that he has not used it in some time. Furthermore, the man clearly suffers from corns and chilblains on his feet, and his shoes look to be a fraction too tight for him. Unless a man is expecting company, if his dress shoes cause him discomfort, he will remove them upon reaching his own house. He has transferred his wedding ring from his left to his right hand, indicating that he is a widower. Given the care with which this button was resewn to his cuff, I think it likely that he keeps a manservant. Now coming back to the handkerchief..."

Holmes unfolded the square of white cloth in front of me with a dramatic flourish. "It bears the initials "T.M." Clearly our guest's initials. His pocket watch..." Holmes pressed the latch and opened it. "Contains a telling inscription. To Thaddeus, a wonderful husband and father on our 25th anniversary. Love, your darling Jewel." Jewel is clearly his late wife, and our man is Thaddeus M. We must track down this man's child or children, Watson. If he has been here for three days, they might be aware of his absence and worried."

"Is there nothing else you can deduce, Holmes?"

My friend looked the unconscious man up and down a few times, before uttering a quick exclamation of triumph. "Observe, Watson! A foreign hair clinging to his own hair. White horsehair that has yellowed. From its length and the curls on it, it comes from a judge's wig! Watson, examine our copy of *Who's Who*, go to the M's, and see if you can find a judge named Thaddeus with a wife named Jewel, though upon further reflection, "Jewel" may be pet name for his wife."

I obeyed and began scanning pages while Holmes applied his standard level of scrutiny to T.M.'s hands and feet. A few minutes passed, until I finally found an entry that met our specifications. "This could be him, Holmes! Thaddeus Merridew. High Court Judge, his wife Jillian passed away two years ago."

""Jewel" might feasibly be a sobriquet for "Jill," Holmes noted. "The usual information on his residence is present?"

"Yes. 2218 Guilders Lane. Not much more information, other than a couple of clubs and the fact that he has a son currently working in Belfast and a married daughter living in India."

"Then we have a solid thread to follow," Holmes replied. "I could not find much more of use on his extremities, save for the fact that he was in the habit of carrying a silver-headed walking stick that he needed for a limp in his left leg."

Why fight it? I asked myself. "And how did you deduce that, Holmes?"

"The scuffing on his left shoe indicates a limp. When a cane is carried to alleviate leg pain or damage, it is generally held in the opposite hand from the afflicted leg. On his right hand, I found traces of silver polish. Clearly, he lost his walking stick soon after the attack. As the cane was not merely decorative, he would not have left it at the door along with his coat and hat."

A knock at the door showed us that the ambulance had arrived, and the presumed Mr. Merridew, who was just starting to emerge from his stupor, was eased onto a stretcher and carried away to the hospital. At Holmes' suggestion, I continued making my way through the "M's" just in case there was a second potential name that fit our profile. There was none, and so, once the remaining scones and tea were consumed, we left to investigate.

A knock at the door of Justice Merridew's home brought a ruffled-looking valet to the door. After explaining that his master was not at home, Holmes informed him that we were aware of the fact that his employer had been missing for the last few days and that the judge had been found and was now in the hospital. Our request to be allowed in to ask some questions was accepted. As we entered, Holmes tapped the address plate on the pillar by the door.

"This may explain why Justice Merridew came to our residence and had the fixed impression that it was his house, Watson. He had been wandering the streets of London for some time before he reached our room, probably for the better part of a day, given the very slight about of the dust and dirt of the city on his clothes, and the fact that he was not at death's door from dehydration. His brain was damaged, and what remained of his mental faculties was devoted to finding something, anything with a semblance of familiarity to his home. When he saw our address plate for 221B, he misread it for his own 2218, and in his impaired mental state he became convinced that he had reached his own dwelling."

Since he was to talk to us, the valet was clearly uncertain as to whether he should allow us into the main sitting room, where the judge's guests were welcomed, or if he should lead us into the small back room where he was allowed to meet with his own acquaintances. Holmes, no doubt correctly deducing that the chairs would be far more comfortable in the judge's siting room, settled into a plush chair, and I followed suit.

"Your name, please?" Holmes asked after introducing ourselves.

"Tenners, sir."

"How long have you been working for Justice Merridew?"

"Just over four years, sir. I started working for him right after Mrs. Merridew fell ill with her long ailment."

"When was the last time you saw him?"

"Just a few days ago, sir. He had a dinner engagement at The Golden Nectarine, and I prepared his clothes and polished the silver handle his walking stick."

"Can you describe the clothing and cane?"

"An ordinary long black dinner dress coat, a white scarf, and a black top hat. Exactly the same garments worn by thousands of other gentlemen, sir. The walking stick had a handle shaped like a lion's head."

"Do you know who the judge was going to meet for dinner?"

"I do not, sir. My employer is not in the habit of providing me with any details besides what I absolutely need to know for my duties. I was told to expect him back by midnight. I was waiting up until three for him, sir. When he didn't arrive I made some discreet enquiries, but I was waiting to inform the police out of fear of a scandal. The judge would not have liked that at all, sir. He was most reluctant to cross paths with the police unless it was absolutely necessary. He considered it ungentlemanly."

"You ought to have come to me," Holmes replied.

"You were away investigating a case until an hour ago, with no information on how to find you," I reminded him.

"True enough," my friend conceded. "Do you have any knowledge as to anyone who might want to do the judge harm?"

"None, sir," Tenners answered. "He had no enemies that I know of, but perhaps someone at the Old Bailey might have had a better idea. I dare say a magistrate upsets a lot of people with his rulings, but he never shared any details with me."

"No angry or threatening letters?"

"I don't open his mail, sir. I just gather it. He keeps his recent correspondence on that salver there, if you'd care to look."

Holmes examined the stack of envelopes, and found nothing of note. Thanking Tenners for his time, we took a hansom to The Golden Nectarine, where we were told that Merridew had a reservation for two that night, but he had never arrived. Another man named Ivers had arrived and asked for Merridew, but after an hour passed with no sign of the judge, Ivers had left. Having learned almost nothing of use, we travelled to the Old Bailey to investigate at the judge's chambers.

On our way, we passed two men, a young fellow in his early twenties, and a distinguished-looking mad in his mid-sixties wearing a barrister's robe. We would not have given them a second look had we not heard the younger man refer to the elder as "Mr. Ivers." It took only a few moments to introduce ourselves and explain our purpose. Ivers expressed concern and stated that he was happy to do whatever he could to assist us, and his young friend murmured a polite goodbye and slipped away.

"I suspected that something was terribly wrong," Ivers declared. "Thaddeus is never late and he would never miss an appointment. I was certain that *I* had made a mistake of the date, but I was informed at the restaurant that Thaddeus had reserved a table. I was quite certain that something had happened, but I was not sure what to do– I didn't have his home address handy, and when I didn't see him around here the last few days, I had a word with his clerk, although he's an elderly fellow and prone to letting things slip his mind. Thaddeus should have forced him into retirement years ago, but they've worked together for most of their professional lives, though Thaddeus has kept his mind sharp as a tack."

Holmes shook his head. "Unfortunately, his mental powers have probably been forever destroyed by the attack." Ivers asked for details, and the lawyer grew horrified as he learned of the damage to his friend's mind.

"Good heavens! How distressing!" Ivers patted his face with a handkerchief. "Is there any hope of a recovery?"

"Unlikely," I said. "In any case, given his overall bad health… I don't know if you were aware…"

Ivers nodded. "He was diagnosed with cancer about seven months ago. They said it would be unlikely that he would make it to Christmas. Poor fellow. We'd often talked about what we'd do during our retirements. Thaddeus thought of moving to a warmer climate. And now… Would you happen to know which hospital they took him to? I should like to visit him."

I provided him with the requested information, and Ivers nodded and excused himself, noting that he had to meet with a client. As he walked away from us, Holmes called out to him, "By the way, Mr. Ivers. Did you never think of talking to the police about your missing friend?"

Ivers looked horrified. "Of course not. A gentleman never has anything to do with police if he can help it."

Once Ivers turned around the corner and out of sight, Holmes murmured to me, "He's lying, of course."

"Whatever makes you say that, Holmes?"

"A man like that doesn't just assume that his missing terminally ill friend will be all right and does nothing, no matter how much he dislikes the police. No, there's more to it than that. He's hiding something important, and I rather suspect that he's bribed the valet Tenners as well."

"Do you have a reason for those suspicions?"

"Tenners was nervous, and clearly had something weighing on his conscience. My guess is that Ivers wanted to keep Tenners from raising the alarm. Perhaps he made a threat, or more likely, suggested that it was not in Tenners' interests to create a potential scandal, and slipped him a little money to assuage his conscience."

"Do you really think that Ivers harmed his friend?"

"No," Holmes frowned. "I don't. First of all, Ivers is not the sort of man who allows his own hands to get dirty, especially not with blood. I have a feeling that there's a significant link or two or three in the chain that we're missing." He paused and looked reflective. "Watson, do you remember the positioning of the wound? The direction of the thrust of the ice pick?"

I needed a moment to search my memory. "The bit of metal was pointing downwards, wasn't it?"

"It was. And Merridew was a small man. The stab came from an upwards direction. Which means that either his assailant was diminutive, or…"

At first I thought that Holmes was pausing for dramatic effect, but after time passed with no continuation, I realized that my friend was concentrating. After a few people stared at Holmes for acting like a statue, I gave him a little nudge, prompting him to say, "What I can't understand is, why didn't the assailant follow Merridew to finish the job? Why didn't he strike again with another weapon, or why not restrain him somehow? After all, the odds were likely that his erratic behavior would catch the attention of a police officer. Surely the villain could have caught up with an elderly, injured, seriously ill man. Unless…" Thankfully, Holmes didn't try my patience with too long a pause. "Watson! I've got it! The assailant was in a wheelchair!"

I begged him for some explanation.

"It makes perfect sense. Why didn't Merridew's attacker follow him out the door and try to kill him again? Because he couldn't, Watson! Whoever did this was too weak in the legs to go after him, though the would-be killer was strong enough to stab him with an ice pick. We must go back to The Golden Nectarine immediately and search the neighborhood."

"For what, Holmes?"

"For a ramp, Watson! A private home with an entrance designed for someone in a wheelchair!"

As we began the journey back to The Golden Nectarine, I informed Holmes that I thought that he was making a logical leap here, and I was surprised to see that he agreed with me. "Indeed, Watson, I may be going beyond the limits of pure logic here. I could be putting two and two together and making five, or even five million. If I get egg on my face, you have my permission to record my humiliation with total accuracy in one of your literary endeavors. In the meantime, let us see what my deductive leaps produce."

We spent twenty minutes walking around the neighborhood surrounding The Golden Nectarine in a spiral, until Holmes yelped in triumph. "A ramp, Watson! This house has a ramp!"

He noticed the ramp from about twenty yards away. As I struggled to keep up with him, I reminded him that there are many people in London in wheelchairs. "I am well aware of that, Watson," he replied, "but if this does not prove to be the domicile in question, then we shall simply have to look elsewhere. If we have beaten the odds and this is indeed the spot we're searching for, then a young, pretty woman wearing rather too much inexpensive makeup will answer the door for us."

I was too intrigued not to ask, "How on earth did you deduce that, Holmes?"

"Did you not notice the mark on Ivers' neck, Watson? Cheap rouge, the kind a young woman of modest background will slather on in an attempt to get the attention she desires. Ivers has a wedding ring, and in any event, a barrister of that standing will have been prudent in his selection of a wife in his youth, but rather more reckless in his selection of a mistress in his later years. A respectable barrister's wife would not coat herself with that sort of cosmetic, nor would Ivers approve of his daughter adorning herself in such a manner." Having reached the house, Holmes immediately bent over the hand rail at the side of the ramp and began to sniff it. "Aha! Silver polish, Watson, a faint but noticeable lingering aroma. This rail is base metal, the only reason for silver polish being there is if poor Merridew gripped it on his way out, having dropped his recently polished cane after the attack."

"Sir? What are you doing?" The front door opened, and a pretty young woman appeared in the entryway. She was tall, with long honey-colored hair and her face was indeed liberally coated with rouge, though I lacked the experience with makeup to tell the cost of this coloring.

Holmes drew himself up with remarkable dignity and replied, "I am here to speak to you, Miss, about your friendship with Mr. Ivers, as well as his friend Justice Merridew."

Even under all of that rouge, it was obvious that the girl had blanched at Ivers' name, though curiously the name of Merridew did not appear to affect her. Indeed, after displaying clear confusion for a few moments, she replied, with palpable honesty, "I've never met a Justice Merridew."

"But you *do* know a Mr. Ivers, the barrister," Holmes pounced. "Come, come. There is no point in denying it. You were seen together."

The girl looked troubled. "What do you want from me?"

"Only the truth, young lady, nothing more. And I think that if you would be so kind as to let us inside, and allow us to speak to the resident of this house who uses a wheelchair, we might be able to clear up this entire unfortunate situation."

The girl seemed hesitant to budge, though I cannot say that I blamed her. My friend was playing an excellent bluff, but if she called it, he would be unable to produce any solid evidence to support his theories, nor would he be able to even identify her by her name.

Fortunately, a reedy voice called out from behind her. "Let them in, Millicent. There's no point in dragging this out much longer."

The girl we now knew as Millicent silently stepped backwards and gestured for us to enter. It was not a luxurious or even well-maintained home, but it was obviously a place of modest comfort. Millicent led us into a small parlor, where a woman sat in one corner in a wheelchair, sipping a lemon squash. This woman could not have been too much older than fifty, but she was clearly in declining health, and if my initial impressions were correct, she was not long for this world. "Cancer," she replied, reading my mind. "It started in my throat and spread throughout my entire body. The doctors give me one to two months. I think that's generous." She sipped her lemon squash. "You're Sherlock Holmes and Dr. Watson. I've seen your pictures in the newspaper. Did the judge's family hire you to find out what happened to him?"

"No, he showed up at my home himself."

"Is he all right?"

"No, he is not. His memory has been utterly destroyed."

"So he didn't accuse me?"

"He could not. He was unaware of his own condition."

"Meaning both the wound I inflicted on him and the cancer?"

"That is correct. You're confessing to stabbing him with the ice pick, then?"

"I might as well. I'll never see the hangman's rope, though perhaps it would be less painful than this. In a way, I might have done him a favor by sparing him some of the knowledge of his own ailment."

"I am not certain that he would see it that way," Holmes replied with evident disapproval.

"No, he probably wouldn't." The woman took another sip of lemon squash. "My doctor tells me to keep drinking this. It's supposed to soothe my burning throat. It does help, but only if it's nice and cold, so I have to keep adding little chips of ice to it. That's why I had the pick handy a few nights ago. Millicent provides me with a small lump of ice, and I keep breaking off little chunks to put in my drink. Or I did, before I broke the implement." She looked at Holmes searchingly. "Do you even know my name?"

"I do not."

"It's Mattie Allend. Just call me "Mattie," not "Mrs. Allend," if you please. I've never been one for formality, and I've never had a husband. I'm just trying to look after my daughter." Mattie pointed at Millicent. "Millie knows nothing about what happened, aside from the fact that there was suddenly a hat and coat and scarf and walking stick she needed to hide away when she came home from babysitting the neighbor's brat. Is that clear? She's totally innocent. Of attempted murder at least. I suppose you've noticed that she's five months in the family way." I had observed that, but I had thought it indelicate to mention it.

"That was my doing, you know. I told her, Millie, you're a very pretty girl, but you're not very clever and husbands are more trouble than they're worth. If you want to be taken care of, you find yourself an older, prosperous career man with a wife and an

86

impeccable reputation, and you get yourself in the family way and make him take care of you and the kid. Not a nobleman, though. Those titled yobs are often flat broke, and they've no sense of paternal responsibility. I learned that the hard way with my first kid, my son. With Millie, I was cleverer. I found a Harley Street physician who liked me and didn't care much for his wife, but couldn't afford a scandal. Luckily for me Millie's the spitting image of him."

"That was your goal with Mr. Ivers?"

"It was. And a good plan, too. Ivers was besotted with her, and a few nights ago she told him he was about to become a father again. Well, he promised he'd take care of her, but she had to promise to never let his wife know about her or the baby. That was easy enough. She needs an income, not a scandal. It all would've been all right, but then that judge saw Ivers kissing her on the front stoop a few nights ago. The judge stopped his carriage and hurried out, but he was sick and slow. By the time he crossed the street Ivers was long gone, and Millie was on her way to babysit at the neighbor's. He must not have seen her leave, because the judge started pounding on the door, demanding to speak to her. He was making such a fuss, I felt I had to let him in. He hung up his coat and hat, and we had a nice, civilized talk for a while. He didn't approve of me, but I couldn't care less about a judge's opinion of my character unless I'm standing in the dock. Then he started insisting on going to

Ivers' wife and telling her everything. I told him not to be a woolly-headed fool, that he would ruin everything for Millie, but he insisted, he said Mrs. Ivers was his cousin, and he couldn't keep the news that her husband was going to have a baby out of wedlock from her. We argued, things got a bit heated, and I panicked a teensy bit and struck him with the ice pick. Next thing I know, I'm holding the handle in my hand, and he's stumbled out the door before I can get to him. I expected him to collapse and die right in front of the house. I've no idea how he managed to make his way to your home."

Mattie drained her glass. "Well, that's all, then. Millie came home an hour later and wanted to know what the clothing and cane were doing here, and I told her that at my age, a woman doesn't have to explain or justify her relationships with men. As she was gathering up everything, Ivers came back to the house, saying his friend hadn't come to dinner. He saw the clothes and cane, I took him aside, and told him for Millie's sake, he mustn't ask too many questions about Merridew. I implied that Millie might be unjustly blamed for his disappearance, so Ivers kept mum and paid the manservant a bit to do the same. So now you know everything. This was all for my daughter. I wanted to see her taken care of before I died. What'll happen to me now? It seems a waste of taxpayer money to pay for a trial. I'm going to a much more final courtroom soon enough."

Holmes gave her a long, penetrating gaze that was not completely devoid of sympathy. "I shall tell the authorities everything, and perhaps they shall be merciful."

They were. After a doctor confirmed that Mattie was not long for this world, Scotland Yard decided not to make an arrest, and the unfortunate woman died just over a week later in her own home. Merridew was placed in a nursing home, and passed away from complications connected to his cancer six months later. By the end, his memory grew more and more abominable, until he finally was unable to finish a sentence more than three words long without losing his train of thought. It was a tragic end to a reportedly brilliant legal mind.

Holmes did not expect a fee for his efforts, so it was a pleasant surprise when a substantial check arrived in the mail a week later. Its sender, Mr. Ivers, thanked us for finding out what had really happened to his friend, minimizing the fallout of the scandal, and asked us to protect the feelings of his wife and children. Holmes, caring little for the check but understanding the need to protect the innocent members of the Ivers family from embarrassment, agreed. And so, I write this account of the case solely for myself, and as soon as I finish, I will take it down to the vaults of Cox and Co. bank and lock it away in a battered tin dispatch-box, where it will rest in peace with dozens of other cases.

Intruders at Baker Street

"When a woman thinks that her house is on fire, her instinct is at once to rush to the thing which she values most. It is a perfectly overpowering impulse, and I have more than once taken advantage of it. In the case of the Darlington substitution scandal it was of use to me, and also in the Arnsworth Castle business. A married woman grabs at her baby; an unmarried one reaches for her jewel-box. "

— "A Scandal in Bohemia"

It is with some surprise and a bit of pleasure that I acknowledge that 221B Baker Street has become inextricably linked in the popular imagination with my friend Sherlock Holmes and myself. With the exception of certain politicians and members of the Royal Family, is there anybody else in England whose address is so well-known and iconic?

Recently, I realized that I had no idea who the inhabitants of 221B before my esteemed colleague were. We never received mail in any of their names, and Mrs. Hudson never mentioned them. I thought of asking our dear landlady about them, and then realized that I really had no interest in Baker Street B.H.– Before Holmes.

It was late January of 1887. After my marriage and my moving out of 221B, my visits to Holmes and the old homestead were far more infrequent than I would have liked. It was with great pleasure and some confusion that I received a note from Holmes one evening, telling me:

COME TO 221B THIS EVENING– CANCEL ALL OTHER PLANS.

–

S.H.

If there was any trace of resentment in me at being ordered about by my friend, it was far overshadowed by my excitement at the prospect of another adventure with Sherlock Holmes. And so, after informing my wife that I would not be home for dinner and assisting a rather querulous old woman with her chilblains, I made my way to 221B to see my friend.

As I knocked on the door, I expected to see the familiar face of Mrs. Hudson greeting me. Instead, a much younger, taller, and lankier woman answered the door, speaking in a high-pitched Cockney voice that was utterly unlike anything that ever came out of Mrs. Hudson's.

"What're ya doing 'ere?" Mrs. Hudson would never have addressed a caller in such a manner.

"I'm here to see Sherlock Holmes," I informed her, wondering if Mrs. Hudson was ill and had recruited this person to handle her duties until she had recovered.

"'Oo's that?"

"Sherlock Holmes. The detective."

"Never 'eard h'of 'im. 'Oo're you?"

"I'm Doctor Watson."

"We don't need ya. No h'one's sick 'ere."

I was beginning to detect a touch of asperity creeping into my voice. "Now see here, I lived here for over five years, and–"

"Well, 'ow h'am h'I supposed t'know that? Hi've only been 'ere since this mornin', 'aven't h'I?"

My initial suspicions appeared to be confirmed. "Where is Mrs. Hudson?"

"Never 'eard h'of 'er."

"But this is her house. She's the landlady here."

"H'I don't know wot to tell you, Doc, but I never met a Mrs. 'Udson. No h'one mentioned 'er name h'all day. The Darlingtons 'ired me. This h'is their 'ouse."

I was completely blindsided. Could Mrs. Hudson have sold 221B without my knowledge? Who were the Darlingtons?

"Young lady, I realize that you cannot be aware of the history of a house where you have just become employed, but I can assure that that Mrs. Hudson has owned this building for years, and Mr. Sherlock Holmes is the well-known resident of these rooms. I should like to speak to him."

"'Oo can't. There's no wot's-'is-name 'ere. Just Mr. and Mrs. Darlington and 'is brother. And they've left orders not to be disturbed."

My patience with this woman had just reached its limit. "What is your name?"

"Hi'm Mrs. Turner. Least, h'I think h'I still h'am. "'Aven't seen him h'in h'a long, long time, but that don't mean my name changes back, does h'it?"

I was fairly certain that abandonment didn't necessitate a return to a woman's maiden name, but I was in no mood to ponder the intricacies of marriage law and customs. "Mrs. Turner, it is of the utmost importance that I should be allowed into 221B. Please allow me to come in. I shall make sure that you are not blamed for anything."

Mrs. Turner pursed her thin lips. "Well… h'I don't know…" Frustration started to seep into every fiber of my being, until I noticed that Mrs. Turner's right hand, dangling at her waist, was clenching and unclenching. Picking up on the hint, I rummaged in my coat pocket, extracted a few shiny coins, and slipped them into her outstretched fingers. With a triumphant smirk, Mrs. Turner stepped to one side, saying, "H'if h'anybody h'asks, you pushed past me."

"Fair enough." I took the stairs two at a time, and when I reached the door, I knocked on it. When no one answered after several moments, I seized the knob and entered. What I saw astounded me.

Three strangers, two men and a woman, were seated around the fire, surrounded by papers. Few of Holmes' possessions remained in their normal places, as the entire room looked as if it had been well rifled-through, though nothing was broken. The coal-scuttle had been dragged out to between the chairs, and all three invaders were smoking the cigars Holmes habitually kept there. From the large quantity of butts and ash littering some glass dishes that Holmes used for scientific experiments, and the emptied Persian slipper thrown into one corner of the room, they had nearly gone through Holmes' supply of tobacco.

"What are you doing here?" I asked.

At first, all three appeared unsettled. Then the larger of the two men stood up, attempting to appear calm and controlled. "I'm Roger Darlington. This is my home."

"It most certainly is not. This is Mr. Sherlock Holmes' home. I know this for a fact. You have no business being here."

"Nonsense! We've lived here for months!" This high-pitched declaration came from the woman, who was presumably Mrs. Darlington.

As I was aware that there was absolutely no truth to this statement, I knew at once that the three were liars. I was about to step forward and demand answers, when I abruptly realized that Holmes and Mrs. Hudson were very likely in danger. I immediately stepped out of the room and called down to the substitute housekeeper. "Mrs. Turner! Please go out immediately and fetch the nearest policeman. We need the authorities immediately." At first Mrs. Turner looked disinclined to leave, but I dipped into my pocket, selected the largest coin I could find, and tossed it down to her. Mrs. Turner sprinted out of the house the second the money touched her palm.

I whirled around to confront the interlopers, only to see a very large revolver pointed directly at me. The other man, not Roger Darlington, was pointing it at me. "Come back in here and don't make a sound," he snarled.

I had no choice but to reenter the room, and sat down when the man gestured me into a chair.

"Who are you?" he asked.

"I am Doctor John Watson. I am a close friend of Sherlock Holmes, and I lived at 221B with him for many years. I know that this is his home, I know that you have no business here, and now I wish to know who you are and what you are doing here." I was in no position to make demands, but I was in no mood to cower in front of these people.

The man with the gun made the most unpleasant smile I've ever seen. "You can call me Jack Darlington. You met Roger, and that's Eva there. And what we're doing here is none of your business."

I wasn't about to be cowed into silence, even if he was holding a gun. "Where are Holmes and Mrs. Hudson? Are they all right?"

"They're fine for now."

"Jack! Don't tell him any more!" Roger Darlington crossed the room. "We'll tie him up, and as soon as we can we'll put him with the others."

"Don't bother with that! Just take care of him!" If this was representative of Eva Darlington's character, I did not envy Roger for having this vicious creature as his wife.

"That would be most unwise," I informed them. "The walls here are definitely not soundproof. Do you see those bullet-holes in the wall there? Mr. Holmes is in the habit of practicing his pistol-shooting in this very room. Every time he has done so, he has drawn a great deal of unwanted attention. Pull that trigger, and a hundred angry neighbors will come rushing to 221B to complain. Can you fend off all of those people, with at most five bullets left in that gun? I should remind you, they all know who Holmes is, and they'll be wondering why you're here instead of him." This was a bluff. The neighbors have grown used to Holmes' pistol-shooting, and they stopped complaining about the noise years ago. Gunshots had long ceased to raise eyebrows in the neighborhood. But the Darlingtons didn't know that, and they appeared unsettled.

Presently, we heard the front door slamming. "That's the police," I informed them. "Can you really afford to risk a constable coming in and seeing you holding a gun?"

Roger tugged at Jack's elbow. "Go into the back room. We'll handle this." Jack obeyed, and disappeared into Holmes' bedroom just as Mrs. Turner and a policeman appeared in the doorway.

"Hello! What are you doing here?" Roger asked.

"This woman here says you needed a policeman," the officer of the law replied.

I didn't want to waste any time. "Sir! These people are criminals. This is the home of Mr. Sherlock Holmes, and they have kidnapped him and his landlady. I don't know what they're doing here, but there is a third member of this gang of crooks in the room back there, and he has a gun. Mrs. Turner, please run out and get as many policemen as you can! I will pay you for your efforts later."

Mrs. Turner turned to go, but the policeman stopped her. "Just a minute. Stay where you are while I ask a few questions. What's going on here?"

Roger Darlington affected a worried air. "I'm so glad you've come here. This man is clearly deranged. He burst into my home half an hour ago, rummaged through our things, and he refuses to leave."

Mrs. Darlington started sniffling. "He tried to take advantage of me! Fortunately my husband fought him off!"

"Did he now?" The policeman started growling at me.

"Sir, they are lying to you!"

"Are you calling that lady a liar?"

She's no lady, I thought to myself. I was starting to feel some trepidation. Perhaps something about the Darlingtons was more convincing to this policeman than I was, and I feared that unless I could completely win over this fellow, it was more likely than not that I would be dragged to the police station and kept there until I could prove that I was telling the truth. And in the meantime, what of Holmes and Mrs. Hudson? It might be hours, even days before I could vindicate myself, and for all I knew, my friends could be in mortal peril.

I decided to prove my story quickly. "Sir, I have worked with Inspector Lestrade of Scotland Yard on many occasions. He can verify the fact that this is truly Sherlock Holmes' residence."

There was a flicker of a response in the policeman's face, but it only lasted a moment. "I'm not familiar with an Inspector Lestrade. But it seems to me that this is a well-dressed couple. They don't look like burglars."

"Don't you see the mess in here? They've been searching this place!"

"That's true," Eva Darlington answered. "We're looking for... a little diamond that fell out of one of my rings. I know it must be somewhere in our home, but we don't know where. I don't want a precious gemstone to be thrown out or lost forever, so we're performing a careful and methodical search. I admit things are a bit messy, but we'll straighten everything out once we find my diamond."

I couldn't believe it. That mutton-headed oaf in a helmet was nodding. "That sounds reasonable to me."

"Don't you see they changed their story? First they lied and said I rummaged through their things, then they said they're looking for a mythical diamond. They're clearly lying!" If the young bobby heard a word I said, he didn't show any signs of having done so.

Roger Darlington seized the opportunity. "This man is clearly not in his right mind. He's been blathering on and on about his imaginary friend and we cannot get him to leave, and he's threatened my wife. I'd be very grateful if you could be kind enough to take him down to the police station."

"I'll do that, sir. Sorry that you've been troubled by this man." The fool put his hand on my arm. "If you'll come with me, mister!"

"Just a minute!" I whipped Holmes' letter out of my pocket. "Look at the return address on this envelope! Sherlock Holmes! 221B Baker Street!"

This stopped him. He stared at the envelope for a moment, and for the first time in a while I had hope that I might be able to convince him that I was in the right.

"He probably wrote that himself," Eva Darlington scoffed.

I have never felt such feelings of loathing towards a woman as I did at that moment towards Eva Darlington.

"Yes, he probably did, didn't he?" The moron's face actually brightened.

I was reminding myself that it would be unwise to descend to the use of physical violence to extract myself from this situation when inspiration struck me. "Look here, the Darlingtons claim to have lived here for years. Can they produce a single piece of mail with their names on it that was delivered to this address?"

The look of horror on the Darlingtons' faces told me that the tide was turning in my favor. My eye wandered over to the fireplace, and I spotted my salvation. Turning back to the policeman, I confidently informed him, "These frauds claim they've never heard of Sherlock Holmes and that I've only been here a short while. Take a look at the center of the wooden mantelpiece. You see that jack-knife sticking out of it? Look at all of the envelopes that have been pierced with that blade. Take a good look at them, and see who they're addressed to. And if you still doubt me, check the postmarks. You'll see that they were delivered at least a couple of days ago, long before the Darlingtons claimed that I first darkened their doorstep."

The policeman shuffled over to the fireplace, extracted the jack-knife with some difficulty, and peered down at the name written on the envelopes in the addressee section. "Mr. Sherlock Holmes," he muttered with a look of pure incredulity on his face.

Before I could cry out a warning, Roger Darlington seized the fireplace poker and swung it through the air, striking the policeman on the back of the neck.

It looked to me as if he'd moderated the force of his blow, just enough to knock the man out, but not enough to kill. Mrs. Turner started screaming, and I moved towards her, but Eva Darlington practically flew across the room and knocked Mrs. Turner to the floor, ripping the cap of Mrs. Turner's head and stuffing it into her mouth.

I made a very quick decision. I could try to disarm Roger Darlington, or I could try to save Mrs. Turner from Eva Darlington. But whichever Darlington I attacked (and my sense of honor reeled at the thought of fighting a woman), there was another factor in play. The third Darlington, Jack. At any moment, he could burst out of Holmes's room with a loaded gun.

I chafed at the prospect of retreating, but I realized that I had no choice but to flee and gather reinforcements as soon as possible to rescue the policeman and Mrs. Turner. I rushed out the door as fast as I could, realizing that Roger Darlington was running after me, brandishing the poker.

Practically flying down the stairs, I sailed out the front door and down the street. After sprinting another hundred yards, I became aware that Roger Darlington was no longer chasing me. I sought out familiar faces and competent members of law enforcement as quickly as I could, and a little over ten minutes later I returned to 221B with a passel of allies in tow.

The policeman was still lying in front of the fireplace and I confirmed that he was merely unconscious and not in mortal danger. There was a nasty lump on Mrs. Turner's forehead, almost certainly inflicted by the brutish Roger Darlington's poker. Mrs. Turner was not badly injured, and as I examined her, one of her eyes fluttered open and she muttered, "'Oo wouldn't be thinkin' about taking your coins back from me while hi'm h'out cold, would'oo?"

I smiled. Despite my initial misgivings, I was starting to like Mrs. Turner.

The policemen, far more competent than their knocked-out colleague, searched 221B, and then the rest of the building. There was no trace of any of the Darlingtons. Holmes and Mrs. Hudson were nowhere to be found, either.

The injured policeman and Mrs. Turner were taken to the hospital for observation, and I started searching for some clue as to why the Darlingtons had installed themselves at 221B, and what they might have done with my friends. As I sorted through the papers that had been strewn about, I realized that they had completely torn apart Holmes' index of assorted people and subjects. The index was so vast and comprehensive that it was impossible for me, who had only had a brief glimpse of its contents now and then, to identify what, if anything, was missing.

The police officers and my other colleagues had left, confident that I was safe on my own. I spent the better part of an hour poring through 221B, not knowing exactly what I was looking for, but hoping for the best. Finally, I thought to look inside the wastepaper basket, and discovered a small paper bag with the name "Bunder's Bonbons" stamped on it. Inside were a few fragments of a sickly-floral-smelling hard candy. I had never known Holmes to partake in that sort of sweet, and after a minute's reflection, decided that it was the closest thing to a clue that I had.

A few inquiries, and I had the address of "Bunder's Bonbons." I decided not to inform the police, as I had no solid proof that this was anything more than a scrap of litter that had inadvertently blown into the house, and Holmes had disposed of it.

Still, if there was any chance at all that it might lead me to my missing friends...

I hired a carriage and asked the driver to speed as fast as humanly possible to my home, where I informed my wife of my destination and instructed her to call the police if I did not get in touch with her within three hours. After making sure that my service revolver was fully loaded and securely in my pocket with a supply of additional ammunition, I returned to my carriage and requested that the driver travel more quickly than he had ever done before in his life.

In half an hour I had reached Bunder's Bonbons, a seedy little shop in a run-down part of London. After instructing the carriage-driver to wait for me, I stepped inside, where an acne-scarred young man slouched behind the counter.

"Can I get anything for you, sir?"

I sized him up, and decided to confront him with a blunt question. "Do you know anybody by the name of Darlington?"

"Sure, they rent part of our basement. Why do you ask?"

I was astounded. Part of me expected this young man to be in league with the Darlingtons, and I hadn't expected him to be so obliging with his information. Wary of a trap, I asked him to describe the Darlingtons. His words exactly matched the three people I had seen. When I inquired as to why they rented rooms in their basement, he shrugged, and replied:

"They say they need the space to house some things of theirs. We've got more room than we can use, and we need the money, so it's a good deal for us. Would you be interested in renting some space down there? I can give you a good price."

I expressed an interest and asked to be shown down there. I made sure the young man went first. He seemed harmless enough, but I was prepared for a sudden attack, so as we made our way down the rickety, dark stairs into the moldy basement, I kept my hand on my revolver, just in case I was being led into an ambush.

The passageway was quite narrow, and I was trying to keep my coat from brushing against the stone walls, which even in the dim lantern light were covered with dust and grit and cobwebs. A few doors were spaced out on either side, but my guide led me to the very end of the corridor, to the only door that was fastened shut with a lock.

"I don't have the key," he informed me. "But this is the Darlingtons' storage room. Can I show you one of the other empty rooms?"

Before I could answer, I heard a couple of thumps behind the door. "What was that?"

"Couldn't tell you. Maybe it's rats. There were a couple of big ones a couple of months ago that got into the peppermint rock. I thought I got rid of 'em, but you never know with rats now, do you?"

My instincts told me that the noise in question wasn't being made by rodents. I pushed past the young man and rapped on the door. I heard more thumps in reply, and despite the fact that I used none of Holmes' famous methods of deduction, I was quite certain that I knew what was behind that door.

"Holmes! Mrs. Hudson! Get away from the door if you can!" I withdrew my service revolver, advised my young colleague to cover his ears, positioned the gun, and shot open the lock. The door remained slightly stuck, so I planted my feet, delivered a mighty kick to door, and sent it swinging backwards.

A pair of muffled voices came out of the darkness. Taking the lantern, I inched into the room, and found Holmes and Mrs. Hudson lying on the floor, separately bound and gagged. The knots were a challenge, but fortunately my young associate lent me the use of his pocket knife. I cut Mrs. Hudson free first, and it only took a few more moments to release Holmes.

My friends were unharmed, but sore and dirty, and it took a bit of massaging to get the blood flowing back into their legs, allowing them to rise to their feet. We all made our way upstairs, and after Holmes and Mrs. Hudson had seen to some pressing needs and cleaned themselves up a bit, I started to recount my experiences that evening to them. After just a few minutes, Mrs. Hudson was shocked at hearing of strangers in her house, and highly suspicious of Mrs. Turner, so she insisted on returning to 221B immediately in order to examine how much damage the Darlingtons had done. I placed her in the carriage and sent her back home, while Holmes and I made our way to a nearby public house for some refreshment.

Holmes helped himself to a plate of dark brown bread and very pale cheese with rather more delight than I felt this simple fare deserved, though I could understand his hunger. I explained my experiences in more detail as Holmes ate and we both drank, and by the time I finished, not a crumb of bread or a speck of cheese remained on the plate.

"I must congratulate you," Holmes told me right after he downed the remaining contents of his glass. "You have performed admirably tonight. I freely admit that you have distinguished yourself far better than I have this evening."

"Holmes, what happened to you? Who are the Darlingtons and why did they take over 221B?

"This will take a bit of time. I suggest that you take a moment to write out a note informing your wife that you have found us and everybody is quite all right, and that she shouldn't worry if you don't come home tonight until quite late. I believe I see an old acquaintance of mine in that corner over there who will be happy to serve as a messenger in exchange for five shillings."

Realizing this was a good idea, I followed Holmes' suggestion, and noticed that Holmes was scribbling a note of his own. I was about to ask him what he was writing, but I reasoned that he would tell me as soon as he was prepared to tell me. As soon as the messages were written and sent on their ways, Holmes returned to the table with another pair of drinks and leaned back in his chair. "I shall begin by answering your second question first. The Darlingtons are a family of con artists, two brothers and one brother's wife. I'm quite certain that Darlington is not their real name, and the first names Roger, Eva, and Jack are just as likely to be spurious, but that does not matter at present. For the moment, we can use those titles. The Darlingtons specialize in a very specific branch of fraud. They are professional substitutes."

"What on earth are professional substitutes?"

"The word "imposters" would be just as apt a term, I suppose. The Darlington collect their ill-gotten gains by pretending to be other people, and they insert themselves into unsuspecting people's lives in order to enrich themselves at others' expense. They find prominent people whose faces aren't very well-known, and assume their identities in order to get ahold of as much money as possible. They like to specialize in titled individuals living abroad. Lord and Lady Eggmere have lived in India or nearly twenty years, and the Darlingtons posed as the Eggmeres for a few days, claiming that they were back for a brief visit to take care of business matters. They wound up cleaning out one of the Eggmere's bank accounts, and took out several enormous loans from both respectable financial institutions and shady dealers in the Eggmere's names. As soon as suspicions started being raised, they went into hiding. In another case, a Mr. and Mrs. Totnurse left some valuable heirlooms at a jeweler's to be reset while they were off for a month-long holiday in Paris. A couple of days before the real Totnurses returned, the Darlingtons arrived at the jeweler's, disguised as the Totnurses, and collected all the necklaces and rings. They have been in business for over three years, and they are very careful to space out their crimes with four to six-month breaks between them, so as to avoid suspicion. I believe they have accumulated a considerable fortune by now."

"How did you learn about them?"

"One of their victims is a member of an extremely prominent family, who was temporarily exiled to Kenya for some potentially embarrassing indiscretions. It was hoped that after a couple of years of managing a coffee farm, this reckless young man could be allowed back into polite London society. However, one of the Darlingtons pretended to be him, and visited some of the most infamous moneylenders around, taking out loans that ran into tens of thousands of pounds. Well, the family, who for reasons I am sure you will understand I will not name even to you, worried that even though their prodigal son was completely innocent in this matter, that any sort of scandal attaching to his name might lead to an extended delay in the errant young man's return to England, where he would make a prudent marriage to some well-off young woman. The family in question, though very respectable, is in somewhat limited financial circumstances, and they lack the liquid assets to pay off the debts the Darlingtons racked up recently."

"Surely the family would not plunge themselves into bankruptcy in order to pay off loans taken out by criminals under false pretenses."

"You forget the delicate bubble reputations of high society, Watson. In these circles, the slightest connection to a crime is a most fearful scandal, even if one is called into court solely as a witness. The merest connection with wrongdoing is to be avoided at all costs. If false loans were taken out in the errant scion's name, it might potentially affect the family's credit, and they need to take out a perfectly respectable bank loan in order to pay for the repairs to the roof of their family estate. Not only that, but the loan sharks do not care one whit for the fact that the person who borrowed money in the young man's name was an impostor. The loans were taken out four months ago, and they are accumulating interest by the week. The moneylenders want to be paid back immediately, and they're willing to make quite the fuss if they don't get recompensed sooner rather than later."

"That hardly seems fair."

"It isn't. That is why the eldest daughter of the family in question came to me, asking me to help them track down the criminals and retrieve the money if possible. That way, the ill-gotten funds could go back to the moneylenders, and the family would be willing to swallow the costs of the additional interest payments."

"So what happened?"

"I interviewed a handful of the loan sharks, and they managed to provide me with some useful information from snippets of small talk the imposter had made with them. He'd mentioned lunching at the Savoy, and when I spoke to the maître d' and gave him a description of the man and his clothing, he told me that the man dined there regularly. I frequented the Savoy for a few days, until the maître d' pointed out that the man in question had returned. After he had finished his meal, I followed him to the house he shared with his brother and sister-in-law. I wondered if they kept their ill-gotten gains at their home– after all, they could not deposit their stolen funds into a bank without drawing unwanted attention, so I fancied that I would try to make them retrieve their hidden cache of loot through a ruse. I wrote a quick note and sent it to you, thinking that I might need your help later in the evening. After surreptitiously looking in the window and finding all three of the Darlingtons there, I decided to climb up to the roof and block the top of their chimney. It didn't take long for the house to fill with smoke, but my hopes of seeing the three of them run out of the building carrying enormous sacks of stolen cash were dashed. I did notice that Mrs. Darlington was clasping her jewel-box close to her heart. I suspect that the box was filled with illicitly-obtained jewelry. The larger of the Darlingtons noticed the plank of wood I'd placed over their chimney, and immediately started climbing up the roof to remove it. While he was up there, he must have seen me crouched in the hiding place that was not as secure as I'd hoped. When he climbed down, he slowly ambled in my direction, calling out something about buying some cigarettes, and then lunged at where I was hiding, catching me off guard and pinioning me. I might have been able to fight him off, but before I could do anything the other two Darlingtons surrounded me. Mrs. Darlington identified me at once– how she recognized me I'm not sure, but I suspect that she read one of your colorful accounts of my investigations. They knew I was after them, and when Mrs. Darlington asked what they were going to do with me, one of the brothers growled "This!" and struck me firmly on the back of the neck. When I regained consciousness, I was hopelessly tied up in a room with no light and no way of figuring out where I was. After an hour or so, the door opened and the infernal family threw a similarly bound and gagged Mrs. Hudson into the room with me. With the light that the Darlingtons brought, I could see that the room was filled with several large steamer trunks. From the way the Darlingtons handled some of them, I suspect that some were filled with cash, and others were filled with heavier items. At a guess, I'd say that one of them held the equipment they used to create the false identification papers they used in their impostures, and others contained jewelry and other valuable items they'd stolen over the years. They said nothing to us, and I had no idea if they intended to have someone come to rescue us as some point, or if they simply decided to leave us there and let us die of starvation. I spent hours trying to free myself, gaining nothing but a few rope burns in the process. Then you came by and saved the day, my dear fellow, and for that you have my eternal gratitude. Thank you."

I savored the complement for a moment. Eventually, my curiosity triumphed over my need to bask in this rare bit of praise. "Why did they move into 221B? What did they hope to accomplish by that? And why did they hire Mrs. Turner?"

"They must have learned my address from your surprisingly popular accounts of our exploits, and they may have thought it wise to

114

look through my belongings to see if I'd left some notes to tell them just how much I knew about their crimes, and how safe it was for them to remain in England. They are sufficiently inured to violence to knock out innocent people and to threaten them with firearms, but to the best of my knowledge and belief, they have never actually killed anybody, and they may not have the stomachs to torture someone for information, either. They probably figured it was easier and more effective to search my rooms than to interrogate me. As you told me, Watson, they were rummaging through the contents of my comprehensive index. When they discovered it, they realized that it could potentially be a gold mine of information for them, as it contained valuable information on many people, including potential new victims for them to impersonate. In any case, they didn't know if I'd told anybody about the location of their home, so they decided it was not safe for them to return there. At some point, Mrs. Hudson caught them and knew they were up to no good, so they incapacitated her and smuggled her to their hideout. I dare say they selected the basement of the candy store to hold their ill-gotten gains because it was cheap to rent, the owners are not inquisitive, there's a back door leading to an alley that they could use to sneak in and out, and the basement of a sweet shop is the last place the police would look for a fortune in ill-gotten gains. The Darlingtons knew that they needed a little peace and quiet to sort through my index, so they quickly found a housekeeper who would turn away anybody coming to consult with me, and bring them some refreshment as they needed it."

"So now what will happen?"

"As you saw, I wrote a note that my acquaintance will deliver to Lestrade. They know that their home, their hideaway, and 221B are no longer secure for them. They retrieved several large trunks, and they cannot simply lug them around. Unless they have another hiding-place, which I think is unlikely, they will head for a port and set sail overseas, probably to Canada or the United States, though I cannot rule out some other location. Scotland Yard is best equipped to track them down, though we should make ourselves available to the authorities in case they need us to identify the Darlingtons."

Holmes was completely correct. Within two hours, Lestrade's men had caught the Darlingtons aboard a ship scheduled to set sail for Nova Scotia in the morning. In addition to the trunks filled with money and valuables, they found many of Holmes' notes from his index. They were clearly planning to continue their schemes by exploiting some prominent Canadians. Though they'd spent a fair portion of the stolen cash, the victims of the impostures all received the lion's share of their stolen goods back, and Holmes was able to prevent a scandal from impugning the good name of a prominent family.

116

Holmes and Mrs. Hudson suffered no lasting ill-effects from their confinement, and after interviewing Mrs. Turner, Holmes took a liking to her, and over the coming years, Mrs. Hudson routinely hired Mrs. Turner to take over her duties when she was out of town visiting relatives.

The young policeman who'd nearly sided with the Darlingtons over me spent a few days under observation in the hospital, but suffered no ill-effects. He had little talent for his profession, but he had influential relatives, so he was swiftly promoted to a supervisory position where he could do little harm.

I spent much of the next day helping Holmes straighten up his rooms, and after several hours of tidying, sorting, and re-alphabetizing Holmes' index, 221B looked exactly as it did before the Darlingtons took over the place. As I looked around 221B, I realized that not only could I not imagine anybody else living in this place, I never wanted anyone other than Holmes to live there, either.

The Heinous Half-Crowns

As I climbed the steps at 221B Baker Street that dreary autumn afternoon in 1899, I had no inkling that an adventure from a decade earlier would be continuing that evening. My work that day consisted of dealing with a half-dozen people with singularly unpleasant physical complaints, and I was looking forward to a quiet night in front of the fire with a hot dinner and a good book. My tiredness had made me forget that my long association with Sherlock Holmes meant that adventure could strike at any moment, especially when I was in most need of peace and quiet.

Just as I reached the second-highest step of the stairs, Holmes opened the door and met me with an excited gleam in his eye. "Evening, dear fellow. Are you hoping for a restful, relaxing evening? If so, you may want to go back down the stairs and visit your club. If you do choose to come inside our rooms, you will undoubtedly be drawn into a case that will take up the majority of the night, and you may not be able to get any sleep for quite a while."

If my wits had been sharper, I would have given Holmes a curt nod and turned on my heels. Instead, I walked straight into our rooms, barely hearing Holmes say, "Delighted you made the decision you did, Watson."

After I hung up my coat and hat and turned around, I became aware of a mountainous presence in the room. Holmes's brother Mycroft was sitting in our most comfortable chair, with the remains of a plate of Mrs. Hudson's rock cakes at his side. Mycroft met my gaze and asked. "Hello, Watson. A woman with boils, twins with colic, a man who cut himself shaving and got infected, and an elderly gentleman with a case of phlebitis. Am I correct?"

I was about to confirm his deductions, ask how he knew about my patients' complaints, and inform him that he had missed the middle-aged man with gout, but then I realized that patient confidentiality issues prevented me from saying anything, and told him so. Mycroft smiled, turned to his right, and said, "You see, Mr. Dacres? I told you that Doctor Watson can be trusted to be discreet."

I hadn't noticed Mr. Dacres until then. There could not have been a sharper physical contrast between the two men. Dacres was a tiny man, no more than five foot two, and he looked as if he'd never had a proper meal in his life. His voice was raspy and wheezy, and I immediately got the impression that he had a very low opinion of me. "How do we know that the doctor won't put everything he hears into one of his tawdry stories?"

Before I could take issue with his use of the word "tawdry," Mycroft informed him, "I can assure you that Doctor Watson has never published a word that hasn't been approved of by me. I can

119

name no fewer than thirteen cases connected to the British national interest where I have asked Watson to refrain from publishing a story, and he has always complied."

Dacres fixed a suspicious glare upon me, creating the impression that if an angel came down from Heaven and told him to trust me, he would still view me with suspicion. While I appreciated his need to be cautious, I was starting to feel a bit insulted when Holmes stepped in to defend my honor.

"Mr. Dacres, either you can decide to trust Watson, or you can kindly leave my rooms at once. If you wish my help, you must accept Watson's assistance as well. The choice is yours."

Despite Holmes' declaration, Dacres still seemed reluctant, until Mycroft slapped his beefy hand against the end table. "Enough prevarication, Dacres! We have an urgent matter at hand. Will you introduce yourself, or shall I?" When Dacres sulked, Mycroft groaned and turned to me. "Mr. Dacres is part of a department of British Intelligence that technically does not exist. The handful of individuals who know about it refer to it as the MPS. The Ministry for the Prevention of Scandal. For the last two decades, whenever a prominent member of the Government or the Royal Family does something reprehensible, Mr. Dacres jumps in to hush it up completely."

"Is he usually successful?" Holmes asked.

Mycroft shrugged. "About sixty percent of the time."

Holmes leaned back in his chair. "How much taxpayer money does the MPS spend covering up scandals?"

As Mycroft drummed his fingers, I could see the numbers and calculations flashing across his eyes. After a couple of moments, he pronounced, "About two million guineas a year. We usually chalk it up to war expenses." He turned to me. "Do you remember reading in the newspapers about how we had to send troops to Mount Kosciuszko last year to quell an uprising?"

"I did."

"There was no war there. We simply picked that area because it was far away and no one was going to visit it and discover that everything was perfectly peaceful. I wrote the dispatches from the frontlines myself under a pseudonym, and we gave a couple of dozen soldiers we could trust a handful of medals each in exchange for telling fictional war stories about the Battle of Mount Kosciuszko in public places. We needed to invent that military intervention in order to square the books after the MPS hushed up an incident involving three minor members of the Royal Family, two tiaras from the Crown Jewels where the diamonds had been removed and replaced with rhinestones, and two dead tigers at the London Zoo."

I had so many questions to ask, but Dacres was determined to leave my curiosity unquenched. "That's enough!" he barked.

"How many times have I told you never to speak to me in a tone like that?" Mycroft asked calmly. "Still, I can understand why Dacres might be reluctant to reveal have the details of the latest scandal revealed to the public."
"Thank you, Mycroft."

"I can understand your feelings, Dacres, but I don't agree with them in the least. If my brother is to help you out of a problem of your own making, he's going to need to know exactly why he's being called into the case." Mycroft continued, projecting his voice over Dacres' shrill protestations. "A week ago, a young man working as a secretary for a back-bencher Member of Parliament was kidnapped. His abductors requested a hundred pounds for his safe return, in gold or silver coins. Now, that young fellow was worth a ten-pound ransom at most, but unfortunately his mother is a very... *close friend* of several Cabinet members and some prominent members of the House of Lords. She threatened to kick up a nasty fuss if her darling boy wasn't returned home immediately and in perfect condition, so the MPS was called in to settle the matter."

"Is the man all right?" Holmes asked.

"Perfectly fine. The problem was with the ransom money. Dacres has been spending the public funds like water lately, and given his subpar performance record and the fact that he recently wasted over a million guineas on a failed attempt to cover up an unfortunate indiscretion involving the ambassadors of four other countries, for the first time in recent memory, Dacres found himself devoid of funds. The Victorian Age was excellent for his business, wasn't it, Dacres? But alas, there's an unfortunate permissive streak running through society lately, enough to make members of the government start putting profits over principles. In any case, after a string of spectacular failures, Dacres' name is mud, and they're no longer willing to give him *carte blanche* for anything less than a scandal that will bring down the monarchy."

Holmes sighed. "I'm not inclined to use my investigative powers to save the rich and powerful from embarrassment, unless there's a compelling national interest to do so."

"This is a different situation," Mycroft explained. "The kidnapping victim is home safe and his mother is no longer threatening to reveal her life's story. The problem is the ransom money and the need to retrieve it."

"Why are you so concerned about a mere hundred pounds in coins?" I asked.

"It's not the amount of money, it's the specific coins that are a matter of national security." After adjusting his position in his chair, Mycroft continued. "Surely you remember the case that you dubbed "The Adventure of the Engineer's Thumb?"

That grisly case was forever etched in my memory. "Of course."

"You recall, then, that though my brother managed to track down the location of the criminals' home base, the criminals were never brought to justice. At least... that's the narrative that I wanted you to tell the world." Mycroft gave Holmes a little nod, and Holmes gave his sibling a thin-lipped smile.

I turned to my friend. "Holmes, is there more to that story?"

Holmes chuckled. "I'm afraid I withheld the final chapter of that adventure from you, my dear fellow. Did you never think it odd that I failed to make more of an effort to track down the criminals?"

I made no reply. I was concerned that I might say something to offend Holmes. Truth be told, I *had* wondered why the investigation had stopped at that point, but when Holmes seemed content to let the matter rest at that point, I set my personal concerns to one side, and allowed myself to believe that the "Adventure of the Engineer's Thumb" ended with us looking over the burnt-out remains of a house.

I don't know if Holmes was able to follow my train of thought, as he often has in the past. Whatever he guessed about my musings, he continued, saying, "Within an hour of the conversation that ended your colorful recounting of the case, a young man who I recognized as one of Mycroft's many emissaries bumped into me on the street, slipping a note into my hand as he passed on by. Upon reading it, I discovered that it was from Mycroft, telling me not to pursue the villains, and that a team of operatives under his supervision were in the process of tracking them down, where they would face justice, though not in the courts."

"Are you saying that they were executed without trial?" I asked, unable to keep the indignation out of my voice.

"Of course not!" Mycroft snorted. "Whatever you may think about the secret workings of the British government, I can assure you that the rule of law is always followed... except in certain emergencies. In any case, the man you knew as Colonel Lysander Stark and his confederates were captured two days after the events that ended your narrative, Doctor. We rounded up the gang and confiscated all of their counterfeit half-crowns. Given their skill at duplicating the coin of the realm, we offered them a special deal. Either they could go to trial and almost certainly be convicted for counterfeiting– I didn't threaten them with execution for the death of Jeremiah Hayling, the young hydraulic engineer who was almost certainly murdered by Stark and his gang, as we didn't have his body, and empty intimidation would have made me appear to be a paper tiger– or they could accept a special deal where they would be imprisoned in a slightly more comfortable prison in exchange for working with the government to use their counterfeiting skills to serve the interests of Britain."

"Do you mean finding ways to protect British currency from counterfeiting?"

"No, Doctor. To help us find ways to counterfeit the currency of other nations. If we can demonstrate to our rivals that we possess the ability to replicate their money, it gives us a distinct advantage in various negotiations."

"I beg your pardon!"

"You are shocked, Doctor, but I can assure you, by finding inexpensive substitutes for gold and silver, and duplicating the molds for coins, we have prevented ten wars in as many years and have managed to set up countless favorable trade agreements that have solidified England's prosperity."

I was far from convinced that the ends justified the means, and my face must have betrayed my moral outrage, but before I could speak again, Holmes reentered the conversation. "By the way, Watson, you may be wondering about what happened to the young woman in the case. As she had helped save Mr. Hatherley and was more of a hostage than an active participant in the counterfeiting ring, Mycroft's associates gave her a new identity and a fresh start in one of the colonies. She is, I understand, quite content with her second chance at life."

This was welcome news to me, though it did not thoroughly quench my indignation. "So the Colonel and his gang are now living a comparatively comfortable life behind bars, finding ways to replicate the coinage of other countries?"

"Yes. The talents of evil men can be redirected to serve the greater good of the nation." Mycroft cleared his throat. "Dacres, would you care to continue the story and explain how your latest attempt to prevent scandalizing the British public went wrong?"

Dacres made a face like he'd just swallowed strychnine, and Mycroft continued as if he hadn't noticed his associate's expression. "As you will recall, Dacres needed a hundred pounds in gold or silver coins for the ransom. Had he asked a week earlier, the Treasury would have provided him with what he requested with no questions asked. Unfortunately, a recent report on the incredible losses the nation has suffered due to his extraordinarily expensive cover-ups has itself caused a minor scandal and it's costing the government a small fortune to keep it out of the papers. Therefore, the powers that be were debating a plan to have the money deducted from his salary."

"It was completely unfair! I wasn't to blame for the plans not turning out the way I'd hoped! Why should I be forced to pay for mistakes beyond my control? And time was of the essence! By the time those bureaucrats were agreed on how to make me the victim, the mother of that dratted kidnapping victim could have endangered the reputations of some of the most prominent members of our government! I am a man of action, and I did what I had to do in order to save the nation."

Mycroft was not impressed by Dacres' outburst. "You could have gone to the bank and withdrawn a hundred pounds of your own money. I've seen your account total. Your savings could withstand the blow."

"It's the principle!" Dacres squeaked. "If I paid out of my own pocket this time, they'd keep making me fund projects out of my own pocket until I went bankrupt! And in any case, I'm not to blame–"

"Yes, yes, so you've said." Mycroft sounded horribly bored. "So Dacres, in need of a hundred pounds in silver or gold coins, and having insufficient funds in petty cash, decided to loot a storage room in the building where he works, one that just happened to contain several chests full of the counterfeit half-crowns produced by Colonel Stark's gang."

"It was one of my secretaries' ideas. It seemed like an elegant solution," Dacres quipped. "Pay off the criminals with phony money, and possibly we could track them down when they tried to spend it and we caught them with the fake coins."

"Yes, but as some of my spies have recently informed me, the goal wasn't to make a hundred pounds. The kidnappers must have coached your secretary to make that suggestion. Their real objective was to obtain a considerable sample of the nickel and tin amalgam that Colonel Stark's gang used to replicate the silver used in half-crowns. That's the trickiest part of counterfeiting coins. You need to use a metal that looks just like real silver and weighs approximately the same amount as silver, but which only costs a fraction of the price of silver. That was the particular genius of the Stark gang. By combining nickel, tin, and a few other substances, they were able to create an alloy that replicated real silver so closely that only time-consuming laboratory tests could prove definitively that it was not actually silver." Mycroft grimaced. "It is my belief that a foreign power wishes to gain an advantage over us by gaining the ability to replicate our silver currency. I've been aware of a project along these lines for some time, but our enemies have never been able to come up with a convincing substitute for silver. Somehow, they must have found out about the Stark counterfeit half-crowns and organized this kidnapping and the subsequent manipulation of Dacres in order to gain possession of eight hundred coins made out of the silver substitute alloy. That would be enough to run sufficient tests to determine the formula and replicate it, thereby allowing one of England's enemies to gain the upper hand with us in negotiations and possibly disrupt our economy."

Holmes finally appeared interested in this situation. "So you wish for me to track down the counterfeit half-crowns before they can be melted down and analyzed by a rival country?"

"Precisely."

"I don't see how you can expect to be of much use, Mr. Holmes," Dacres sulked. "After all, by this point, the villains may already have spirited the fake coins out of the country and into the hands of whoever recruited them."

"Possibly, possibly." Holmes performed a few quick calculations. "Given the weight of a standard half-crown, eight hundred of them would weigh a little less than twenty-five pounds... I am not using the troy ounce system because we're referring to the alloy here and not actual silver. Given the size and weight, it should be fairly easy to smuggle. Coins could be stacked inside thick walking sticks, slipped into hidden compartments in luggage, or melted down and molded into any shape desired. Indeed, it would be nearly impossible to track down." His eyes flashed. "I need to see if the kidnappers have left any evidence of their location. Do you have the ransom letter?"

"I do." Mycroft handed an envelope to his brother.

Holmes picked up the envelope by one corner and carried it over to his laboratory table. He removed the letter and scrutinized it with his magnifying lens. After several minutes of examination, Dacres lost his patience.

"What the devil are you doing? You're not going to find anything of interest on that note. I've already looked over it."

"Perhaps you should've looked under certain portions of the letter." Holmes said, peeling one of the words that had been pasted on to the paper off with a pair of tweezers. "This slip of newsprint here provides a valuable clue. It's a larger piece, but I believe it must have been cut from the second page, because the letters are a considerably bigger than the standard headline. I suspect that they came from the title of the newspaper. Even through the thin layer of glue, I can tell that the letters are "PSW.""

"That's an unusual combination of letters," I remarked.

"Indeed, Watson. From the font, I would guess that the letters come from the town of "Ipswich," and that this is from a local newspaper there. The Ipswich paper isn't easily found in London, so whoever used this paper may have just been passing through Ipswich and bought a paper, but more likely than not, he has ties to Ipswich."

"Sounds reasonable to me, Holmes," I agreed.

"From the way these papers are cut, I can tell that the person holding the scissors is right-handed."

"That hardly narrows it down," Dacres blustered.

"No, you're quite right there. But these indentations on the undersides of the cut-out words indicate that a heavy, flat object was pressed repeatedly against all of these slips of paper while they were cut. It suggests that the person doing the cutting wore a large ring, possibly a signet ring. Furthermore, I can find a small clipping of hair trapped inside the glue under this word here. It's steel gray. If this letter was prepared a week ago at the time of the kidnapping, the person who cut these letters is a gray-haired man who had his hair cut about a week ago."

"Thousands of men fit that description, Holmes!"

"True, Mr. Dacres, very true. But right now only one man who fits the profile of the person I just described interests me."

"Oh?" Dacres was perspiring. "And who is that?"

Holmes strode casually up to the agitated civil servant. "You yourself, Mr. Dacres. You are right-handed, I can tell from how you're mopping your brow with your handkerchief right now. Your hair is a metallic gray, and it's clearly been cut sometime in the last week, give or take a couple of days. But the most notable point is that signet ring on your right hand."

Dacres tried to yank his hand away, but Holmes gripped his right wrist firmly and twisted the large signet ring from his finger. After a moment's study under the magnifying lens, Holmes smiled grimly. "As I suspected. Traces of glue."

"That's sealing wax!" Dacres spluttered.

"True, there is wax on the seal, but there's glue as well, and a chemical analysis will match it to the glue on the letter. Watson, consult my copy of *Who's Who*. See if our guest here has any family connections to Ipswich."

"I can spare you the trouble," Mycroft replied. "Dacres' family estate is in Ipswich. He goes there most weekends."

Dacres began squirming in his chair, and the blood was draining rapidly from his face. With every twitch, I expected him to jump up and sprint for the door in an attempt to escape, so I rose and made my way between him and the door. Looking at the wretched man, I was pretty certain that the expression on his face radiated guilt.

Holmes' gaze was locked onto Dacres. Without warning, Dacres suddenly became very still, and his right hand started inching its way into his jacket. "None of that!" Holmes shouted, lunging at Dacres, who was momentarily frozen by the sharpness of my friend's exclamation. Holmes's hands gripped Dacres' wrist tightly, and with a quick twist, he extracted a small pistol from Dacres' hand.

Sinking back into his chair, Holmes pocketed the pistol, and remarked, "That's as close to a confession as one can get without the culprit actually admitting his guilt. You were right, my dear brother."

"Right?" I asked. "Holmes, are you saying that Mycroft suspected Dacres from the beginning?"

"Of course, Watson. As I have freely admitted many times, Mycroft's powers of deduction are far superior to my own. His shortcoming stems from the fact that he lacks the initiative to follow up on his own conclusions. Mycroft simply dragged Dacres here so I could interview him, examine the ransom note, and confirm Mycroft's hypotheses."

"Which were?"

Holmes gestured to his brother, indicating that it would be best if he were to answer my question himself. With a faint but obvious trace of reluctance, Mycroft took over the conversation. "It's quite simple. Part of my job requires me to review the accounts of

134

several secret departments. A couple of months ago, I took a look at the Ministry for the Prevention of Scandal's numbers, and it occurred to me that this wasn't just a case of profligate spending. I had a strong suspicion that someone was padding the numbers. All those millions spent covering up the filthy secrets of our politicians and titled figures! All those guineas spent when a handful of shillings would do. I knew that someone was running sticky fingers through the till. But was it a secretary, a mid-level employee, or did the rot start at the very top? I didn't have a definite answer to that, so I turned to my brother."

"I should tell you, Watson," Holmes explained, "that I have been investigating Dacres' financial institution for some weeks, and while I discovered a couple of secret accounts held by Dacres under an alias in Switzerland, I could not account for the lion's share of the money. I recently discovered, however that Dacres and both of his sons share a passion for the gaming table. Some discreet inquires prove that the family's losses over the past year have been dramatic, even crippling. Yet the family has exhibited no decline in their standard of living whatsoever. Why is this? Either the people they owe money to are remarkably forgiving, or, much more likely, they have a heretofore unknown source of income that is allowing them to cancel out their considerable debts."

"Excellent investigative work, my dear brother, but I must say that you may have missed one significant detail. While Dacres has been funneling some of his ill-gotten gains into banks overseas, he's also been smuggling a king's ransom of cash into a special, gigantic, hidden safe in the basement of his estate in Ipswich. Of course, he'd have to be very careful about drawing attention by spending it, but his embezzlement has made him one of the wealthiest men in the country. At least, he was. My men are poised to raid his home to recover the funds. A rather different approach will be used to drain his Swiss bank accounts."

As is often the case when the brothers Holmes overwhelm me with a considerable quantity of information, my head began to lose its equilibrium a bit. I still had enough lucidity to ask a question. "But if Dacres has amassed such a considerable amount of money, why would he engage in this farcical subterfuge about a kidnapping and counterfeit half-crowns?"

The brothers made eye contact, Holmes gave his elder sibling a very faint nod, and with some reluctance Mycroft answered my question. "His sons, as we mentioned, are gamblers with terrible luck. A few weeks ago the pair of them participated in a card game with the ambassador of a country that will remain nameless. They didn't just lose their shirts, they figuratively lost every stitch of clothing at Harrods as well. The debt was so massive that it would have wiped out their not-so-proud father's nest egg and would probably have necessitated the sale of the family estate to boot. Indeed, though I have no proof, I'm quite sure that the card game wasn't completely aboveboard, and that the youths were well-plied with alcohol to bet far above their station. I fully suspect that this was all a carefully orchestrated plot by the government in question to gain a sample of our imitation silver alloy."

"But now they do have it," I interjected.

"My dear Watson, please try to give me a little credit. I did not achieve my current role in the British government by being unable to anticipate oncoming threats. For months, I knew that a foreign power was after our collection of counterfeit half-crowns. So some time ago, I had the imitations replaced in order to protect the secrets of the alloy."

"So you replaced them with real half-crowns? Excellent! That means that the government's only out a hundred pounds."

"Not even that, Doctor. I am by nature a parsimonious man. I replaced the imitation half-crowns with more counterfeit half-crowns. However, this second batch were not cast with a secret alloy, but rather with plain tin. I should very much like to see the expressions on the faces of the members of the nameless foreign government's face when they learned that all they've gotten for their trouble is a few pounds of scrap metal."

This statement seemed to galvanize Dacres. "But... but... They'll think I betrayed them! They'll seek vengeance!"

"Tut, tut, sir," Holmes replied disapprovingly. "You'll be safe enough in prison."

"No!" Dacres sat bolt upright. "Here are my terms. You will allow me to keep every farthing of the money I've... accumulated over the years. I've earned it. I've kept the nation solid and respected. Then you'll set me and my family up under new identities in a comfortable estate somewhere in the colonies with a decent climate. Probably the Caribbean."

"And what makes you think that they'll comply with your ridiculous requests, you scoundrel?" I scoffed.

"Because if they don't, I've arranged for a dossier of the most humiliating secrets of some of the most powerful people in England to be released to the public! The government won't survive the scandal, and if my associate doesn't see the signal by seven o'clock tonight, he'll drop the parcel off at the rooms of a reporter I know who won't be bullied into silence."

Dacres' face flushed with triumph, only for this new confidence to fade as Mycroft's face remained impassive. Mycroft calmly removed a large blue handkerchief from his jacket pocket and waved it casually in front of the window to his left.

"What are you doing?"

"Signaling, Dacres. Surely that's obvious. Don't bother getting up. If you get up and run you'll only get caught sooner."

Moments later, three men in dark suits burst into the room. "Take him," Mycroft declared, folding up the handkerchief.

"You're making a terrible mistake! England will be doomed!" Dacres yelled as the men grabbed him and dragged him away from us.

"I doubt it." Mycroft turned to Holmes. "Will you settle the matter?"

"Of course. Watson, will you join me?"

I agreed, even though I had no idea what I was expected to do. The next thing I knew, we were riding in a carriage, heading west.

"You see, Watson, Mycroft and I anticipated his last desperate gambit. We knew he had a secret signal to tell his confederate when to release the package of damaging information.

Since Dacres rarely went anywhere besides his offices and his flat, it stood to reason that the signal was based at his home. My Irregulars have kept a careful eye on the place, figuring that the secret sign must be visible from the street, and within the first three days they discovered that each night, when he returns home at a quarter to seven, he hangs a small piece of stained-glass artwork in a window facing the main road. And then shortly before he retires to bed, he removes it, and repeats the process the next day. The Irregulars have been on the watch for someone who walks by every night and looks up at the window. I trust that they'll be able to help us tonight."

Holmes, as usual, was right. As soon as we stepped out of our carriage, a young street urchin hurried up to us. "You're just in time, Mr. Holmes. The fellow that we're pretty sure is our man arrived ten minutes ago. He looked up at the window and looked shocked when that piece of colored glass wasn't there. He's been standing there, leaning against that wall for ten minutes, smoking a cigarette and looking up, waiting and seeing if that stained glass appears."

"Well done, all of you! Take your positions, just in case something goes wrong." Holmes directed me to walk four paces ahead of him, and I walked right past the man with the cigarette, only to whirl around as soon as I heard Holmes' voice.

"Are you Mr. Dacres' friend?"

Upon hearing Holmes, the man dropped his cigarette and turned as if to flee, but Holmes and I both grabbed an arm and pinioned him against the wall. Holmes patted his jacket, and after a few moments extracted a very thick envelope from one pocket.

A few minutes later, Dacres' associate was in the custody of the police, and Holmes and I were riding back to turn the envelope over to Mycroft.

"I say, Holmes, who would have ever thought all those years ago that when that poor engineer came to me with his thumb severed, that it would lead to a case like this a decade later?"

Holmes shrugged and leaned back into his seat. "I dare say that Mycroft could have anticipated such a possibility. He has the sort of mind where every event, no matter how trivial, can be connected to the general health of the government. I consider myself fortunate that I can dedicate my mental powers to the investigation of crime, rather than applying them to realm of politics."

The Switched String

"There are some intriguing potential crimes in the newspaper, Holmes."

I had expected Holmes to reply with a nonplussed "*Potential crimes, Watson? What do you mean by that?*" Instead, he remained completely focused on playing his violin. I cleared my throat a couple of times, trying to catch his attention, but he continued to play a complex and fast-paced piece for the next three minutes. When he finally lowered his bow with a flourish, he turned to me and said, "Indeed, Watson. I counted no less than sixteen likely crimes that might take place in the coming week."

I had only discovered three, but I was reluctant to reveal this fact to Holmes. "There's a new exhibition of Vermeer paintings at a local gallery, which might lead to a potential theft. I see there's a report of a gang of anarchists that are targeting prominent manor houses for arson. And there's that ambassador from Eastern Europe who is making a speech tomorrow. He's considered very controversial, and there are rumors that he's been targeted for an assassination."

"Quite right, Watson. Of course, you've overlooked how a construction project might provide cover for robbing a local bank; the wedding announcement for a terminally ill duke to a woman forty years his junior– his nephew, who is currently the heir to the title, certainly has a motive to see his uncle pass before he can sire a son; a seemingly benevolent charity that on closer examination appears to be a confidence scheme…" Holmes continued for several minutes, leaving me feeling like I'd been out in the sun for far too long. No one has a better premonition of impending crime than Holmes.

Once Holmes finished his lengthy list of potential lawbreaking, there was a twinkle in his eye that forewarned me that he was about to issue a challenge that I had little chance of passing. "If you'll allow me to change the subject, Watson, did you notice anything amiss with my violin playing just now?"

I thought for a moment. "I don't believe so. You sounded just like you normally do."

"Nothing amiss or discordant?"

"I said that your playing sounded normal to me, Holmes."

"Hmm. I suppose that I have an advantage on you, as I was able to use not just my hearing abilities to identify the problem, but my powers of sight as well. Observe, Watson, the "A" string here."

"What of it?"

"Examine it, dear fellow. What differentiates it from the other strings?"

At first I saw nothing, but then Holmes tilted the violin very slightly, allowing the light to reflect off of the strings. "That "A" string... it's a slightly different color from the others, isn't it?"

"It is indeed, Watson! What else?"

I took the violin from Holmes and scrutinized it more thoroughly. "It's rather hard to tell using just my vision, but doesn't that string look a tiny bit thinner that the others?"

"Most certainly, my friend! Also–" Holmes extended a finger and tapped the string in question. "If you will use your sense of touch, you will note that it is decidedly less supple than the other strings." I ran my fingers lightly over the strings and confirmed that this was indeed the case.

"Holmes, my ears are not so trained and musical as yours are. How does the quality of this string compare to the others?"

"It is decidedly inferior. The pitch is off, and any note played in this string lacks resonance. It is a cheap string, the kind no one with any appreciation for music or pride in performance would use. Young children might use strings like this when they are learning how to play for the first time, when they need to learn technique."

"Then you would never place a string like this on your violin?"

"It would be akin to slapping Stradivarius across the face."

"Then how did it get there?"

"Ah! That is the question I've been asking myself for the last several minutes."

"What are your theories, Holmes?"

"The first question centers around opportunity. Who had the chance to defile my instrument in this manner? I know that I had nothing to do with it. The violin's strings were perfectly fine yesterday. We have had no clients visiting our rooms in the past twenty-four hours. There is only one other man with access to this violin. His motive? Perhaps he wished to play some sort of practical joke, or perhaps he sought to provide me with an unexpected and irresistible puzzle?"

There was a twinkle in Holmes' eye, but I felt no merriment whatsoever. "I can assure you that I had nothing to do with changing the string on your violin."

"Are you certain of that?"

"I am not in the habit of damaging musical instruments in my sleep, Holmes."

"No, you are not. I realized that you had nothing to do with this as soon as I saw your facial expressions when I queried you about the string. But if you are not responsible, then that means that someone else must have done this. So who had the opportunity? Could someone have crept into our rooms while we slept? It's possible. I didn't lock my violin away, and locks can be picked."

"It would have had to be an outsider. Mrs. Hudson would never do anything like this."

"I agree, but I think we should question her. Remember, we went out to dinner at Simpson's Divan last night. We were gone for over two hours, it's possible that someone could have crept inside without our knowledge, but that means that someone would have had to come inside without Mrs. Hudson observing him as well."

Holmes summoned Mrs. Hudson, and she confirmed his conclusion that she knew nothing about what had happened to his violin. When asked if anybody had been inside 221B while we were gone, she replied in the negative.

"At least, not as far as I know," she added. "I wasn't here all evening. Around half past seven, a neighbor down the street came to me for help. Someone had smashed two of her windows and she needed help cleaning up the shattered glass in her living room."

"How far away was this?" Holmes looked interested.

"Just three houses down, sir. Mrs. Ardor's been a friend of mine for years, but I don't think that you know her."

"Did you find any stones or bricks in the house? If I could examine them…"

"We found nothing like that, Mr. Holmes."

Disappointed, he muttered, "Perhaps they struck the windows with a cane or something like that so as to leave fewer clues behind." Raising his voice, he asked, "Can you describe Mrs. Ardor?"

"About my age, sir, though her eyesight isn't good, and her rheumatism means it's difficult for her to sweep up a mess. That's why she needed to call on me for assistance, sir. I also helped her cover up the broken windows with some cloths, as a glazier couldn't come until the morning. Luckily it was a warm night."

"Does she have any other friends nearby?"

"Not to my knowledge. She doesn't get out much, and she's on a very limited income, living off her late husband's pension. She didn't have enough to cover the cost of replacing the glass, so I had to lend her a wee bit of my housekeeping money to pay the bill."

"So if someone damaged her home, she would almost certainly come to you for assistance," Holmes mused. "When did you return?"

"Not for over an hour. Perhaps twenty minutes to nine."

"Seventy minutes. More than enough time to perform this act of vandalism."

"Not really vandalism, is it, Holmes?" I questioned. "After all, it's easily fixed."

"Yes, and once again, the question is "why?" What could be gained by this? Why go to the trouble of damaging our neighbor's home just to lure Mrs. Hudson away? If this was a practical joke, why arrange it in a way that no one could see my reaction save you, Watson?"

"It's not like you were planning to perform at the Royal Albert Hall."

"Exactly. I can see no other acts of disruption around our rooms. This is such a tiny thing…"

After a few minutes of silence, I asked, "Whatever happened to the original string?"

"An excellent question, Watson. It had no particular value. No one would have any reason to steal it."

The three of us searched our rooms for the missing string. The hunt only lasted for three minutes before Mrs. Hudson discovered the string in the wastepaper basket.

"Hmm!" Holmes studied the string, which had been coiled up into a little ring. "It's been cut. Too damaged to restring. Yet as it was left behind, then the goal was to affect the violin rather than gain access to the string itself."

"If someone had theft in mind, why not take the whole violin?" I asked. "After all, it's quite valuable, even if you did purchase it for a fraction of its value."

"Precisely." Holmes picked up his violin and examined it further. "I wondered if someone tried to hide something inside the holes, but I can see nothing, and light shaking provides no sounds. No, I do not believe that someone removed the string in order to facilitate the insertion of some unknown object into this violin. Holmes gently laid down his instrument and then began examining the lock to the door. "Hmm! There are some new scratches here– faint but clear. I think it's reasonable to conclude that someone skilled at picking locks was here. And…" He hurried downstairs and examined the front door. "Yes, there are similar marks around the keyhole here. We can now confirm that someone was here last night while we were all away, and that someone has a good deal of training in housebreaking. An amateur would have left clearer traces of his entrance, as well as of his exit when he re-locked the door, for that matter."

"Unfortunately, we know absolutely nothing about him."

"Not quite, Watson. We know that he has large, nimble hands, is probably reasonably young and healthy, is musically inclined, and is carrying a handkerchief with cream-colored smears on it."

I balked at asking the question Holmes wished me to ask, "How could you possibly know that, Holmes?" before succumbing to the inevitable and inquiring.

"Remember the original string we found in the wastepaper basket, Watson. Most likely he wrapped it around his finger several times to form the ring we found. Given the size of the circlet, he must have rather large hands. Yet they must be quick and nimble, given the dexterity needed to pick some high-quality locks and restring an instrument. Obviously no arthritis has set in yet. Additionally, he had to have smashed our neighbor's windows and hurried away sufficiently swiftly so as not to be noticed by other people on the street, again indicating a younger man in athletic condition. He was able to unstring and restring my violin without much difficulty. While the replacement string is of a markedly inferior grade, I could not have attached it to my instrument better myself. It takes practice to develop this skill, especially when one considers that under the best circumstances, one should not have to replace violin strings too frequently."

"So he's both a trained lockpicker and a violinist?"

"We can proceed under that assumption."

"And the stained handkerchief?"

"The smears are violin polish, Watson. I applied a thin coating of it before dinner last night when I had finished playing. I noticed no finger-marks or other signs of disturbance to the veneer before I began playing. Tying a string to a violin is difficult enough with bare hands, it is far more challenging when gloves are worn. The culprit almost certainly touched this instrument with bare hands, and then wiped it down, almost certainly with a handkerchief, thereby removing both any finger-marks and most of the new polish as well. I shall need to polish it again. I rather resent having my possessions handled by an intruder."

I had almost forgotten that Mrs. Hudson was still there when she asked, "Are you sure that the violin is the only item that was touched, Mr. Holmes?"

"My initial cursory examination of our rooms has revealed nothing out of order, but it's quite possible that something equally subtle has occurred." With that, the three of us began a close, detailed examination of our possessions. Mrs. Hudson carefully flipped through every book on the shelves, checking for torn-out pages or scribbled messages. I scrutinized our furniture and found nothing amiss. Holmes was the most active of all of us, darting from corner to corner, sniffing his laboratory equipment, pulling each cigar out of the coal-scuttle and examining it, rifling through his files, shaking out the curtains, and otherwise darting around with remarkable energy.

Fifteen minutes into our search, there was a knock at the front door and a young man handed Mrs. Hudson a telegram. When she tried to give it to Holmes, he tossed it onto a side table without even glancing at it, and continued to hold his pipe-tobacco up to the light, sifting it through his fingers.

Hours passed, and I eventually became convinced that we had confirmed that every carpet fiber and floor nail was exactly where it should be. Mrs. Hudson was compelled to go to bed shortly after midnight, and I reached the point of total exhaustion a bit before three in the morning. Holmes showed no signs of weariness, and continued to give our rooms the fullest possible scrutiny. He pored through his massive index, checking to see if any or his records were added to, altered, or removed. He sifted through every article of clothing he owned, including his substantial collection of disguises, examining everything minutely for added or removed buttons, items sewn into the lining, holes, or stains. All of his chemistry supplies were tested to make sure that they had not been tainted, as was his stage makeup. Even mementos from previous cases were checked from every angle under a magnifying glass to see if they had been damaged in any way. Naturally, this painstaking search took a very long time, and several hours later, when Mrs. Hudson brought in breakfast, I realized that he had not slept at all that night.

"Did you discover anything, Holmes?"

"Nothing. I had wondered if an inferior cigarette might have been slipped into a box, or if a bottle of one of my chemistry supplies had been emptied and refilled with flour, but as far as I can tell, the violin string is the only item that is amiss."

"And you're quite sure that there's no one who would perform this sort of practical joke on you?"

"In all the time that you've known me, Watson, have you ever suspected that I am the sort of person who cavorts with merry pranksters?"

"But Holmes, what possible motive could anybody have for this?"

"Are you doubting that it happened?"

"No, I know that somebody replaced your violin string. I saw the false string, the original was rolled up and deposited in the wastepaper basket. That is undeniable. It wasn't you, I had nothing to do with it, and Mrs. Hudson would never had done anything like that in a thousand years. But the chain of events, while I do not doubt it happened, still beggars belief. Think about it. Someone waits until we have left 221B. That person then breaks our neighbor's windows and runs away. The vandal knew that our neighbor would walk to 221B and ask Mrs. Hudson for help cleaning up the broken glass, knowing that she'd be gone for the better part of an hour. The culprit hides in a place where he can watch our neighbor walk to 221B and soon after Mrs. Hudson leaves, he rushes to the door and carefully unlocks the front door, being able to do so sufficiently quickly to not draw any attention."

I paused and reflected for a moment. "It is surprising that no one saw a strange man picking the lock of the front door of 221B."

"Not really. It was dark at that time, and it was a chilly night. Few people would have been idling around the street, watching the area. Additionally, I often enter and exit our home at all hours of the day and night, wearing all sorts of disguises. A strange man fumbling at the lock is not such a rare occurrence."

"Fair enough. Then the villain hurries upstairs, picks the lock to our rooms, locates your violin, removes one string, replaces it with an inferior string, and hurries out of 221B, locking the doors behind him as he goes. He then disappears into the night, having achieved his only objective." After a deep breath, I concluded. "Do you agree that is an accurate summation of events, Holmes?"

He tented his fingers and leaned back in his chair. "I believe that it was accurate until your final sentence."

"Are you saying he didn't disappear into the night?" A wave of horror swept over me. "Holmes, do you believe that he's still here, hidden somewhere in the building?"

"What? No, Watson, that is not what I mean, and that is not the portion of the sentence that I found suspect. I meant the five words, "having achieved his only objective.""

"Is there something we missed?"

"The intruder did not want the string itself. That is proven by the fact that it was tossed in the wastepaper basket. In any event, the string has no intrinsic value. Just because it was used on a Stradivarius does not make it any more valuable than any ordinary fiddle string. I certainly did not plan to audition for a position in an orchestra. No public embarrassment or any direct negative consequence could come to me from this. And we have agreed that a practical joke becomes less amusing to the prankster when the person initiating the supposed humor is not there to witness the results.

Which raises one distinct possibility. The purpose of substituting a string was to generate an indirect consequence."

"But what sort of indirect consequence could result from switching a violin string?"

"What did happen, Watson?"

"We wasted a day searching our rooms."

"Precisely! From the moment I noticed how my instrument has been defiled, I have obsessed over who might have done this and what the goal of this stunt might have been. I have been focused on this string at the expense of everything else. If I am correct in my deductions, then that means that this entire charade was meant as a distraction. A bagatelle that would demand my full attention. Something that would keep me away from something more important. Like one of the potential crimes in the newspaper we discussed earlier!"

It took me a moment of reflecting, and then everything made sense. "You mean that someone was planning a major crime, became afraid that you would become involved, and created this subtle, mystifying distraction?"

"Doesn't that make perfect sense to you?"

"I cannot say that it does."

"Consider, Watson, that a clever criminal is in the process of planning a major crime. The villain in question is aware of my existence, and for reasons that I will theorize about later believes that it is probable that I will be called into the case either immediately after the crime occurs or perhaps right before it occurs in an attempt to prevent it. Do you see a flaw in my logic?"

"After all we've been through together, Holmes, you should know how unlikely such an occurrence might be."

"My blushes, Watson. Therefore, if my involvement is not wanted in this theoretical crime, then the perpetrator must find a way to prevent my investigation. Open threats would not work. Such aggression would only serve to make me more determined to insert myself into the case. If I cannot be bullied, then perhaps I can be distracted. The only way to keep me away from a very important case is to provide me with an irresistible problem. Perhaps the person in question attempted to come up with an impossible murder or some other baffling crime. Maybe this individual's powers of creativity were not up to the task, or perhaps this plotter feared that the mystery would not be interesting enough to attract me, or I might solve the case too quickly. Perhaps after much thinking, the criminal at the heart of this mystery realized that the best way to catch my attention was to personalize the problem he created for me. Instead of planning an additional complex crime solely for the purposes of distracting me, why not derail me with a simple question?

"Why would someone change out one of your violin strings?"

"Precisely. It is reminiscent of Lewis Carroll's famous riddle in *Alice's Adventures in Wonderland*: How is a raven like a writing desk?" Holmes paused for a few moments, and I pondered before admitting defeat.

"There is no answer. Carroll deliberately proposed a riddle that he didn't have a solution for. Of course, over the years readers have proposed their own solutions, such as "they both produce notes," "they both have inky quills," and my personal favorite, "Edgar Allan Poe wrote on both." But the point is that when Carroll wrote that riddle, it was designed to go unanswered. So it is with the violin string substitution. There is no rhyme or reason for the action *in itself*. It is the *consequence* of the switch that is of paramount importance. The person involved might have put pepper in my tobacco, or gold sovereigns in my dressing-gown pockets, or even left an actual wild goose in my bedroom for me to chase. The point is that I was meant to become obsessed with this ridiculous, pointless charade, and my opponent triumphed spectacularly. Full marks to him."

"But who would do such a thing? Who would not only plot a terrible crime, but go through all of this rigmarole just to prevent you from getting involved?"

"Once we find the crime, my dear fellow, we will have our answer. We have not have any potential clients knocking on our door, have we? Could the solution to this puzzle have been turned away?"

"No one has been to 221B since that boy delivered that telegram–" Scarcely had the words escaped my lips than Holmes leapt up, sprinted across the room, and retrieved the missive. "It is from a Baron Culmond, a man who has worked with my brother Mycroft on many previous occasions. It seems that he is hosting that Eastern European ambassador you mentioned yesterday. He's concerned for the diplomat's safety, and if I am correct, he has every right to be."

In less than a minute, Holmes, who was disheveled from the previous night's escapade, had thrown on a coat and had summoned a hansom cab. As we drove away from Baker Street, I asked him, "But you can't be certain that this is *the* crime you think you were distracted from, can you?"

"No, but seeing as how no one else has tried to hire me lately, and given the importance of this ambassador, it is by far the most likely option. The ambassador in question here is pivotal to resolving a trade dispute between England and his home country. If he were to die on British soil, then the negotiations would fall apart, and someone who was well-positioned in the business world could conceivably make hundreds of thousands of pounds from the resulting economic chaos."

A half-hour later, we arrived at Baron Culmond's home, and after some very terse words with the butler, the Baron met us in the hall. "Mr. Holmes. You never responded to my telegram, so I assumed that you had no interest in my worries."

"I apologize, sir. I was caught up in a very clever scheme orchestrated by the man who I believe is planning to assassinate the ambassador at any moment."

After a few words of shock and concern, the Baron led us into the ballroom where the ambassador was addressing an audience of about fifty guests. Holmes scanned the room, and after about seven seconds, he spun around and sprinted out the door. I hurried after him, but I was so far behind Holmes that I could barely hear my friend declare, "He's outside, Watson! He's in the oak tree!"

When I finally caught up with Holmes, he was crouched behind a shrub in the courtyard. He placed a finger over his lips and then pointed upwards. I could see a shadowy figure sprawled out on a very thick branch halfway up the tallest tree, pointing a rifle at the window. Holmes' eyes darted around the ground before discovering a rock the size of his fist, and upon grabbing it, he hurled it upwards at the gunman, striking him on the head. The man and his rifle hurtled to the ground with an unsettling thud.

"Is he alive, Watson?"

After a brief examination I nodded. "He's unconscious and I suspect one arm and both legs are broken, but he ought to survive."

"He shall live long enough to be tried and convicted," Holmes declared, and he was right. We summoned the authorities, who carried the gunman away on a stretcher, managing to do so without disturbing the guests inside the house.

Upon learning of our actions, the Baron and the ambassador were both effusive in their thanks. The agents of both governments decided to speed up their negotiations, and a deal was struck and signed shortly after midnight. The ambassador returned home the following day without incident.

Holmes and I returned to Baker Street as soon as the treaty was signed. "There's just one unanswered question, Holmes."

"Oh? What's that?"

"Who was behind all of this? Who not only planned the death of the ambassador in order to profit from the resulting chaos, but who knew that you would be involved, and that you would be distracted by a little adjustment to your violin? Who would break our neighbor's windows, knowing that Mrs. Hudson would be called away to help?"

Holmes sighed. "You ought to know the answer to that, Watson. Only one criminal in all of England knows my character so well, realizes the danger I pose to him, and could position himself to turn international upheaval into a small fortune. I suppose I should be flattered that he only sought to distract me instead of killing me. I have no strength to discuss my nemesis now, as I am spent. I have not slept in over forty hours. If you will excuse me, my good fellow…"

And with that, Holmes staggered into his bedroom for some well-deserved rest.

The Bitter Gravestones

Sherlock Holmes was not having a happy Christmas. He was tired, a little bitter, and would much rather have been back with his honeybees.

He had not wanted to spend the holiday at an isolated manor house in the countryside, but his brother Mycroft had requested that he make the visit and protect the nation's interests at a top-secret conference there. Although I cannot go into details as the event is still a state secret, by the morning of the twenty-fourth of December the matters being decided were satisfactorily resolved and the assorted diplomats had left hurriedly in order make their way home in time for the holiday. Holmes was under orders to remain at the manor house until Boxing Day to tie up loose ends and await the arrival of a government agent for further instructions.

Holmes had invited me along, privately warning me that my presence was necessary to preserve his sanity. He had previously met the Blurdells, the family who owned the manor, and they were not the sort of people who Holmes would willingly spend time with given the option. Once Holmes had done his duty to King and Country and sent the last of the diplomats on his way, Holmes retreated to his room and asked that his meals be delivered to him on a tray.

"Surely, Holmes, you don't intend to spend the entirety of Christmas in your room? I'm aware that you aren't feeling particularly warm towards the Blurdells, which, having gotten to know most of them over the last two days, I can rather understand. But Christmas is Christmas, and wouldn't you rather share your goose and pudding with other people?"

The glare on Holmes' face was far more chilling than the icy winds whipping around the mansion. "I can assure you, Watson, that having devoted all of my energies to maintaining peace on earth, I now no longer have the strength to muster any goodwill to all men. I have done my part to prevent the recurrence of those horrors that plagued our continent for four long and violent years recently. I do not deserve the torment of having to pull Christmas crackers with Lord Derek Blurdell or listen to Horace Blurdell's tired jokes as he drains a decanter of port. I have a quiet room, a couple of books, and enough paper and writing equipment to begin work on the monograph I have been planning for some time. Should for some reason I desire conversation, I can always speak to you, dear fellow. Otherwise, I shall be perfectly happy being left to my own devices."

I chose not to argue further with Holmes, as in my heart I knew he was completely correct. For most people, any company is better than none at Christmas. Not so for Holmes.

We spoke little over the next few minutes, and I was about to return to my room and take a little nap before dinner when there was a knock at the door. Before Holmes could utter a response, a thirteen-year-old boy hurried into the room and shut the door behind him. It was Duncan Blurdell, the only surviving son of Lord Derek Blurdell, his older brothers having perished in the war. "Mr. Holmes? Doctor Watson?"

"Yes, Duncan? What is it?" I asked.

"I need to talk to you about the gravestones."

"What's wrong with them?" Holmes asked, not bothering to hide the asperity in his voice.

"They're so *bitter*, sir. It doesn't make sense."

"How can a gravestone be bitter?"

"It's what's inscribed on them, Mr. Holmes. Six relatives I've never met or even heard of. They all died on Christmas, one a year for the past six years. And what's written on the gravestones is truly vile, sir. Not Christian at all. But if someone's died every Christmas for over half a decade, well, what if the pattern holds and someone else dies tomorrow? I don't know for sure, but it can't be a coincidence that six members of the family died on that date so regularly, sir. If we could find out what's going on, maybe we could prevent tomorrow's death, sir."

Holmes' facial expression and posture altered completely, and I noticed that familiar spark of interest that he gets whenever he decides that a problem is worthy of his skills. "Can you lead us to the gravestones?"

"Yes, sir. They're not far from the house."

"Get your coat, Watson, and meet us outside my door. I very much want to see these gravestones."

As I rummaged through the hall closet for my coat, I felt my eyes water from the abundance of pine. Multiple large trees had been installed in the entryway, and evergreen boughs festooned the archways. A few minutes later, we were walking along a lightly trampled pathway in the dead grass, wrapping our coats tightly around us to protect ourselves from the blustery wind. "How long have you been aware of these gravestones, Duncan?" Holmes asked.

"I just discovered them twenty minutes ago, sir. I don't like to visit the graveyard, it's not a pleasant place. But I was playing with my dog, Rex. He's a spaniel. We were playing near the edge of the woods, about a quarter-mile south of the family cemetery, and all of a sudden he started running off. Well, I followed him, and when I got there Rex was sniffing around these six gravestones in the corner. I tried to shoo him away, but he started howling, and he drew my attention to what was written on them, sir. Gave me the chills, it did. That's why I came to you, thinking you might be able to make sense of it all."

The wind grew steadily stronger as we made our way to the cemetery. It was a small square of land surrounded on three sides by the woods, and completely enclosed by an iron fence. Unlike every other portion of the estate, there were no Christmas decorations to be found around the graveyard. We pushed through the unlocked gate. There were about seventy gravestones scattered around the graveyard in no apparent order. Most of them were large, ornate slabs of shining marble. Duncan led us towards the back of the area, where six gravestones stood far apart from the nearest markers.

The first four gravestones in the line were small pieces of cheap tan rock, each about a foot tall. The first gravestone read:

Elspeth Blurdell Hill

June 3 1881 – December 25 1919

She Will Not Be Mourned

"Who would write that on a gravestone?" I asked.

"Wait until you see the others," Duncan informed me.

The words on the second gravestone were:

John Blurdell

March 3 1884 – December 26 1920

Good riddance to bad rubbish

I was flabbergasted.   Holmes looked fascinated.   As we moved to the third gravestone, we read the words:

Alicia Blurdell White

December 15 1900 – December 25 1921

Liar

Adulteress

Murderess

"Murderess? Who is she supposed to have killed?"

"We shall have to look into that, Watson."

The fourth grave was no less malicious or baffling.

Gregory Blurdell

August 11 1847 – December 25 1922

S.I.T.

Suffer In Torment

The fifth gravestone was a bit larger than the first four, and was made of much nicer material.

Thomas Blurdell

February 27 1898 – December 25 1923

If only he had been stillborn, the world would have been a happier place.

"What a heartless thing to write!"

"Possibly, Watson. Observe this sixth gravestone."

The sixth gravestone was by far the largest and most ornate. It was the only one to resemble the other prominent markers in the cemetery. This one actually had a poem inscribed on it:

Daniel Blurdell

January 2 1897 – December 25 1924

Here rots the corpse of Dan Blurdell

The worst sinner since Adam fell

His breath gave off a loathsome smell

If he had virtues none could tell

Not once in life did he mean well

We hope the bastard roasts in hell

"How appalling!" I blurted out uncontrollably.

"Not appalling, Watson, so much as intriguing. The odds of six people in the same family dying on Christmas over the course of six consecutive years defies the odds."

"Why would someone carve such sentiments on a gravestone, where anybody can see it?"

"Not anybody, Watson. Remember, this is a private graveyard in the middle of the countryside. The only people likely to ever see this are the Blurdell family and their servants."

"And not many of either group you mention, Mr. Holmes," Duncan chimed in, "Most of the family and servants don't much like to spend time in the graveyard. It's an unsettling place, sir. Every now and then someone comes in on an anniversary or something, but more often than not we never visit. There's a gardener who comes in once in a while to tidy up everything, but not many other people."

"Interesting. When was the last time you were in here before today, Duncan?"

"For my brothers' joint funeral back in 1919. They were all killed in the war, but we didn't get their bodies back until long after all the battles had ended. I've been at school when all of the other family members' funerals were held." Duncan pointed across the graveyard at four headstones, each with a stone bust on the top. "They all died during the last six months of fighting, sir. If the war

171

had just ended a couple of months earlier, maybe a couple of my brothers could've made it home."

"I'm so sorry, Duncan."

"It isn't your fault, Mr. Holmes. I know I should come here more often, but, well, I just don't like it here. I'm away at school most of the time anyway. I didn't know them all that well because they were so much older than I was, but that didn't mean we weren't close, sir."

"You do not have to explain yourself." Holmes started walking around the other gravestones. "There seems to be a clear disparity in these monuments to the dead. The holders of the earldom, those who died in battle... most of them receive enormous headstones, often with some sort of tribute inscribed on it. Others, mainly women and those who died young, get smaller headstones, with much simpler inscriptions, just the names and dates. Still, the rest of these are made out of high-quality material, unlike those four stones there, which might crumble over a relatively short period of time when exposed to the elements. You can see the first of the bitter gravestones has already developed the first hints of a crack. It won't last another decade. So the point arises– someone loathed these people enough that they were willing to carve their venom onto a slab of rock, but they didn't care enough to buy sufficiently durable material so that their rancor would last throughout the ages."

"And why are the last two headstones nicer than the others?" I wondered. "Do you think that whoever purchased them loathed the deceased, but thought that they deserved a lasting monument to their awfulness?"

"My father would have bought those headstones," Duncan noted. "As the head of the family, it's his job to handle all of the major purchases."

"Duncan, you understand that I have to ask these questions, even if they are rather personal," Holmes explained. "Are there financial reasons why your father might have been compelled to scrimp a lot on those headstones?"

"Not really, sir. He certainly spared no expense for my brothers' graves. He's complained about the cost of my school fees, but he's never been unable to pay them. The staff doesn't seem to be any smaller than it was in the past. I haven't noticed any paintings missing from the walls, and as far as I can tell my mother still has all of her jewels. Actually, my father's bought her an enormous diamond necklace for Christmas this year, but please don't tell her and spoil the surprise until tomorrow."

"I see. What do you know about the six people in the graves?"

"Nothing, Mr. Holmes."

"Surely you must have heard something about them?"

"Well, I can't be sure, because when my grandfather was alive before the war, he was always telling long and rambling stories about the family, but I never really listened, so it's certainly possible that he mentioned them at some point but they didn't stay in my mind."

"Did you ever meet any of them?"

"No, sir, not as far as I can remember, but there are a great many family members that I've never seen. You see, a lot of my relatives have led rather... *scandalous* lives. Plenty of them have run off with lovers, some have wasted massive amounts of money gambling. and there's no shortage of cousins who bear the family name, but whose parents were never married. There's probably dozens of relatives who are considered embarrassments. I suppose the official family policy is that if someone's not considered sufficiently respectable, they are *persona non grata*. Their names are never mentioned, there are no pictures of them anywhere, and they're never invited to the manor house. Every now and then the family lawyers may send them some money, but I don't know why. Maybe they've been very good, or maybe they're in terrible trouble, or perhaps they're threatening to make an embarrassing scene and my father bribes them to mind their manners." Duncan shuddered. "We're a rather idiosyncratic family."

Holmes shrugged. "You're really not that different from other wealthy and prominent families."

"Do you know any other families who write messages like this on gravestones?"

"No. Which makes this situation all the more intriguing." After a moment's pause, Holmes asked, "How many of these estranged relatives have been buried in the family plot?"

"As far as I can tell, none of them, at least since I was born. I've looked around, and I recognize the names of everyone who's died in my lifetime." Duncan gestured. "I see my grandparents and some great-aunts and uncles, and of course my brothers. I never met my great-aunt Cicely, who lived in Paris since she was twenty-one, but she was mentioned all the time before she died four years ago. Our cousin Gerald, who comes from the branch of the family with no money of their own, he works in the family archives and traces the family genealogy. My parents often sit me next to him at family dinners, possibly because no one else wants to listen to him talking about our ancestors and distant relatives. Just last night at dinner, he was talking about someone rather high up on our family tree who fought at the Battle of Bosworth Field. I don't remember what side that person was on, though."

"Hmm. Let's take another look at the gravestones." Holmes walked back to the start of the line of markers. "Elspeth Blurdell Hill. Indicating that she was married, or possibly was the daughter of a Blurdell daughter who married a Hill and wanted to make sure the Blurdell name was not lost. A little under forty. Can you think of any other relatives named "Ellie" or "Ella" or any other potential derivatives?"

"No, sir. I have a distant cousin named Eleanor, but she's only six or so."

"Very well. Five words in the epitaph. "She Will Not Be Mourned." Simple, terse, but vague. That is notable, especially when paired with some of the other headstones."

I was a bit confused. "What do you mean, Holmes?"

"Simply put, writing an angry epitaph on a gravestone is the ultimate way of having the last word in an argument. It's a means of shaming the person you held a grudge against long after death. The deceased can't respond. So why not be more specific? Why won't she be mourned? What did she do wrong? We can't tell from this gravestone, only that no one is going to miss her. But that leads to other deductions. If she was married, then it assumes that her husband is either deceased or than they were not on warm terms. If she had children, something so terrible must have happened that the maternal bond was absolutely severed. Surely what she did would have to be utterly horrific if it were to cut her connection with her own parents, unless of course they were already dead."

"That seems reasonable, Holmes."

"But that ignores a major question. What is she doing here? Why is she buried here? Duncan, since you have no knowledge of her, can she really be that close of a relative? No matter how estranged she was from her family, they allowed her to be buried here. And if she wasn't that close to the Lord Derek Blurdell, why would he have so much rancor towards her that he would carve those words on her gravestone?"

"Perhaps whatever the reasons for that estrangement, Lord Blurdell didn't want to expose the family to scandal?"

"Then why put those words on the headstone at all, Watson? If he wanted to hush up the scandal, all he needed to do was put her name and the relevant dates on the stone. Nothing more. A comment like this is enough to raise eyebrows. If he had those words carved on the headstone, he must have wanted someone to see them. He clearly didn't think enough of Mrs. Elspeth to spend much money on a headstone, yet he willingly paid the engraver extra money to carve that vicious comment. Why pay for a that, and use a low-quality stone that is likely to crumble within a decade? I repeat, if someone wanted to immortalize their bitterness in stone, why not spend a little extra money to make the anger last? It's contradictory, Watson."

"True." After listening to Holmes' reasoning, I was feeling a little dizzy.

"The same principle applies to the grave of John Blurdell. Once again, Duncan, you know nothing of him?"

"I don't believe so, Mr. Holmes. I know an uncle and a couple of cousins named John, but they're all alive and on good terms with the rest of the family."

"I see. The same questions from the first gravestone apply here. The inscription is cutting, cold, and completely devoid of context. The grave of Alicia Blurdell White is far more promising. Only twenty-one years old. Hmm! A liar? That can be said for most of us. Adulteress? That implies that she was married to a Mr. White, but why would Mr. White want to advertise the fact that he was cuckolded? Why would anyone else want to advertise that fact in such a manner? And "Murderess?" Who did she kill?"

"Perhaps she killed her husband so she could marry her lover, Mr. Holmes. Or maybe she killed her lover to prevent a scandal," Duncan theorized.

"Possibly, possibly. But why advertise this? In any event, I am extremely well-informed as to the crime news in this country. I am aware of every person who met a sticky end on the gallows over the past few decades. And I am quite certain that Mrs. White's name is not on that list. Therefore, she was not hanged. Of course, she might have been tried and executed overseas, but would they have shipped the body back here? I suppose that could be true. Might she have committed suicide, or met a violent end at the hands of someone avenging the victim? Twenty-one is a young age to die of natural causes, though of course it happens all the time. And how are we to know that she was really guilty of murder? I know of no trial. It's possible that this woman was falsely accused."

"Not just of murder, but of adultery as well," I mused.

"Very true, Watson. We have to bear in mind that these gravestones may not be telling us the absolute truth. It's quite possible that they're only telling one side of the story. Or rather, one side of six stories." Holmes cleared his throat. "And now, we need to address a critical issue, the dates on the tombstones. Not the birthdates, though there may be some points of importance there that might be unearthed through further study. It's the death dates."

Duncan nodded. "I was wondering that myself, sir. How come all of them died on Christmas? If this happened once, it's perfectly understandable, and twice is a coincidence, but it can happen. But six deaths, all on Christmas? It just seems to be beyond the realm of possibility."

"Left to pure chance, then I agree with you, Duncan. However, there's also the possibility of design, as well."

"You mean they were murdered, Mr. Holmes? All on Christmas?"

"That is one of multiple possibilities. It is also perfectly conceivable that the death dates are a fabrication made out of convenience."

"What do you mean, Holmes?"

"Sometimes when it's not clear when people have died, a date is picked somewhat randomly. This happened a lot during the war. Often for various reasons, it could not be determined exactly when a person was killed. Perhaps it was in the middle of a late-night skirmish and no one knew whether the fatal bullet was fired before or after midnight. Maybe a solider was shot while travelling through the countryside and his body was not discovered by his comrades until a week later. Often, just to get the necessary paperwork out of the way, one date would be selected because it was just as good as another."

"That happened with two of my brothers," Duncan nodded. "They were in the Asian-Pacific theatre of the war, and one got captured and the other got separated from the others in an attack. When their bodies were found, no one knew when they'd died, so in both cases the authorities just went with the date the corpse was discovered. Luckily the legal question worked out without much confusion."

"What legal question?" I asked.

"Their wills, sir. My brother Timmy divided his possessions amongst his four brothers, and my brother Arthur said that his gold watch went to Timmy unless Timmy predeceased him, in which case the watch would go to his wife– Arthur's wife, I mean. Widow, now. Well, even though officially Arthur was supposed to have died a couple of days before Timmy, the bodies had clearly been dead long before they were found, so we just don't know for certain who died first. If Arthur died first, Timmy would get the watch, and since Timmy and my other brothers are dead, the watch would go to me. But if Timmy died first, Arthur's widow got the watch. It could've led to a big court battle if a lot of money had been involved, but Arthur's widow, she's a nice lady, and she told me she wanted me to have the watch." Duncan pulled a pocket watch from his jacket. "I'd much rather have my brothers back, though. Arthur's widow got married again a couple years ago, and just had a baby girl. That's nice for her." He replaced the watch and turned away. I suspect a tear was forming in his eye and he didn't want us to see.

I believe that Holmes wanted to change the topic of conversation in order to provide young Duncan with some time to compose himself. "The remaining graves do not provide us with much additional information. "Suffer in torment?" A particularly piercing emotion, telling us exactly where whoever requested that epitaph believed Mr. Gregory's soul is now. What did he do that led the person who ordered the gravestone to come to such a conclusion?"

"My father must have ordered those words," Duncan noted. "No one else would have done that or allowed such a thing to be inscribed without his approval."

"Hmm, yes. No point in trying to theorize was Mr. Gregory might have done. Not enough evidence to draw any sort of conclusion. But what of your father, Duncan? Is he the sort of man to hold a powerful, burning grudge, so much so that he would flaunt the rules of decorum and the custom of never speaking ill of the dead?"

"No, sir, not at all. He's a most restrained man. He never has been much of one for showing emotion. That's why I can't explain this at all. It makes no sense whatsoever. He's a fierce believer in keeping family secrets away from outsiders. When his sister's daughter got– well, I mustn't say, sirs. You understand the need to keep things private." We did. "He'd never order grave markers like this. It's completely out of character."

"As you noted, this is a fairly private place," I noted. "It's not like your standard church graveyard where any Tom, Dick, or Harry can walk in off the street and start scrutinizing the gravestones. And I don't think that most of your guests will ask to see this portion of the grounds."

"True enough," Holmes conceded, "But all it takes is one person to wander in here and start asking questions. In any event, there are plenty of options that could retain privacy. If one's malice towards a deceased person was so violent that they wanted to carve out a final parting shot upon a tombstone, why not have the body cremated and have the attacking words inscribed upon an urn? An urn could be hidden in a far more private place, even indoors, and since expenses were clearly spared in the first four cases, why not save even more money by choosing cremation over burial? If money was no object, why not build a crypt and keep the bitterness sagely locked inside solid walls?"

Neither I nor Duncan had any response to this, so Holmes continued. "Here is where the situation becomes even more perplexing. These last two headstones are far larger and of much better quality than the first four. The fifth headstone is of a size usually dedicated to the maiden aunts of the family, whereas the sixth headstone is almost the same size as one of your brother's markers, though without the bust atop it. Not cheap. An insult carved upon an obelisk like these will last for decades, perhaps centuries. One more point I forgot to mention about the four smaller stones. You can tell from the dead plant matter surrounding them that the grass has been allowed to cover them during the warmer months. So the groundskeeper has almost certainly been specifically ordered not to tend to those graves, which means for much of the year, the inscriptions would be unreadable. Why go through all the trouble of putting those comments upon the headstones, only to neglect the tending, meaning that the comments are only readable in the winter? Most perplexing."

Holmes coughed and adjusted his coat. "Moving on. The fifth stone's inscription is filled with loathing but is low on specifics. What did the deceased do to warrant such antipathy? It does not say. Perhaps the reference to his being "stillborn" means that he was a nasty piece of work ever since he was a child, but there is insufficient evidence to draw a solid conclusion. Hem! The final inscription is the longest and the most intriguing of all. A bit of doggerel devoted to telling the world what a rotter Dan Blurdell was. You know nothing of him either, Duncan?"

"Not a thing, Mr. Holmes."

"Hmm. Interesting. If a man is referred to as a "sinner," it's most probable that he was given to various forms of dissipation. Women? Alcohol? Gambling? All of the above? Prone to violence?

Halitosis is unpleasant, but not necessarily an indicator of poor moral character. The previous headstone, "Suffer in torment" also expressed a desire for the resident of this grave to reside in the depths of Hades. And to refer to him as the "worst sinner" is perplexing. Surely the worst sinners are the murderers, but if he had killed someone, why not mention it? Recall Alicia Blurdell White's gravestone. If she was identified as a killer, why not Daniel? Therefore, whatever his crimes, Daniel probably never took another human being's life, at least as far as the author of this inscription knew." Holmes paused. "Is your father of a poetic disposition, Duncan?"

"No, sir. He hates poetry. Mother loves it, though. She's always writing poems for our Christmas cards–" Duncan drew in his breath so hard he whistled. "I just realized, sir. My father might not have been able to have bought the gravestone last year."

"Why not?"

"Family business, sir. He was called away to Canada in late November. He didn't get back until well after Twelfth Night."

"Then perhaps your mother ordered the stone and wrote the inscription herself. It seems that your parents share antipathy towards these people." Holmes took a step forward and slapped a hand against the sixth headstone. "No, it won't do. It won't do at all. It doesn't make sense." He stooped down, withdrew a folding knife from his pocket, and began digging in the dirt in front of the sixth gravestone. After carving out a little cone, he eased it out and studied it. "Just as I suspected. Observe, Watson. The ground's hard-packed, some layering is clear. I highly doubt that someone actually dug up the ground here a year ago in order to bury a coffin."

"But if no one's buried here…"

"Then perhaps the other five graves are empty as well." I did not care for the gleam that appeared in Holmes' eyes as he spoke these words. "Duncan, do you know where we can find ourselves a shovel?"

"Holmes, you can't! It's indecent!" A memory flashed through my mind. "And probably illegal, too. Remember Mr. Frankland's comments during the Baskerville case? How it's against the law to disinter a corpse without the permission of the next of kin?"

"I'm a member of the family, aren't I?" Duncan observed. "If I say it's all right, that might take care of any legal issues, couldn't it?"

I was torn between feeling aghast and thwarted, and admiring Duncan for making a clever point.

Holmes allowed himself a little chuckle. "I dare say we should be able to make a compelling defense should the matter ever come into court, yet at this stage of my life I feel the desire to spend as little of it in a courtroom as possible. In any event, at my age I should avoid the heavy manual labor of digging a minimum of six feet into the ground. No, upon further reflection I shall not seek out the use of a shovel."

"I'm delighted to hear that, Holmes."

"I am, however, in need of a bit of exercise. Would the two of you care to join me for a brisk stroll into town? I believe the village is just over half a mile down the road."

As we walked away from the graves, I asked Holmes, "What exactly is your destination in the village, Holmes?"

"The local monumental mason, Watson. The person who designs and carves the gravestones. I noticed his shop next door to the undertaker's a few days ago, although I believe he self-styles as a "memorialist."" Holmes froze and turned around. "Just a moment. There's one further point that I observed earlier but never got around to mentioning." He pointed at the headstones. "Take a closer look at the lettering on the markers. Compare the first four to the most recent two. Pay particular attention to the letters "J" and "L" and some of the others."

Duncan's eyes were much younger and sharper than mine. "The lettering doesn't match, sir! The person who carved the first four tombstones, the ones on the poor-grade rock, he's clearly a different person from the one who covered the other two stones. And... Duncan ran around the graveyard, peering at some of the more recent headstones. "Whoever did the last two stones also did my brother's grave markers, as well as some other relatives who died over the past decade!"

"Indeed. I would very much like a word with our village memorialist."

Fifteen minutes later, we reached the village, and it looked as if everybody who lived there was filled with the Christmas spirit. Mistletoe dangled over many doorways, lit candles stood in most of the windows, and paper daisy chains were festooned everywhere. A quartet of carolers were strolling down the street singing "God Rest Ye Merry Gentlemen," and a man on one corner was selling freshly roasted chestnuts from a little cart. I purchased a small bag and shared them with Duncan. Holmes declined my offer.

Eventually, we reached the memorialist's shop, one of the few stores in the village that was not decorated for the season, which made sense given the somber nature of the business. Holmes tapped on the door. Louder knocks produced no answer, but when Holmes tried the knob, the door swung open.

"Are you sure you should be entering?" I asked as Holmes strode inside the shop.

"There is no "Closed" sign, and if he didn't want people walking in, he ought to have locked his door," Holmes replied. A moment later the three of us were wandering around the shop. Holmes pushed through a second door and found himself inside the memorialist's workroom. "Well, well, well. Watson, Duncan. Come here and take a look at this fascinating discovery, please."

We followed him into the workroom, where a substantial obelisk stood in the center of the room. Traces of stone dust were strewn all over the floor. The room was rather dark, so Holmes struck a match and held it to the marker so we could read it.

Nancy Blurdell Jones

May 5 1901 – December 25 1925

The epitaph was in huge letters that filled the rest of the stone.

THE WORLD IS A BETTER PLACE WITHOUT HER

Holmes chuckled, and I turned to him. "Do you find this kind of bitterness funny?"

"I am in awe of this memorialists' powers, Watson. Not only is he a skilled craftsman who knows how to neatly carve words into stone, but he is also a psychic. How on earth does he know that Mrs. Jones will die tomorrow?"

I had a few seconds to reexamine the stone before Holmes' match burned down to his fingertips. "You're right! How on earth could he know when she'll be passing away? Even the best doctors wouldn't dare to predict when a terminally ill person will die more than a day or two before it happens. People have an amazing ability to linger longer than we'd expect– and sometimes they die much quicker then we think. Is she planning to commit suicide on Christmas? Or is someone planning to murder her?"

Though the light was dim, I could still see Holmes shaking his head. "No, Watson. I don't think that anyone can possibly kill Mrs. Jones. She can never be murdered, nor can she commit suicide."

"Why not?"

"Because she never existed."

"I think you're right, Mr. Holmes," Duncan replied. "When I was little, all the young relatives came to the house several times a year. Even the children of relatives who were estranged from the family came, because the children weren't held responsible for what their parents did. But I never met a cousin named Nancy."

"And I'm quite willing to wager every bee in my hives that all six of the names on the other remarkable gravestones are similarly fictional."

"I believe you've got it, Mr. Holmes"

I was utterly flummoxed. "But why? Why go through all of this absurd rigmarole? Why carve out such vile hatred onto six tombstones–"

"Seven, Watson, including this one."

"Seven tombstones, all for seven supposedly hated relatives who never existed? What could possibly be the point? Is this all some sort of dark practical joke?"

"I am reluctant to cast aspersions upon Duncan's parents in front of him, but I believe that his father and mother have a fairly reasonable motive for their actions."

"His parents?" I realized the truth of this observation as the words left my mouth. "Of course. His father bought all the headstones, except for last year's, when his mother had to handle the transaction."

"And the poem on the sixth one, sir. The meter. The rhyming. It's exactly the sort of thing mother would write. It sounds exactly like one of her Christmas card poems, only with much more negative sentiments. I'm sure it's her work."

"I would not be surprised if other members of the family were aware of what is going on here."

"But what is happening, Holmes?"

"Unfortunately, I still do not have enough facts to draw a reasonable–"

He stopped at the sound of a door shutting. Wordlessly, he motioned us into a corner, and the three of us hid as best we could in the shadow of a tall shelf. A moment later a man and a woman entered the workroom.

"He's probably at the tavern drinking. He'll probably have to spend all of Christmas sleeping it off," the man grumbled.

"Well, he can wait for his money. While we're here, we might as well take a look at his work," the woman replied.

Holmes stepped forward. "Do you often come here on Christmas Eve, Lord and Lady Blurdell?"

Even in the weak light, the surprise and embarrassment on their faces was clear. Lady Blurdell was the first to regain her composure. "Mr. Holmes. Dr. Watson. Duncan. I'm rather surprised to see you here."

"That is understandable, Lady Blurdell. Please accept my condolences on your relative's passing, which will apparently happen tomorrow. Very sad. I must say that I admire your efficiency on ordering the headstone. But please, if you will excuse my overwhelming curiosity, what exactly did Nancy do to make your believe that the world is better off without her?"

Lady Blurdell rallied, and responded to Holmes' question with frigid hauteur. "I consider that a most improper question, Mr. Holmes."

"With all due respect, Lady Blurdell, you do not. In fact, you are anxious to know how I came to ask that question in the first place. A display of false indignation might work on many gentlemen, but quite frankly putting on airs of being insulted has no effect on me whatsoever. You make cast whatever aspersions you like about me based on my words. I can assure you that I am not moved one tiny bit."

Holmes' comments had a remarkable effect on Lady Blurdell. It was rather like watching a balloon deflate in a few short seconds. Lord Blurdell had the appearance of a schoolboy who had just gotten caught in a bit of mischief. "Perhaps we can work out some sort of deal, Mr. Holmes," Lord Blurdell murmured.

"Much wealthier men than you have tried to bribe me, sir, and far more powerful men have tried to threaten me. The thing you can give me now that I most desire is information. I want to know exactly what is going on with this little charade."

Lord Blurdell appeared to have no more strength left in him than his wife. "Please, not here. Anyway, how much do you know and how much have you guessed?"

"I shall recount the events of the last hour to you on the ride back to your estate. Once there, I expect you to answer all of my questions fully."

Lord and Lady Blurdell were both very quiet as Holmes informed them of everything that had happened since Duncan had come to us. Once we arrived at the manor house, the tension was cut a bit by the wonderful smell of roasting goose and cakes baking in the oven. The Blurdells led us into the library and locked the door securely.

"Would you care for a drink, Mr. Holmes?" Lord Blurdell asked.

"No, just information." Holmes caught my eye and read my thoughts. "Watson will take something, though. A whiskey, dear fellow?"

I agreed, and Lord Blurdell poured me a whiskey and soda, and prepared a particularly strong one for himself. The glass was nearly filled with whiskey, and there could not have been more than a teaspoonful of soda-water mixed in with it. Lady Blurdell took a small tumbler of brandy, and Duncan had a glass of plain soda-water. Lord Blurdell swallowed his drink in two gulps, and poured himself another of equal strength. Holmes took the glass from him and set it aside.

"I need you to be in a fit condition to answer my questions, sir. Now, you can start by confirming my suspicions. There are no bodies buried in those six graves, are there?"

Lord Blurdell shook his head. "No."

"And the names on the gravestones. They never existed, did they?"

This question caused Lord Blurdell to look up at us with a surprised expression. "Oh, no. They were all real. They just didn't live for very long. Over the years, there have been many Blurdells who died in infancy. The seven names we've used so far, they all passed away within a few days of being born. Most were born premature. It helped to have genuine birth certificates, though."

"I see. That makes a great deal of sense. The married names of the women were pure fictions, of course. Hill. White. Jones. You picked the most common names possible just to make it harder to track down their husbands if anyone was so inclined."

"Correct. We could have left them unmarried, I suppose, but... we thought that it might help to pair them up with wealthy husbands."

"In order to explain your inheritances, I suppose."

Lord Blurdell's face paled. "You guessed?"

"I did. Thank you for confirming my suspicions. At this time, many members of the landed aristocracy are pinching pennies. Many of them are suffering financially due to increased taxation, death duties, and all sorts of unwanted expenditures. You are doing quite well for yourselves. I see no spaces on the walls where priceless portraits have been sold off, no gaps on the shelves for missing antiques, no housing developments where large tracts of land have been put on the auction-block. Your staff is massive, your wines top-notch, and I have been informed by a reliable source that your Christmas present for your wife is absolutely extravagant. What does this mean? You are enjoying an impressive source of income, something that's allowing you to indulge in extravagances. I know that your home is used by the British government to entertain foreign dignitaries on a near-monthly basis. I believe you get some recompense for your hosting duties, but just enough to cover expenses. Unless, of course, you are finding ways to pad the bills?"

A very ugly smile passed over Lord Blurdell's face. "Blackmail, Mr. Holmes. It's been easy to stand aside and watch these powerful politicians lounge about our homes like they own the place. I've seen who they smuggle in at night, I know what substances they consume, and I hear them talk amongst themselves about how they've been skimming off the top of the various public funds at their disposal. Oh yes, Mr. Holmes. Our Parliament and Foreign Office are full of depraved and venal men. They do not govern our nation wisely. They simply live in the pursuit of pleasure, filling their pockets and living better than the King at the nation's expense."

"And you are particularly offended by this," Holmes replied. It was a statement, not a question.

"Those wretched degenerates killed nearly all of my sons!" Lady Blurdell finally broke her silence. She was a small woman, fragile in build, and the violence that coursed through her body gave the impression that the force of her rage would tear her to pieces. "My four eldest boys all died in the war, Mr. Holmes. And for what?

Is the world any better than it was in 1913, before the conflict started? Are the nations of the world wiser and more humane? Did all those untold numbers of people make the ultimate sacrifice for the greater good? If they did, Mr. Holmes, I can't see it! And who started the war? It was foolish, short-sighted, arrogant, pompous politicians like the ones who tell us they're commandeering our home at a moment's notice, and expect oysters and lobsters and thick steaks and the finest wines and liquor. We must find African violets for the Swedish ambassador's room, they're his favorite. It doesn't matter that it's January, we need to find some strawberries for the Spanish consul. This mattress won't do for the Italian delegate's wife. Get another of the finest goose down right away. And speaking of the beds! They turn our home into a den of iniquity that Caligula himself would be ashamed to enter! These are the men who govern the nation, Mr. Holmes. These aren't statesmen, they're confidence tricksters who are addicted to power and dissipation. They ran us straight into four years of hell on earth, and at the end of it, when we were burying caskets full of our children and wondering if we'd ever be able to stop crying, these men made glorious speeches about how they were going to keep the world safe and secure, and while they bankrupted our friends with new taxes, they used those funds for their own endless revelry. Well, can you really blame us, Mr. Holmes? We had the chance. We waited until they made their way back to their homes. I won't tell you who we recruited, but we managed to blackmail them in a way that they never suspected we were involved. So several years ago, we started, and soon we collected a small fortune from them. But then we were stuck with a problem."

As Lady Blurdell seemed reluctant to continue, Holmes prompted her. "How to explain the money? You needed to spend it. And so, like the American criminals who buy small legitimate businesses in order to turn their ill-gotten gains into income they could pay their debts with and put in the bank, you needed a seemingly respectable avenue as a cover for your financial chicanery. It is a lot easier for a gangster from Chicago to buy a laundry and pretend to profit handsomely from it than it is for a British aristocrat to run a business. So how to account for the funds? You claimed to inherit them."

"I shan't give you the names of the people who helped us!" Lord Blurdell's voice showed defiance for the first time. "I won't get these decent people in trouble. They understood. They'd lost children of their own, they knew we were just getting our own back, and we paid them well to compensate them for the terrible suffering they endured. But you're right. At the end of the year, we totaled up all the money we'd collected over the past twelve months, and claimed that a long-estranged relative left us everything. To fund the maintenance of the family home– we figured that they might not have cared for us, but they had loyalty towards the house and grounds. The people who might have investigated were paid off, and after all of our expenses and dispensations, we were still enjoying a hefty profit."

"Yes, we paid a small fortune in death duties, but it was all going back to where it came from," Lady Blurdell explained. "The thieves in the government had less money, and much of it went back in, where hopefully some of it managed to find its way into actually helping the country. Of course, the bloodsuckers took some of the money right back, so we just had to take it from them again the next year."

"It was rather fun," Lord Blurdell mused. "But every now and then there was somebody– someone from the government who would ask us about what was going on. It happened immediately. That's when I realized. English "gentlemen" hate to pry into people's personal scandals. Perhaps it's because they're afraid someone else will start asking about their own private affairs. And I do mean "affairs." So what better way to silence questions than to imply that these people who died were terrible people we couldn't bear to talk about?"

"Surely you didn't have to carve those words on their graves?" I wondered.

"Actually, that was the icing on the cake," Lord Blurdell grinned. "Whenever some official started inquiring, we'd show them to the headstones. When they saw those graves, they figured that something absolutely awful had happened in the deceased people's pasts, and being well-trained since birth to avoid other people's unpleasantness, they said their goodbyes pretty quickly. They figured that if I were to allow those words to be carved on a headstone, then the story must be too shocking for human ears. The looks on their faces! I've lost count of all the times I had to bite my tongue to keep from laughing! The first time a tax employee saw "She will not be mourned," his pince-nez fell off in shock and shattered on the stone!"

"But something went wrong two years ago," Holmes countered. "That's why you had to buy more expensive gravestones."

"The local memorialist was in the graveyard for an aunt's headstone being installed, and he saw the four cheap stones. "Why didn't you come to me?" he asked. He knew something was wrong by our faces. So we bought a nice, big gravestone from him the next year to keep him quiet. The next year he dropped more hints, saying he got paid by the letter. So my wife wrote that little poem, bought that huge slab of rock, just to keep him happy. It cut into our profits a bit, but not too much. This year– you saw what we ordered. I don't mind. We're spreading the wealth around to people who need it. The memorialist lost two brothers and three of his seven children in the war. That's a reason why he drinks so much. I don't fault him."

"Why did you have all the "relatives" die on Christmas?"

"We came up with a story about a Canadian branch of the families. Ne'er-do-wells who married or gambled or otherwise connived their way into considerable fortunes, and after leaving England as expatriates, they wanted to be buried back home. We said they had interests in the Yukon gold fields, but the mail there only came out rarely, and as they'd died in cabins in the middle of nowhere, no one knew exactly when they'd died, but we just said Christmas for convenience, as that was about the time we'd receive a news update from our Canadian family members. We'd learn about their death on Christmas, so we'd say it just to have a date. People understood. Plus, we could claim that we'd held the memorial service when all the family was here for the holiday. No one else wants to come to a funeral at Christmastime. It was an easy way to keep the burials quiet."

"What do you intend to do now?" Holmes asked.

"Why, exactly what we've been doing," Lord Blurdell explained. His demeanor had changed. The beaten, embarrassed man was gone. "We're not going to stop. This is just compensation for the loss of our sons. And you won't tell anybody. Otherwise we'll provoke a scandal that will bring down the government. Given what we know, we'll never see a day in prison."

"We can't let this continue!" I blustered.

"You don't have a choice." Lord Blurdell had regained his backbone. "This is rough justice, and we're not going to back down just because you have qualms about a little justified extortion."

"No, you won't!" Duncan yelled. "This is wrong, and you taught me to always do the right thing. I'm ashamed of you both!"

This started a huge argument. The three Blurdells all forgot that Holmes and I were there as they launched into a no-holds barred shouting match. Father, mother, and son all screamed and fought, losing all sense of decorum and hearing none of what Holmes and I were saying.

After ten minutes, I can only explain what happened next as a true Christmas miracle. The butler pushed open the library doors, muttering, "Your lordship. Your ladyship. I can't believe it..." Behind him limped a young man. He was gaunt, haggard, and looked as if every step caused him great pain. But the sight of him had an incredible effect on the Blurdells.

"Timmy!"

"Timmy?"

"My God! My son!"

The long-lost son gulped down a little brandy, and soon told his amazing story. He had been captured in the waning days of the

203

war in Asia, and an enemy agent who resembled him superficially had been recruited to assume his identity. Apparently he had been killed soon after embarking on his mission, and his body had been mistaken as Timmy's due to the identification papers. Meanwhile, Timmy had languished in prison, not knowing what had happened or even that the war had ended. Due to all sorts of oversights and inefficiency, he hadn't been released for many years, and the government, thinking he was dead, hadn't made efforts to rescue him. When he was finally released a month ago without money or identification papers, he was compelled to beg until he had enough to buy a steerage ticket on a ship headed home. He would have sent a telegram, but he had no funds. He'd picked up some tropical disease in prison, anyway, and spent most of his days aboard the ship in a mild state of delirium. I examined him, and though he was in poor health, after proper treatment and plenty of rest, there was no reason why he shouldn't make a full recovery.

There is little more to say. Holmes spoke to Mycroft to apprise him of the situation. Over the coming months, there were a great many resignations from the government. I was not made privy to the details, but I assumed that the Blurdells went unpunished in exchange for their silence. Apparently, the Blurdells' thirst for vengeance faded with the knowledge that one of their lost sons had survived. The family wasn't whole, but it was happier.

Young Duncan was the happiest of all, and he wasn't the least bit upset that he was no longer the heir to the family fortune. His brother's survival was more than enough for him, and I was delighted for Duncan and Timmy. Duncan had tried to give the watch he'd inherited from his other brother to Timmy, who refused it, and they eventually agreed to share the watch, though the details weren't clear. In a letter I received shortly after New Year's, Duncan told me how he and his family had celebrated the coming of 1926. That night, the Blurdells, with the help of some members of the staff, had taken eight gravestones and hurled them into a lake on the estate. Seven of the headstones were the ones with bitter epitaphs. The eighth was Timmy's. I am told that the cheering was deafening as the stone bust on Timmy's grave marker sank beneath the water.

Part Two: Crossovers and Alternative Histories

Of Course He Pushed Him

"See him?" Battlecruiser Barry jabbed a finger with a cracked, filthy nail at the pub window, pointing at the dignified-looking doctor hurrying down the street.

Florrie leaned forward, causing Battlecruiser to involuntarily recoil backwards. Six years earlier, when women of Florrie's profession were being slaughtered on the streets of Whitechapel, a rumor circulated that Jack the Ripper had come up to her, taken one whiff of Florrie's breath, and then run away screaming. A slightly nastier version of the rumor suggested that Florrie's halitosis had proved lethal, which is why the Ripper's reign of terror finally ended.

"Oh, I know him-- his picture used to be in the papers all the time. Not so much now that his friend's dead and he's spending all his time seeing patients instead of solving crimes." Florrie shuddered. "So sad about his friend. Such a brilliant man. Terrible that he fell off that cliff in Switzerland three years ago."

"Yes... fell..." Battlecruiser put special stress on the second word.

"What do you mean by that?"

"Mean by what?" Battlecruiser tried to look innocent. It didn't suit him.

"You were being very coy when you say "fell." Of course, it wasn't an accident. He went off the cliff because of his fight with that professor, didn't he?"

Battlecruiser shrugged. "Well, that's the official line."

Florrie scraped her chair forward, causing Battlecruiser to scoot further back. "That's what the doctor said in his account, didn't he? Don't you believe his story?"

A contemptuous sneer spread across Battlecruiser's face. "The doctor would want everybody to believe that his pal was killed by a master criminal who's conveniently also dead and can't defend himself."

"Are you saying that's not what happened?" Florrie looked incredulous.

"I've got a distant cousin who works at that Swiss hotel where the doctor and his friend stayed, and my cousin told me that the so-called good doctor was acting very shifty the day his friend and the professor died."

"No! I can't believe it!" Florrie made an effort to sound indignant, but it was obvious that juicy, scandalous gossip delighted her. "You think-- you're saying that the doctor pushed his friend over the cliff and into the waterfall?"

"Of course he pushed him. It's obvious, really. There's something not quite right with the doctor. You can see it in his eyes, he's a wrong'un, he is."

"What about the professor? Are you saying the doctor killed him, too?"

Battlecruiser shrugged. "Who knows? You know that the doctor was in the army in Afghanistan. Some men go a bit wrong after a war. And not to be too crude to a lady, but there was always something a bit amiss with his relationship with his... "friend." Not surprising it turned violent. I suppose they quarreled, the doctor shoved his pal, and perhaps he took care of the professor as well because that distinguished old mathematician witnessed the crime. Then the doctor came home and wrote that ridiculous story to explain away the deaths."

Florrie continued to express skepticism about the doctor's guilt, but still paid close attention to Battlecruiser's theories. It was obvious that the possibility that the doctor was a killer, possibly a double murderer, had latched into her imagination. By the time she finally left to go in search of paying clients, she was not only convinced of the doctor's guilt, but she was itching to spread her suspicions to everybody she met.

Battlecruiser smiled when he saw Florrie whispering to one of her colleagues. Truth is sluggish, but malicious gossip is quick as lightning. He knew that if he spread the rumor to all of the names on the list, in a matter of weeks all of London would be convinced that the doctor had shoved his best friend off a cliff and into a central European waterfall.

Battlecruiser checked his watch. He had just enough time to make his date with the scullery maid, Polly.

•••

"I never liked him. There was always something uncouth about that doctor. I never trust a man who writes about himself. There's something vulgar about that sort of self-aggrandizement." Mrs. Talmidge sniffed disapprovingly, and adjusted her cards in her hand.

Mrs. Dinell tittered softly behind her cards. "I always liked the doctor's stories."

"Pure sensationalism! That's what they are!" Mrs. Talmidge had read plenty of the doctor's stories herself, but she was not about to admit that to the members of her bridge group, especially now that she had publicly implied that the doctor was a cold-blooded murderer.

"Wherever did you get the idea that he killed his best friend?" Mrs. Opaline inquired.

"Oh… a <u>very</u> reliable source. Someone who knows a lot of secrets, someone who I trust <u>completely</u>." Mrs. Talmidge had heard it from her lady's maid, though she wasn't about to reveal that fact to her friends. Her lady's maid, incidentally, had picked up the story from Mr. Talmidge's valet, who'd heard it from the parlormaid, who'd been told the rumor by the scullery maid, Polly, though the parlormaid had been sworn to secrecy.

"You mark my words," Mrs. Talmidge declared, laying down another card. "The police will arrest the doctor any day now. I'd bet my grandmother's pearls on it!"

•••

"Oh, you <u>mustn't</u> go to that horrible man!" Mrs. Opaline pleaded to her cousin, Mrs. Wellner. "It's simply too dreadful to think about! I hear that there is a witness who actually <u>saw</u> him push that marvelous detective over the cliff, and that professor as well-- they say that he was jealous of his friend's success, I think. I couldn't bear to have that man touch me for a second! No, dear, you really ought to go this other gentleman in Harley Street to look at your throat. He's very talented, very respectable. I have his address in my handbag here…"

•••

The doctor's wife was an affable woman, and she was rather surprised when her so-called friend Mrs. Wellner cut her dead in the street.

Running up to Mrs. Wellner, the doctor's wife tugged at her sleeve and cheerfully said, "Juliet? Didn't you see me?"

Juliet Wellner drew herself up to her full height (which was not very imposing, as she was a tiny woman), and with glacial hauteur replied, "I should consider it a favor if you would not approach me with such unwelcome familiarity, madam."

The doctor's wife was stunned by this frigid reception. "Juliet, what on earth has gotten into you?"

"I have no desire to continue any acquaintance with a woman who has chosen such a disreputable husband. Good day and goodbye." Mrs. Wellner flounced down the street, and the doctor's wife stared at her open-mouthed.

•••

"You can come in now, Inspector."

The Inspector cautiously crept into Superintendent Dilys' office. It was obvious that there was tension in the air, but the

Inspector wasn't aware of having done anything wrong. The Inspector was about to lower himself into the chair in front of his superior officer's desk, but Superintendent Dilys snapped at him.

"Don't sit down."

The Inspector remained standing.

"You know why you're here, of course."

"No, I certainly don't."

"Don't be a fool. I know you do."

"I assure you, sir, I haven't the faintest idea."

Dilys snorted and leaned back in his chair. "Then you're an even bigger fool that I suspected. It's about that shady pal of yours."

"You'll have to be more specific, sir."

"That bleeding writing doctor! The one with that meddling dead detective friend!"

"Oh, him. What about him?"

"Just so you know, we're starting an investigation into him, and if you try to warn him off, I'll see you stripped of your rank. You understand me?"

"An investigation? For what?"

"Murder, of course. The London underworld is buzzing. Apparently every pickpocket and prostitute knows for a fact that he pushed his… roommate off that cliff a few years ago."

The Inspector nearly choked. "That's utter bosh, sir!"

"Is it? Well, whether it's true or not, we have to look into it. It's dashed inconvenient for us. Especially since the murder didn't happen on British soil. If it turns out a murderer has been involved in investigations for over a decade, that could lead to some pretty awkward situations. The Home Office is already asking some sharp questions about that bludgeoning in Herefordshire five years ago. We had the victim's son dead to rights, and that bleeding know-it-all detective and his shifty doctor friend got the boy acquitted, didn't they? And that other medical man who died. Who the bloody hell dies of a snakebite in Surrey? That stinks of rotten fish to me. Well, I knew that pair was up to no good from the beginning, sticking their noses where they didn't belong. And you're hand in glove with them, aren't you? Are you a dirty copper, Inspector?"

"What? No! I'm not!" The Inspector felt his face turning crimson, as the volatility of the situation suddenly became fully apparent to him.

"Well, I don't trust you half an inch, you little rodent-faced plodder. You can consider yourself on desk duty until further notice, do you hear me? Now get out of my office!"

The Inspector stormed out of Dilys' office, trying to control his rage. The situation was blatantly unfair, and he was helpless to clear either his own name or his friend's.

•••

"I'd like to try on that hat, please," the doctor's wife asked the milliner.

The milliner glared at her. "No."

"Why not?"

"We don't want your type in this establishment. This is a respectable shop."

The doctor's wife turned chalk white. "I assure you, I am a respectable woman. My husband is a doctor--"

"Oh, I know all about your murdering husband," the milliner sneered. "I'm sure he'll be on the gallows before the month is out. Now get out of here before I call a copper and have you thrown out!"

The doctor's wife hurried out, trying to keep her dignity. This was the fourth time in three days that she'd had a confrontation like that. But she hadn't told her husband. It would only upset him, she reasoned...

As she shuffled down the street, she felt the stinging sensation of a steadily worsening pain in her head. She had been getting so many headaches lately, she was starting to worry...

•••

By the end of the following week, the doctor was quite possibly the only man in London who hadn't heard the rumor that he'd pushed his best friend to his death.

It was therefore with great bewilderment that he noticed that he was being snubbed.

On Monday, he received a letter informing him that his invitation to speak at a medical conference had been rescinded. No explanation was given.

On Tuesday, an old friend of his from the army had politely but firmly refused to have a drink with him.

On Wednesday, three of his patients cancelled their appointments with him, and informed him that they were changing doctors.

On Thursday, the doctor lost four more patients, and he noticed that a friend of his wife and her husband hurriedly crossed the street when they saw him walking towards them.

Normally, the doctor would have wondered about the cause of this sudden coldness, but his mind was preoccupied with other matters. He was worried about his wife. She had been looking very pale and fragile lately. Her health had never been robust, but lately… there were signs detectable to an experienced medical man that she was under severe strain. He had tried to talk to her in the hopes that she would unburden herself to him, but she had airily refused to admit that anything was wrong.

And so, instead of wondering why he was rapidly becoming a social pariah, the doctor focused his attention to his wife exclusively on Friday, when she suddenly collapsed with a burning fever and a devastating migraine.

•••

Battlecruiser chuckled. "Thanks for the money, Colonel. I must say, this is one of the easiest jobs you've ever offered me. No safecracking, no rough stuff, just a little bit of rumour-mongering. Will this be a regular thing?"

The Colonel did not look up from polishing his gun. "I'm afraid, Battlecruiser, that this will be a one-of-a-kind project. Step one of my plan for total revenge."

"Are you trying to get the doctor hanged?"

"Certainly not. That would be too merciful for him. I've lost a bloody fortune due to him and his friend meddling in the Professor's affairs. I'd be a millionaire now, vacationing in my private chateau on the French Riviera if that precious pair hadn't interfered. So, I want him to suffer. But if you really want to hurt an Englishman, you don't kill him. You humiliate him, and the best way to crush a really respectable Englishman's spirit is to shatter his reputation. Men can hold their heads up high when they can excuse away their personal sins, but they crumble when people believe they did something they didn't do. By the time I'm through with him, his practice will be in tatters and he'll wish he had a noose around his neck."

"I wonder if his wife will leave him."

"I dare say you're right, Battlecruiser, but not in the way you mean. My spies say that the doctor's missus has taken ill, and I suspect that the rumour-mongering has played a part in her sad decline. They tell me she's had some sort of seizure, and may not survive the week."

Battlecruiser chuckled. "Dear me, how sad."

"Yes, isn't it a tragedy? The moment her coffin is lowered into the ground, you can start a new fleet of rumours, suggesting that the good doctor may have contributed to his wife's demise. Perhaps some rare, untraceable poison he discovered while serving in Afghanistan. Won't that be delightful?"

•••

Superintendent Dilys strolled into the Assistant Commissioner's office. He wasn't sure why he was being summoned, but he hoped it something to do with the promotion he'd been angling for over the last six months.

It took one glance at the Assistant Commissioner to inform him that he wouldn't be getting promoted anytime soon.

"Dilys! I understand that you've launched an investigation into that doctor."

"Yes, Assistant Commissioner, that's right."

"Well you're going to cancel it right away, you hear me? Call it off, and bring all your notes on the case to me so I can burn them. Understood?"

Dilys turned purple. "But... But... Why? Doctor--"

"That doctor has a very powerful friend, and if you don't back off him immediately, it's the chop for both of us. So leave him be. That's an order."

"But--"

"I don't have to tell you why or who, Dilys, that's none of your concern. Just call off your dogs, and leave the man be. Oh, and that sly little fellow, the inspector who looks like a drowned rat. You put him on desk duty, didn't you?"

"Yes, I--"

"Well, take him the hell off desk duty. Apologize and tell him he'll be getting an extra fiver in his next pay envelope as an apology. And don't ask me to explain myself, you're not going to get any answers. Now get the hell out of my office before I break you down to a constable!"

Superintendent Dilys limped out of the Assistant Commissioner's office, wondering what had just happened and why.

•••

The fat man folded his hands across his ample stomach and leaned back in his chair. He did not like to show emotion, but he permitted himself a very faint smile as he observed the extreme agitation on Battlecruiser's face. The fat man's associates, Geoffrey and Bertram, both enormous men (though unlike their boss, their bulk was entirely muscle), stood behind Battlecruiser, oozing intimidation from every pore.

"You let me go now!" Battlecruiser tried to sound tough, but succeeded only in managing a plaintive whisper. "You can't keep me here!"

"I can and will," the fat man replied. "I am not pleased with you, Mr. Battlecruiser. You have caused a great deal of distress for my late brother's best friend and his wife. By slandering a good man and destroying his practice, you have caused irreparable harm to a heretofore sterling reputation. Now, why would a low-level criminal like yourself do such a thing? You never crossed paths with my brother and the doctor. You have no reason to spread slander. Unless... someone put you up to it. I believe that it was either the Colonel or the dentist. Which was it?"

Battlecruiser writhed anxiously. "I'll never tell! He'll put a bullet right between my eyes, he will!"

The fat man sniffed. "No need to tell me. I observed your facial expressions as I named my suspects. It was the Colonel who organized this little plot. Thank you for confirming my suspicions, inadvertent as your help may have been. Now, explain to me why the Colonel has initiated this smear campaign against the doctor."

"I won't say!" Battlecruiser moaned.

"As you wish," the fat man sighed. "Geoffrey? Please demonstrate the Baadsgaard method on Mr. Battlecruiser here. Perhaps that will induce him to talk."

"Yes, sir," replied Geoffrey, who knew full well that there was no such thing as the Baadsgaard method. "Do you want me to use the water version or the fire version?"

Waving a pudgy hand, the fat man carelessly replied, "Surprise me."

"You can't hurt me!" Battlecruiser shrieked. "I'm a British citizen! I've got rights!"

The fat man drew a small box of chocolates from his waistcoat pocket, popped one in his mouth, and sucked on it for a few seconds before swallowing it. "For the purposes of this investigations, I am the British government. I can order Scotland Yard to drop any investigation I desire, and I have the right to revoke the citizenship of anybody I wish for whatever reason I see fit, and I do so to you now. So now, dear fellow, you may officially consider yourself a man without a country. And therefore, you have none of the protections that the British citizenry enjoy. Geoffrey, I believe that this case justifies the combined fire and water method, if you would, please--"

"Wait!" Battlecruiser shrieked and started blubbering. His next several sentences rolled out of his mouth rapidly. "The Colonel wants vengeance against your brother. He knows he's still alive. The Colonel's never forgiven your brother and the doctor for breaking up the professor's organization. It cost the Colonel a fortune, and he's out for revenge. He told me to start spreading the rumor that the doctor killed your brother, because that was the best way to bring your brother out of hiding. This was all a ruse to get your brother to re-emerge so the Colonel could kill him for real. When he ordered me to start spreading the rumor, I couldn't say no, could I? Could I? He'd shoot me dead in the street if I didn't follow orders. It's not my fault, sir, don't you see? I had to do what I did. Please don't hurt me, gov, please!"

Battlecruiser started sobbing uncontrollably. The fat man, who had no patience for tears, snapped after two seconds. "Stop your blubbering immediately!"

"Yes, gov. Sorry, gov." Wiping his eyes, Battlecruiser forced himself to stop crying, and lacking a handkerchief, blew his nose directly on the floor, to the horror of the other three men. "So, can I go now?" Battlecruiser asked hopefully as he got up from his chair.

"Go? Certainly not." As the fat man spoke, Geoffrey and Bertram took hold of Battlecruiser's shoulders and lowered him back into his chair. "You will remain here for another two hours, at which point my associates here will escort you onto the *Rialto*, which sets sail for New South Wales at dawn. I have no idea how you'll make your living in Australia, but that is really no concern of mine."

•••

The fat man and his younger brother, the detective, were sitting in the elder brother's room at his club. The detective puffed on a pipe, and the fat man wrinkled his nose and tried not to make his displeasure too evident. From the amused glint in the detective's eyes, his brother was not succeeding.

"Must you smoke that wretched thing?"

"My dear brother, you know that it helps me concentrate my decision-making processes."

"Humph. What's to decide? Just come back to life already and be done with it."

"It's not that simple, as you are no doubt aware."

"Nonsense. You can walk back into your lodgings at any time. You just don't <u>want</u> to return."

"Whatever makes you think that?"

"I believe that you've come to prefer life in the shadows."

"I find that it is infinitely more efficient to destroy a crime syndicate as an essentially anonymous figure."

The fat man ground his fist into the arm of his chair. "Need I remind you, that not only does the Colonel know that you still draw breath, but that your supposed death has been weaponized by your enemies to cause the very genuine demise of the wife of your best friend?"

The detective became very still and quietly put down his pipe. "There was no need to mention that."

"Because you'd rather ignore that discomforting fact?"

"No, dear brother, because I never stop thinking about it." The detective leaned back in his chair and placed the tips of his fingers together. "We've had bodyguards on them around the clock for the last few years. I thought that if the remains of the Professor's gang did decide to go after them, they'd go for a physical attack. I can assure you, it was a humbling and salutary lesson when I discovered that the Colonel had chosen to launch an assault against which we were completely defenseless- rumor and innuendo. A pair of weapons far deadlier than even the most high-powered rifle, especially in the wrong hands."

Grunting in agreement, the fat man added, "But there is a quick and effective way to disarm this weaponized rumor."

"Reveal that I'm alive," the detective replied. "Yes, at this point, it's the only way to completely and thoroughly lay waste to the ridiculous idea that my poor friend killed me! How absolutely disheartening it is to realize that London society, particularly its medical establishment and its so-called "respectable" classes, could be so credulous, so willing to believe the most respectable and reliable man in the world was a cold-blooded killer! Be thou as chaste as ice, as pure as snow, thou shalt not escape calumny, eh?"

"It's a miracle that the doctor hasn't had an inkling of the whisper campaign against him yet."

"No. And he mustn't. Taken on top of the sudden loss of his beloved wife, hearing that all of his medical colleagues and fair-weather friends are looking at him with suspicion might very well kill him. And I can't have that. No, to save a good man's reputation and his life, and to avenge the death of a golden-hearted woman, I must return to a notoriety I have never sought and do not enjoy."

"Excellent. When do you plan to return to the land of the living?"

"No time like the present, I suppose. The longer I put this task off, the harder it will be to resume my old life. Tonight, I rise from a watery grave and simultaneously smash the Colonel's remaining portion of the Professor's gang, and obliterate his vile web of slander as well."

"How will you make your reappearance? An interview in the papers? A speech to Parliament?"

"No, London's reporters will break the story. I shall let my friend tell more in one of his well-intentioned but ultimately overdramatic stories. I think he deserves the opportunity to reveal his own innocence to the world without realizing it. Of course, he'll need a bit of crime to make it a proper story for that very lurid magazine. He might as well focus the story on the Colonel's capture and arrest for that recent fatal shooting. I shall set a trap for him within the hour, and then allow my friend to know that I am still alive."

"Fair enough. What will you do? Knock on his door and reveal yourself?"

"A bit too simplistic for my tastes, dear brother. I think that I must make myself known a touch more quietly, but memorably. You know that I cannot resist a touch of the dramatic. I cannot just show up at the good doctor's doorstep, at least not as myself. I think that I shall introduce myself to my friend in a way that he will not recognize me at first. I have been working on a particularly convincing elderly bookseller disguise…"

The Adventure of the Villainous Victim

I have lost count of all of the occasions where my friend solved a baffling mystery where the official police failed, only to allow the legal authorities to accept all of the credit for the resolution of the case. In contrast, I believe that there is only one instance of a case where my friend desired public recognition for catching a killer, but he was denied it due to a fluke of chance.

In June of 1881, shortly after our initial meeting, Holmes and I took a day trip to Brighton to make some purchases at a new tobacconist's shop that had rapidly gained a reputation for having a special house blend of fire-cured pipe tobacco that had smokers all over London raving about its quality. After making some purchases that severely strained both of our monthly budgets, we walked back towards the Preston Park Station to take a late lunch at a nearby café before catching the three o'clock train back to London.

Our plans for lunch were interrupted when we heard a man's screams coming from the station. We sprinted in the direction of the shrieks, and soon discovered that they were coming from a ticket collector. I am the first to admit that I lack my friend's observational skills, but it did not take a pair of eagle eyes to determine what was causing the poor man's distress. Sitting on the ground five feet away from the ticket collector was another man, whose entire body was covered in blood.

While Holmes delivered a firm yet gentle slap across the hysterical ticket collector's face in order to silence his ear-piercing cries, I examined the blood-covered man. After a minute's study, it became apparent that the blood was not his own. It was a disturbing realization. I shook his shoulder until he finally turned his head and met my eyes. "Look here, my good fellow, do you know what's happened to you?"

He stared at me with glassy eyes until finally he responded to my question. "I... don't remember. Not everything, anyway. After they attacked me..."

His voice trailed off and I snapped my fingers in front of his face to keep his attention. "Listen, sir, please try to stay with me. I'm a medical doctor and I need to find out what's happened to you. You say you were attacked. Who did this to you? What did they do?"

"I don't know. After they struck me, everything's a blank."

My friend's voice made me jump. I hadn't expected him to join in on the questioning. "Perhaps you can start by telling us your name. If, of course, you can recall it."

I couldn't be sure because of all the blood, but I thought I observed a small flash of indignation in the bloodstained man's face. "I most certainly do know my own name."

"And that name is?"

"My name is Percy Lefroy. Two men attacked me as the train started travelling through the Merstham tunnels."

I remained silent, knowing that Holmes was far more skilled in asking questions about crimes than I was.

"Very well, Mr. Lefroy. Did you know your assailants?"

"No, they were strangers to me."

"Can you describe them?"

"Well... no, not really. They moved so quickly, I couldn't get a proper look at them. I remember that they were unusually tall and strong, though."

"You have no recollection of their hair or eye color? Their clothing? Did they have facial hair?"

"I... couldn't tell you. I just can't remember. They just came up to me, beat me, robbed me... and the next thing I know I'm here, and I don't have a clue what's happened to me."

A constable's arrival interrupted the conversation, and the official representative of the law quickly took charge of the bloodstained man, hurrying him off to the police station to lodge a complaint before receiving a full medical examination.

I could tell from the glint in my friend's eye that he had no intention of taking the train back to London. He was far too intrigued by the grisly discovery, and once he was on the scent of a case, there was no stopping him.

"That poor fellow," I murmured.

"Poor? I wonder…"

"Well, surely he's the victim of a terrible crime."

"Nonsense! There's no "surely" about it, Watson. His story is deficient in so many ways, I'm surprised that he didn't blush with embarrassment at his own perfidy. Although, due to all of the blood covering him, it's quite possible that his face did turn crimson without our realizing it."

"Deficient? Whatever do you mean?"

"Surely, my dear fellow, you realized right away that the blood covering that man was not his own."

"Well, yes. That was clear after a brief examination."

"And I realized that after only a second's glance. After all, a man who had lost that much blood would be at death's door and would probably be unable to move. No, that wasn't his own blood. Now it's possible that he had somehow wandered into an abattoir, but

I am never one to embrace a comparatively innocent option when a far more sinister one will suffice. Judging by the spatter on the man we just met, it's entirely probable that the blood came from a particularly violent fight with another human being, and as noted earlier, the loss of that much blood means that the other party involved in the fight is more likely to be dead than alive. Now, you noticed no serious wounds on that blood-covered man. I submit, that when a man is attacked by another man with a weapon that can draw a large amount of blood, the innocent victim is highly likely to be seriously injured, even if that person does manage to turn the tables in the end. But this man sustained no injury, a condition more probable in an assailant than a victim."

"I agree with you that it's more probable, but not necessarily. Suppose he was attacked by a drunkard or a madman. The assailant could have swung a knife or some other weapon about wildly, but his impaired condition could have made it fairly easy for his would-be victim to have turned the tables."

"Possibly, possibly. But did you observe the watch-chain on the bloodstained man?"

I allowed myself to smile a bit. My observational skills have improved quite a bit over the last few months, and I'd noticed that there was no watch or chain in the bloodstained man's jacket or vest pockets when I examined him. I said as much, and my fleeting sense of triumph was crushed by my friend's superior grin.

"The bloodstained man's watch-chain wasn't in his jacket or vest, Watson. It was sticking out of his boot."

"Was it?"

"Yes, a little under an inch of it was visible coming out of the top of his right boot. Now, that is suggestive, is it not?"

"Well, I suppose it's odd, but I don't see how it could be considered suggestive."

"My dear fellow, why would a man shove his watch-chain into his boot? If he wished to consult his pocket watch, he would leave it in his jacket or vest. If it were damaged or if he'd lost his watch, he might conceivably keep the chain it in his overcoat pocket. Under what circumstances might he have placed his watch-chain in his boots?"

"Perhaps if he were trying to protect it from being stolen? If he feared a pickpocket or an armed robber, he might have hidden the watch-chain there in the hopes that no one would look there."

"That is certainly within the realm of possibility, I agree with you. But you're missing a critical point. If an innocent man were taking care to protect his watch-chain, he would make quite certain it was completely hidden inside his boot. And if a man was attacked by a drunken madman, like you suggested, then he would have no time to secrete his watch-chain into a hiding place. A sudden attack would provide him with no opportunity to do so, and as we just discussed a few moments ago, an unexpected attack is by far the most likely way an innocent man might have escaped an assault unscathed. Therefore, the postulation that the watch-chain was hidden in the boot as a precaution will simply not hold water."

"Then why would the watch-chain be in his boot? Are you saying that he tucked away his own watch-chain to bolster his claim that he'd been robbed?"

"I very much suspect that the watch-chain in question doesn't actually belong to him, but to his victim. An intelligent criminal would have accepted the loss and disposed of the watch-chain, and if the chain truly belonged to him, he would have sold or pawned it if he were in dire need of money. It's more likely that he stole the watch-chain, and then hid it in his boot so that he would not have committed his crime for nothing. Being in a hurry to hid his ill-gotten gains, he neglected to conceal the chain completely."

"Then this man isn't an innocent victim of a crime, but a perpetrator."

"That is a reasonable theory at present. I shall need to investigate further in order to verify my theories."

"Will you tell the police to arrest him, Holmes?"

"No point in that, I regret to say. We have no solid evidence that will justify an arrest. I need to collect some more clues before I can make a proper charge. If I were to go about accusing men of committing murders with no corpses, even if I were entirely correct it's likely that I would wind up in court facing a lawsuit for slander. Not my preferred use of time and funds, I can assure you. No, our investigation must commence, and quickly, before our gory friend vanishes. After he makes his statement to the police and cleans himself up, there's nothing to keep him here."

"Then what is our next step?"

"If you'll follow me, Watson, I want to take a look at the train currently waiting at the station. I daresay we shall find some useful information there."

And with that, Holmes led the way to the train and climbed aboard. He worked his way down the train car, glancing into each room of the carriage, until he finally scrutinized one door handle more closely.

"Aha! Here we are, Watson! This is the one we want."

"How can you tell?"

"The smears of blood on the handle, of course. The dark color of the door handle makes them difficult for the untrained eye to see– the casual observer may mistake them for rust. I, however, have made a special study of how blood responds to various surfaces. I have started a very promising monograph that I really must finish some day on how bloodstains appear on various kinds of wood and metals. These little marks that could easily pass for rust? They have a far more sinister meaning, I assure you."

With that, Holmes withdrew a handkerchief from his pocket and gingerly opened the door. He took a very swift look around, and turned back to me.

"This is the scene of the crime, no doubt about that."

"Are you sure?"

"My dear Watson, the copious amounts of blood on most of the surfaces, the damage to the room indicating a struggle, the abandoned, bloodstained personal items, and the three bullet holes in the wall all lead to the unescapable conclusion that a violent crime has been committed here. It is beyond the bounds of probability to suppose that two particularly sanguineous attacks have taken place in the same train car within the past hour. The dampness of the larger patches of blood and the lingering scent of gunpowder prove the recentness of the violence that occurred here."

"Shall we speak to the police and have him arrested now?"

"Of course not. We need to find the real victim of this case. But we will go straight to the authorities and tell them of our discovery."

We could have made it to the police station in less than five minutes, but we had the unfortunate poor luck to be confronted by a pair of train conductors who had wandered into the carriage, spotted the two of us amongst all of the carnage, and drew the erroneous conclusion that we were responsible for the mess. We tried to explain the situation to them, but the dim-witted pair were holding fast to their first impression, and they blew their whistles and summoned the police. Seeing as how they were disposed to make trouble if we attempted to flee, Holmes explained to me that we might as well stand and wait, and we ought to be able to explain away the situation in a matter of minutes.

Holmes' prediction proved overly optimistic, and it took nearly an hour to convince the local constabulary that we had only been investigating a crime. It was only Holmes' repeated pointing out of the facts that neither of us had any wounds upon us that could have caused the bloodshed, that neither of us were carrying a firearm, and that the state of the blood's coagulation indicated that whatever had happened there had taken place sometime earlier, that the police reluctantly but wholeheartedly conceded that we had nothing to do with the carnage. Furthermore, the realization that this was the scene of the crime that had led to that mysterious man getting covered in blood had a galvanizing effect on the Chief Constable in charge of the case.

"Well, I thank you for bringing the possible murder scene to our attention, Mr. Holmes," the Chief Constable told us with a moderate amount of grace. "But we would've found it fairly quickly on our own, I'm sure you know that. And thank you for those very insightful theories about the case as well."

"Will you be holding that man?" I asked.

"I don't think we can, sir. We've interviewed him, and I must say I've had my suspicions of him from the start. We policemen aren't fools, you know. You weren't here when Mr. Lefroy made his statement, but I noticed a fair number of holes in his story, though I did suppose we might be able to chalk them up to mental distress over the incident. It could affect anybody's memory, don't you know."

"Where is Mr. Lefroy now?" Holmes inquired.

"I suppose he's at the hospital. They're giving him a full examination, and we'll see what he has to say for himself after a bit of rest and time to collect his thoughts."

"May we speak to him?"

"You'd have to check with his doctors. If the man's in a state of shock like one of the doctors suspected, they might not allow anybody to question him."

Holmes craned his neck and examined a small cardboard box on the Chief Constable's desk. "Are these Mr. Lefroy's possessions?" he asked, pointing at the label.

"They are. Care to examine them?"

"I would. Holmes picked up a pair of golden coins and held them up, one in each hand.

"Now, why would a man be desperate enough to rob someone else when he had a couple of sovereigns in his pocket?" the Chief Constable mused.

"Oh, these aren't sovereigns," Holmes replied, tossing them on the desk, where they made a dull clunking noise. He withdrew a pocket knife from his coat and scratched the face of both coins, leaving a dark scrape on them. "Gilded lead. These sovereigns are counterfeit."

There was silence for several moments, and I broke it. "At the very least, are you going to arrest him for possessing counterfeit coins?"

The Chief Constable did not respond, and eventually Holmes responded, "It would be very difficult to make a passable case out of that, Watson. After all, we have no proof that Mr. Lefroy actually knew that these sovereigns were not genuine coin of the realm. All he has to do is claim that he was unknowingly given these coins by a bank or business and that is enough to shed a reasonable doubt upon his guilt. In any case, why arrest him for a trifling crime when a much greater crime, possibly mere assault but more likely murder, has been committed?"

"Are you proposing a course of action, Mr. Holmes?" The Chief Constable seemed oddly willing to listen to a non-policeman's ideas for continuing the investigation.

Holmes nodded. "I am. Where is Lefroy?"

"I just got a message from one of my men telling me that the hospital's given him a clean bill of health and that he's on his way to board the next train to London."

"Surely that shows a guilty conscience," Holmes mused. "The man wants to flee as soon as possible. Additionally, he's not bothering to pick up the so-called sovereigns. That's highly indicative that he knows they're counterfeit, and doesn't want to return to the police station to retrieve them. When does that train leave?"

"In just under nine minutes. Perhaps a bit less– my watch runs slow."

Holmes turned to me. "Watson! Hurry to the train station, purchase a ticket to London, find Lefroy, and ride back with him. Don't let him out of your sight. And be on your guard. I believe he's already seriously harmed one man today, I certainly do not want you to be the second. Meanwhile, Chief Constable, will you kindly allow me to assist your men with a search of the line?"

I followed my orders to the letter, and I managed to board the train moments before it pulled away from the station. The train was not particularly crowded, so it was an easy matter to come across Lefroy. He was wearing a clean suit, but it was one of the old, worn, third-hand pieces that hospitals often keep on hand for the indigent. It did not fit him well, and the legs of his trousers were considerably longer than necessary, so the tops of his boots were completely covered and it was impossible for me to tell if he still had the watch-chain hidden inside one.

I maneuvered myself into a seat one row behind and across the aisle from Lefroy, who was slouched down and staring at his

241

boots. My mind raced as I attempted to figure out what the best course of action would be. Did I introduce myself to him? Should I try to strike up a conversation? Twice, my mouth opened in order to speak to him, but a moment's thought led me to clamp my lips closed again, figuring that perhaps it was best to keep my presence a secret. After all, what if he remembered me from the train station? No, it was surely a more prudent course of action to try to follow him unobserved.

The train ride was uneventful, and one station before we reached London, a grubby-faced young boy poked me in the elbow. "This is for you, Doctor." He pushed a telegram into my hand. "Mr. Holmes said you'd have half a crown for me."

I thought it presumptuous of Holmes to dole out my half-crowns without my permission, but I figured that he and I could settle accounts when we met again. As I dropped the coin into the boy's hand, I wondered how he'd gotten aboard the train, but he turned around and vanished before I could ask him the question.

Opening the telegram, I read the message:

WATSON–

BODY FOUND. DON'T LET LEFROY OUT OF YOUR SIGHT. WHEN YOU DO LOSE TRACK OF HIM, WIRE ME IMMEDIATELY.

HOLMES

My first reaction upon reading this telegram was indignation. Holmes has developed a frustrating habit of assuming the worst about my abilities, and the fact that he is often more correct than I'd like him to be is a continual source of irritation on my part. Still, though I had no real experience shadowing other people in the street without being detected, I noted that the sun had recently set, and a light London fog was drifting into the area. I reasoned that these new developments would help keep me hidden from my quarry, though I immediately realized that a tandem consequence of the darkness and fog was the fact that I would have increased difficulty keeping Lefroy in my sights.

I managed to keep an average of ten paces behind Lefroy over the next three blocks, but a throng of churchgoers exiting a small chapel blocked my line of sight, and by the time I made my way through the group of worshippers, I found that Lefroy was nowhere to be found. I hurried ahead in the hopes of catching up with him, but I felt my heart leap up so high it nearly hit my chin when a hand reached out of the alley and gripped my shoulder firmly.

"Who the hell are you and why are you following me?"

I found myself quite unable to speak, and as I turned around, I realized that the man holding on to my shoulder was Lefroy himself. My muteness proved no serious problem, as Lefroy recognized me immediately.

"Here now, didn't I see you at the station in Brighton?"

Mercifully, I regained control of my vocal chords. "Yes. I'm a doctor, you see. My name is Watson. The hospital was very concerned about you and wanted someone to keep an eye on you. Since I was on my way back home to London, anyway, I volunteered to follow you and make sure that you got home safely. I didn't introduce myself because I didn't want to disturb your quiet time to yourself, you see. After a terrible shock like the one that you endured this afternoon, it seems only right that you should be given as much space as possible in order to process everything."

I felt the overpowering desire to keep talking, but I realized that babbling would only serve to raise Lefroy's suspicions, and I forced myself to be silent.

Would he believe what I said? If he was the violent fiend that Holmes suspected him of being, might he attack me? I met Lefroy's gaze directly, and tried to make my eyes unsuspicious and unthreatening, hoping that he would view me as a well-meaning friend.

Lefroy's eyes remained focused on mine for what seemed like hours. His expression was hard and accusatory, but unexpectedly and instantaneously, it transformed, becoming relieved and amiable.

"Oh, I say. How very decent of you."

"Not at all, my dear fellow."

"I do appreciate your going to such lengths to look out for my wellbeing. But I don't want you to go to any trouble. I was just on my way to my relative's boarding-house where I've been staying." He fingered the shabby, ill-fitting suit he was wearing. "I need to change my clothes."

"I don't mind joining you if you don't mind my presence," I replied, trying to sound nonchalant. "It'd give me a clear conscience to make sure that you got home safely."

"All right, then, thank you! But you're in for a bit of a walk, I'm afraid. The boarding house is in the Wallington district."

That was indeed a bit of a trek for me, but I decided that despite my many purchases earlier that day, I could afford a small luxury. "I must insist that you let me pay for a carriage-ride."

He demurred, then agreed with minimal coaxing on my part. Soon afterwards, we arrived at the boarding house. He wished me good night and made his way into the building.

I abruptly realized that I was in a tricky situation. I didn't know if the boarding house had a back exit, and there was no convenient place for me to hide and observe unseen. There was no way that I could make sure Lefroy was resting in his room. I was fretting over the best course of action when a young street urchin jumped into the carriage with me.

"Who are you, young fellow?"

"My name's Cookney, Doctor. I just heard from Mr. Holmes, and I'm to give you this telegram."

I opened it, and read–

WATSON–

VICTIM IDENTIFIED. ISSAC GOLD, FORMER CORN MERCHANT. BOTH GUNSHOT AND KNIFE WOUNDS. HAVE YOU LOST LEFROY YET? IF SO, RETURN TO 221B AND WAIT FOR ME.

–

HOLMES

Once again, my initial response was indignation, but the abrupt realization that I did not, in fact, know for certain that Lefroy was securely in his room tempered my umbrage. After I hastily tossed the carriage driver his fee, I hurried into the boarding house, planning on making up some story about wishing to rent a room there, thereby giving me access to the building.

Before I could reach the door, I felt a faint tug at the back of my coat. Turning around, I saw Cookney.

"It's too late, Doctor. Didn't you hear the whistle?"

"What whistle?" I had been so lost in my thoughts, a cannon could've gone off without my noticing.

"A couple of my pals gave the signal. Mr. Holmes gave us all some special whistles a while back. If you're young– around our age– or if you have unusually sensitive ears like Mr. Holmes, you can hear them. Most adults can't. The whistles are very high-pitched. Anyway, Lefroy went out the window about two minutes after he entered the boarding house."

"We need to catch him!"

"Don't you worry, Doctor. My pals are right on his heels. About an hour ago, I got a message from Mr. Holmes to pick up this special preparation of his from his home."

"What special preparation?"

"Couldn't tell you for sure what was in it, but it smells like a mixture of anise and vanilla extract. Rather nice, really. Anyway, I snuck in through the coal chute, found Lefroy's room, and sprayed all the clothes and boots in his closet with the preparation. Mr. Holmes figured Lefroy would change his clothes and make his escape. But my pals are tracking him. Bobby'll catch him."

"You seem to have a lot of faith in that boy Bobby."

"Bobby's not a boy, he's a spaniel. Best nose in London. Wherever Lefroy goes, Bobby will follow the scent."

I stood silently for a moment, reflecting on both Holmes' ingenuity and his absolute confidence in a dog and a bunch of street urchins. "So what am I to do?"

"Just what the telegram said. Go back to 221B and wait. One of my pals is wiring Mr. Holmes."

"My carriage is probably long gone by now."

"No, I told the driver to wait. May I ride back with you?"

And so, a little over an hour later, I found myself back at 221B, eating one of Mrs. Hudson's hot dinners and wondering just where Lefroy was at that moment.

I was two bites away from finishing my meal when Holmes walked in the door.

"Ah, Watson! Enjoying your meal, I hope? I've asked Mrs. Hudson to send up my meal as well. You won't mind if I eat while I tell you the results of the last few hours, do you?"

"Not at all."

Mrs. Hudson entered and set down a large plate of stew with rolls in front of Holmes, who smiled and began enjoying it immediately.

I allowed Holmes some time to nourish himself, but after a few minutes my curiosity got the better of me and I practically begged him to provide me with some news on the case.

"Ah, yes. I must say, Watson, this case was a great disappointment to me. There was no artistry, no cleverness, no imagination. None of the hallmarks of the great criminal, or even an inspired miscreant. Simply a bare, bland case of brutality and greed, resulting in a wasted life. I tell you, this Lefroy, if that is his true name, which I very much doubt, has done nothing to distinguish himself as a criminal. Nothing more than a modern highwayman, who sacrificed another human being with every right to live for a pittance."

"There was a murder, then?"

"Yes, and it required no real effort of my intellectual powers to resolve the case. It was obvious from the very beginning that a violent crime occurred in that train compartment, and that no man could survive such a substantial loss of blood. That left the question of what happened to the body, and I suspected that the killer had simply pushed it out the window, possibly in a place where it might not be spotted for quite some time. A tunnel might be a logical place for disposing of the body, where it could be jettisoned from the train in darkness and lie undiscovered for hours, even days.

After analyzing the state of the coagulation of the blood in the carriage, I had a fair idea of how much earlier the crime had occurred. I therefore subtracted the amount of time since the train arrived in the station, and after calculating the average speed of the train, determined that there was only one tunnel in the estimated range, and asked the police to check it.

There, they found a body that was quickly identified as one Isaac Gold, a gentleman of mature years who was now enjoying a comfortable retirement. An aged, rather frail man whose clothing illustrated his prosperous condition was a natural target for a marauder. The body suffered numerous bullet and knife wounds. His watch and chain had been ripped from his waistcoat, and all of his money was removed from his wallet and pockets. Poor fellow."

"And you think that Lefroy is the killer?"

"I'm quite sure of it, Watson. The motive was robbery, a crime of opportunity. It was just the late Mr. Gold's bad luck to have been the selected victim. It might have been any one of a hundred other people. Lefroy– or whatever his real name is– will not escape the grasp of justice for long. I have utter confidence that between my ragtag collection of street urchins, the keen nose of Bobby, and the efforts of the police, Lefroy will be arrested within a very short time, and will doubtless pay the ultimate price for his crimes."

Holmes' predictions proved completely accurate. Lefroy was swiftly arrested and charged with the crime. Holmes and I were among the prosecution witnesses at the trial, where it was revealed that Lefroy's true name was Mapleton, and that he'd attempted to rob the unfortunate Mr. Gold, but Gold's refusal to be cowed into compliance led to Lefroy– or rather Mapleton– to turn to lethal violence.

After the announcement of the guilty verdict, Holmes and I discussed the case back at our lodgings.

"A sad crime, but not without its points of interest," Holmes remarked.

"One point still bothers me, Holmes. Why was Lefroy– or rather, Mapleton– sitting down at the station when the ticket collector found him?"

"Most likely, he realized that he was covered in blood and realized that he couldn't get away without attracting attention. So he decided to collapse and act as if he'd been injured in order to deflect suspicion.?"

"That makes sense," I replied. "You know, I can't say that I came across very well in this case. I let him escape out from under my nose."

"You're new to the field of catching criminals, my dear fellow. Give yourself a bit more time and experience. And indeed, if you wish to write up this case, you can always utilize a touch of artistic license to make your role a bit more heroic."

"Thank you for your generosity of spirit, Holmes, but I think that if I do choose to record this case for posterity, I shall adhere strictly to the truth. Accuracy is very important to me."

Holmes laughed. "If only the newspapers were as scrupulous as you, Watson."

"What do you mean?"

Holmes withdrew the evening edition of a newspaper from his pocket and dropped it on the table. "Read the coverage of our case, Watson."

I did so. When I reached the last paragraph, I read aloud, "The police are particularly indebted to the assistance of an independent detective, Mr. George Holmes... *George* Holmes! Wherever did they come up with that name? Who in their right minds could ever mistake the name "George" for "Sherlock?"

My friend smiled. "I have no idea, but I shall take this as a lesson. Never seek out fame in the popular press. Any attempt to catch the public eye is bound to have unintended consequences, especially when reporters have such difficulty keeping stories straight. No, I think that in the future, wherever possible I shall refrain from accepting any public acknowledgement of my role in solving crimes. Unless of course, you decide to record my exploits, Watson. You are the one person who I trust to get all of the details correct..."

Author's note: The murder of Isaac Gold was a true case from 1881, and the basic narrative and most of the characters, including the detective "George Holmes," are taken from history. The idea that the papers got Holmes' name wrong is of course, purely my own invention.

The Chapel of the Holy Blood

It is often said that two heads are better than one, although this is by no means a universally shared perspective. When an acquaintance once repeated this dictum to Father Brown, the priest immediately replied that when two heads of state get together, the result often leads to war. His acquaintance retreated immediately, and from that point forward was noticeably recalcitrant to engage the good Father in any form of conversation whatsoever. Father Brown has never complained about that.

It was a dreary Thursday afternoon, and as the little priest was making his way down Baker Street, he was holding tightly to his umbrella. The weather was so blustery that had anybody bothered to look at Father Brown, they would have worried that a sudden gust of wind would send the priest flying over London. No one was seriously concerned about his welfare, however, as everybody on the street that day was completely engrossed in their own affairs, and there was so little light that a small man clad all in black and covering himself with a black umbrella was virtually invisible.

When Father Brown knocked on the door of 221B, Mrs. Hudson informed him that Sherlock Holmes was currently out and she didn't know when he'd be back, but he was more than welcome to wait in his rooms. Father Brown stood by the fire, waiting for his cassock to dry, and sustained himself with the pot of tea and the plate of Scottish shortbread that Mrs. Hudson had thoughtfully provided for him.

After about twenty minutes, the priest was shaken out of his daydreaming when a familiar voice called out to him. "My dear Father Brown! How wonderful to see you!"

"Holmes! I hope that I haven't arrived at an inconvenient time."

"Not at all. I just resolved a rather disappointing situation involving a banker absconding with funds. His initial trick of using mirrors to make it appear that the vault he'd been pilfering from was fuller than it was had at least a touch of ingeniousness to it, but his getaway plan was shamefully obvious. His disguise was positively laughable. In any case, he is now sitting uncomfortably in jail and the stolen funds have been recovered. I shall not go into any more detail. The crime simply is not that interesting. Anyway, how are you, Father? I haven't seen you since we solved the case of the two Coptic Patriarchs together."

"I'm quite well, thank you. I've been working at the Deaf School along with my usual parish duties, and my old friend Flambeau is coming for a visit next week."

"Good old Flambeau! Give him my best, will you?" Holmes had met the reformed thief Flambeau a few years earlier during the case of the Vatican cameos. Flambeau had been the chief suspect, and Holmes and Father Brown's combined efforts had managed to clear his name and prevent an international uproar.

"Where is Doctor Watson?"

"He's at a conference in Wales now. Won't be back for several hours. He'll be sorry to have missed you."

"And I'm disappointed to have missed him this visit."

The two men helped themselves to tea and shortbread. Father Brown checked his cassock and after he assured himself that it was dry, he settled down in a chair next to Holmes.

"So Father, what brings you all the way to London on this most inclement day?"

"I came to you because I needed your assistance– particularly your knowledge of chemistry."

"Indeed? Is there a matter of science that you needed to discuss?"

"There is. If it isn't too much trouble, I need you to use your famous re-agent."

"The one precipitated by haemoglobin?"

"The very same." Father Brown reached into his pockets and pulled out a rosary, a breviary, four small coins, a whistle, a compass, two sticks of chocolate, and three handkerchiefs (all of different colors) before finally pulling out a small glass jar containing traces of a dried reddish substance.

"Is that blood, Father?"

"I was hoping that you could tell me whether it is or not."

Holmes' face lit up, and he happily snatched the jar from Father Brown's hands and rushed over to his small laboratory. "I shall fill this flask with water, and I just need to take a tiny bit of this sample– as much that will cover the tip of this bodkin here. Now just one moment…" Holmes shook the flask vigorously, dropped some pale crystals into the solution, and then uncorked a bottle full of clear liquid and shook a tiny trickle of it into the flask. After about four seconds the water turned the color of strong tea.

"Is that a positive test, Holmes?"

"Well, yes… and no. The haemoglobin test is positive, but… the color of the test result isn't quite right. It isn't dark enough. Which means…" Holmes drew another tiny sample from the jar, spread it onto a glass slide, and slid it onto his microscope. "If I'm right, the red blood cells will be slightly oval… Yes, by thunder, they are!"

Father Brown's face brightened. "That means that's not human blood, then?"

"I'm afraid I can't be positive, but based on my previous experiments with animal blood like beef and chicken, I'd be willing to give fair odds that this blood came from a sheep."

"That's better. That's very much better." Father Brown smiled, walked back to his chair, and sat.

"Are you at liberty to explain where the blood came from, Father?"

"Oh, yes. The seal of the confessional is not a factor here." Leaning forward, Father Brown turned to Flambeau, who had returned to the chair next to him. "Have you ever heard of Dirus Castle?"

"I dare say I may have come across its name in the newspapers at some point, but at present I can recall nothing about it."

"Dirus Castle was for many centuries a monastery. When Henry VIII seized most of the Catholic Church's property for his own use and gave much of what was left to his powerful friends, he sent a squadron of armed men to seize the monastery, which was located on some particularly fertile farmland. The monks were known for beekeeping and other agrarian pursuits, but they were not trained fighters, and in a very short time all of the monks were slaughtered. What happened next is obscured by legend. According to the story my niece told me, the abbot was the last to be slain, but as he was dying from a mortal blow, he placed a curse on the property, claiming that every so often, the blood of the slain monks would trickle down the halls of the monastery as a reminder of this horrific crime."

Holmes arched an eyebrow. "Do you– er– believe that story, Father?"

"Oh, I'm quite convinced of the veracity of the first bit of the tale– the part where Henry VIII ordered the murder of a lot of members of the clergy and stole their land. That's well-documented, despite the current owners' attempts to hush up the violent history behind what's now called Dirus Castle. You see, the title of Lord Dirus was bestowed upon a particularly brutal fellow who raised a great deal of money and land for Henry VIII and his allies by killing anybody who opposed the King and seizing everything of value. I may say, Lord and Lady Dirus don't like people knowing that the family lands, funds, and titles derive from a massacre of unarmed monks. They prefer everybody to think that their titles derive from antiquity, and that the family's lineage dates back to the Knights of the Round Table. All tosh, of course."

"But what do you think about the curse, Father?"

The priest smiled. "I suppose that given my personal predilections, I'd prefer to think that a dying man of the cloth would choose to spend his dying moments praying for the souls of those who persecuted him rather than using his last breath calling for vengeance through sanguineous haunting. I certainly believe in miracles and the supernatural, but I can also smell a rat. And I believe that some sort of fakery is happening at Dirus Castle at the moment. You see, Holmes, I took that sample of blood from the walls of the castle."

"Are you saying that there really was blood flowing from the walls?"

"Well, not really flowing. Earlier this morning, trickles of a dark reddish substance, presumably blood, were found smeared and splattered all over the walls. I took this sample from the inside of Lord Dirus' study, which was once a room of private contemplation for the monastery known as, ironically enough, the Chapel of the Holy Blood."

"Did Lord or Lady Dirus call you in to investigate, Father?"

"Oh dear me, no. The Dirus family is decidedly antireligious. They have nothing but cold hostility for me and everybody of my faith and vocation. But my niece, Betty, is engaged to the son of Lord and Lady Dirus. A young fellow named Agro."

"Best wishes to her. What is this Agro like?"

"Holmes, I believe that in Doctor Watson's account of "The Copper Beeches" that you discussed how the character of parents can be seen in their children, and vice vsersa."

"I did. In the case that you refer to, I was talking about a particularly nasty and cruel boy, and I postulated that he inherited his unpleasant demeanor from one or both of his parents. Am I right in thinking that your niece's fiancé is... not such a pleasing youth as you'd hope?"

The priest made a face. Even though he couldn't see his own expression, he was quite sure that anybody watching him might conceivably concluded that he was being uncharitable. Anybody familiar with young Agro would have found Father Brown's reaction understated. Dozens of the family's former servants had surreptitiously warned away potential employees with horror stories of the tantrums that the heir to the title was prone to throwing.

Holmes smiled, "My dear Father Brown, you needn't worry about speaking ill of others. It so happens that on a recent case I interviewed a kitchen maid, and though she could provide very little in the way of information useful to my investigation, she told me a great deal about her previous employer. Lord Dirus is an angry man, a womanizer, and excessively fond of the bottle. His son follows in his footsteps, and Lady Dirus is a coldhearted, imperious woman who doesn't just work her staff to the bone, but to the marrow as well."

Taking a sip of tea, Holmes redirected the topic. "How, exactly, did your niece become engaged to that fellow? If your niece's character bears any resemblance to your own, then I doubt that Betty and Agro are compatible."

"They are not."

"Will you take offense to my broaching the possibility that your niece may be... shall we say... blinded by the glamour of lands and a title?"

"Oh, no. Betty is not a golddigger. Her mother, however, has always wanted her daughter to marry "well," and Betty has always tried to appease her mother at all times. In any case, Betty has had bad luck with previous suitors. More than one of these seemingly respectable young men has proven to be a criminal, and the cycle has been going on for rather a long time. Betty has, unfortunately, developed a certain amount of anxiety about her unmarried state, and I believe that she has latched onto this relationship both to please her mother and because she has come to the deeply flawed conclusion that a bad marriage is better than no marriage at all."

"Father, have you come to me for help in breaking up this engagement?"

"No, though that would be a welcome development. I visited you today in the hopes that your test would confirm whether or not the substance on the walls of the chapel was blood or not, and if so, if that blood was human. Depending on your verdict, I was going to investigate further in the hopes of explaining why the blood was decorating the castle walls."

A delighted look spread across Holmes' face. "Would it be presumptuous if I were to offer my services?"

Father Brown immediately accepted Holmes' offer, and half an hour later the pair were on a train bound for Dirus Castle. Once the train was on its way, Holmes asked, "Explain again to me what you observed this morning, please."

"My niece invited me to elevenses at the castle, and I met her in the village and walked with her to visit her intended and his family. When we arrived, we could see at once that there were bloodstains on part of the wall of the entryway. Young Agro showed us into his father's similarly-stained study on one side of the entryway, which used to be the Chapel of the Holy Blood when the structure was a monastery, and rather gleefully told us about the legend– which I was already familiar with– and declared that the abbot's curse was at work."

"Interesting. You say that Agro seemed happy about the blood on the walls. Has he ever, to your knowledge, showed any interest in the supernatural?"

"On the contrary, as I said earlier, Holmes, the family has a reputation for being particularly antireligious. When Agro waxed lyrical about the abbot's curse and the vengeance of the slaughtered monks, his parents were standing there, gritting their teeth and glaring at Betty and myself. Neither of them had anything to say about the blood on the walls. Indeed, they wanted to ignore it altogether."

"Really?" Holmes pressed his fingertips together underneath his chin. "You would think that they would have at least been interested in talking about it. After all, such an occurrence mustn't happen every day. It would have made for some amusing conversation over elevenses."

"I agree with you. Unfortunately, our meeting was particularly unpleasant. Lord Dirus and his son made a few derogatory remarks towards my profession and my religion, and when I contradicted them and defended my faith and vocation, they both became rather annoyed and left the room. As for Lady Dirus, she never said a word to me or to Betty, despite our best efforts to ask her questions about the phenomenon going on in her home."

Holmes permitted himself the faintest trace of a grin. "Far be it from me to criticize a lady, but I rather doubt that Lady Dirus is living up to the highest standards of hostessing. I am surprised that she didn't provide her future daughter-in-law with a warmer reception. Am I correct in theorizing that Lady Dirus is opposed to the match?"

"I should say that assessment is accurate. Betty comes a line of country squires that are rich in family history but poor in funds. I don't know the exact state of the Dirus finances, but people with substantial estates seem to be in constant need of more money to pay for the upkeep of their considerable property. In any case, they've shut up most of the castle to save on maintenance expenses. They're only using a tiny portion of the property, which is why we had our elevenses in the little dining nook right next to the chapel."

"And the landed classes of England realized a long time ago that the best and most reliable way of raising enough money to support one's estates is to marry money." Holmes' eyes glinted with amusement. "I've heard it said that when England's gentry with country estates start their families, they pray for a son to inherit the property, and they pray for a wealthy heiress for their son to marry about two decades down the line. I trust that you will take absolutely no offense when I ask, why exactly did young Agro agree to the match?"

"I regretfully but relievedly concluded a while ago that Betty was not entering into a love match. Agro is close to his parents, but one of his chief joys in life is riling them. I've made some enquiries, though I suppose that it would be ingenuous to call my questioning discreet. Apparently Agro likes to toy with his parents' nerves, and he has a reputation for courting attractive young women without a bean to their names, even getting engaged to them if it suits his fancy. Of course, none of these relationships ever come to anything."

"Wouldn't such behavior leave that pleasing youth vulnerable to the prospect of a breach of promise lawsuit? I know of at least two dozen cases where a wealthy young man has gotten engaged to a wholly unsuitable woman, and when he tries to extricate himself from the relationship, the young woman takes legal action over being jilted, and invariably receives an impressively lucrative settlement without ever having to enter a courtroom."

Father Brown sighed. "I suppose the financial risk is part of the sport for our friend Agro. When he tires of his latest lady friend, he engages in such boorish behavior that the young woman terminates the engagement. He's careful to have a friend of his as a witness at all times. That leaves him well immunized against any lawsuits. Indeed, my sources– most of them former employees of the Dirus family– make it clear that the girl is usually so relieved to be free from that singularly unpleasant young man that she would be willing to hand over her life's savings to her ex-fiancé if it meant that she would never have to see him again."

"I see. Do you think that your niece wants to escape from the relationship?"

"She hasn't said so in so many words, but if past patterns hold, the only reason why she entered the relationship in the first place was to please her mother. She's a very dutiful daughter, although perhaps it's a lot easier for her to pursue relationships with men she doesn't particularly care for than it is for her to listen to her mother complain about her marital status."

Holmes took a breath and redirected the conversation. "How exactly did you get that blood sample? Even if Lady Dirus wasn't speaking to you, I can hardly imagine that she would let you scrape off a bit of coagulated blood without protest."

"Lady Dirus walked away without so much as an "excuse me" when she finished her coffee. She did pause to give a large golden candelabra a quick dusting with her handkerchief before leaving the room. I went straight to the chapel– technically the current Lord Dirus' study, although I dare say that it was never officially decommissioned– and used the edge of a coin to remove a substantial amount of the blood. Luckily, I happened to have an old jam jar with me, though for the life of me I can't remember why I was carrying it with me in the first place. Betty was a bit nonplussed about the whole thing, but she was rather keen on the prospect of me coming to you. Betty's mother has gotten her into a number of excruciating relationships with unpleasant yet wealthy young men, but she's always been able to escape, usually with my help. Young

Lord Agro may be her least pleasant and most intimidating fiancé yet, and she was enthusiastic at the prospect of you getting involved in the situation, even if it was only to analyze the blood sample. In a situation like this, she wants as many allies as possible in her corner."

"Sensible young woman."

Holmes and Father Brown continued their discussion of the case for the rest of their journey. In a little under an hour, their train reached the tiny station on the outskirts of the village closest to Castle Dirus. At the priest's suggestion, they went directly to the Purple Boar, a pub where the former second footman at the Castle had found employment after an unpleasant incident involving an irate Lord Dirus and a tantrum involving a chamber pot and a flaming log from a fireplace.

"I tell you, I wouldn't go back to work at the Castle again, not if you paid me a million pounds. *Two* million," the ex-second footman declared as he poured drinks for Father Brown and Holmes. "They're batty, every last one of them. Lord Dirus is an absolute monster. When he's not drinking up half the wine cellar, he's chasing after girls from the village or the female staff. Not very dignified for a man of his age, is it? He's careful not to do anything untoward in the presence of his wife, of course. She's an iceberg, she is, but when somebody crosses her, that porcelain façade cracks pretty fast, if you get my drift. And the son takes after the father, you know. Chases after anything in a dress, and a fuse so short a single spark would burn it up completely in a half-second, it would. Why, I'll tell you about the time…"

The second footman turned publican continued expounding upon the many personal flaws and offensive aspects of the Dirus family, and Holmes and Father Brown sat and listened quietly, and marveled at the ease at which they were being provided with information on the local nobility's personal foibles. It was a full seven minutes before the former second footman took a breath, giving Holmes the chance to ask, "Do you happen to know how many members of the staff are left at the Castle?"

"Well, when I left last month, there were only four of us left. The housekeeper and both of the gardeners had given notice the week before, after Lord Dirus had gotten good and soused and fired his shotgun through the window at them– the gardeners, that is. And when the housekeeper ran into the room to see what had happened, he fired again at her! If I'd had any sense, I'd have left myself that day, especially considering how scant my wages were. They're not so well-off as they'd like us to think, you know. Lucky for me, I got out of there soon enough, and I found a place here. Not as fancy as the Castle, but a darned sight jollier."

"Who are the four remaining employees?" Holmes asked.

"Actually, only three now. A week after I made my happy escape, my pal, Lord Dirus' valet, decided he'd taken enough verbal abuse from the old… Better watch my language in front of a priest, I suppose. Anyway, he found a place working for a retired army colonel in the next village. Due to the Dirus family being short of ready cash, and the fact that their reputation for being terrible employers is well known for miles around, they haven't been replacing their missing staff members lately. The only ones left are that dotty old butler Bassett, who's half-senile but still manages to do his job. I think the only reason the butler sticks around is because he forgets Lord Dirus' insults the moment after he shouts them, and Lord Dirus keeps him around because his memory's so bad, Lord Dirus can claim he's already paid him his salary for the month, and the poor old fellow can't remember otherwise. Then there's the cook– a real tartar, that woman. The only staff member who can hold her ground against the members of the Dirus family. If she doesn't want to prepare something, she doesn't make it, even if the family demands it. Finally, there's Agnes, the housemaid. Pretty thing, though I'm disappointed to say that I've never gotten anywhere with her."

The former second footman continued to ramble for a long time after Father Brown and Holmes had finished their beverages. Most of what he told them was a rehash of what he'd previously said, although at times he would slip in the name of an unfortunate person, usually a maid or a girl from the village, whose life had been damaged in some way due to coming into contact with the Dirus family. Eventually, the owner of the pub told the former second footman that he wasn't being paid to chat with the customers, and the mildly chagrined man turned to serving other customers.

As Father Brown and Holmes left the pub and walked through the village, Holmes turned to his friend and asked, "Do you remember the first case we investigated together?"

The priest nodded. "The sudden death of Cardinal Tosca. Of course."

"When we were following up on that note we found in the Cardinal's breviary, I told you that we needed to investigate the scene of the crime for clues. You told me that we needed to find out more about the Cardinal's character and what he truly believed him if we were ever going to find out why someone would want to kill him. In the end, we were both right. If we hadn't followed both lines of inquiry right away, we would never have proved it was murder or identified the culprit before it was too late and additional lives were lost."

"What are you saying, Holmes?"

"I mean, my friend, that we need to hurry up and investigate. Can you manage to get another invitation to Castle Dirus? If I can get a look at the bloodstains on the wall, and if you can try to gain some insight as to the family's behavior, I think that we can figure out what's going on here surprisingly quickly."

Father Brown explained that his niece had gone back to her mother in a nearby village, and that the Dirus family would never let him inside if they could help it, but that he was on friendly terms with the cook, and she would help them if they were to approach quietly by the servant's door.

When they arrived at the castle a quarter of an hour later, the cook was indeed happy to help them. Like nearly all of the other servants who had worked for the Dirus family, the cook made no pretense to any claims to loyalty to her unpleasant bosses.

Luck was on the side of the sleuths, and Father Brown and Holmes were able to make their way to the former chapel as stealthily as they possibly could without being seen by the other inhabitants of the castle. Upon reaching the chapel-turned-study, Holmes immediately whipped out a magnifying glass and began scrutinizing the bloodstains on the wall. Meanwhile, Father Brown crossed to the window, where he observed the three members of the Dirus family walking towards the house.

"Better hurry, Holmes. They're returning." After a moment the priest murmured, "I wouldn't have taken Agro for a gardener."

"What do you mean by that?" Holmes did not avert his eyes from the wall.

"He's carrying a shovel and a spade."

"Look at this, Father," Holmes pointed at the bloodstains. "Most of these droplets appear to be poured on the wall, as if someone took a bottle full of blood and gently tipped some of the contents down the sides. I don't think there's anything miraculous about this. Just a gory and unhygienic sight. However..." Holmes squinted. "Not all of these bloodstains follow the same pattern. I have made a study of the shapes blood droplets make during acts of violence. Most of the blood on these walls was gently poured. But here and there are different patterns of blood. Spattered droplets, rather like–"

Holmes was interrupted by the sound of the door clanging, and three pairs of feet came clamping towards the chapel.

"Well, that takes care of that," the gruff voice of Lord Dirus declared. "First thing tomorrow, I'm going to call that fellow and ask him to make good on his boasting and fix up a sixteenth-century document for us. Bassett? Bass-ETT? BASSETT!" Lord Dirus bellowed. "Get down here at once and make me a whiskey and soda. In the largest glass you can find, and don't feel it necessary to go heavy on the soda."

There was only one door to the former chapel, and nowhere to hide, not that Holmes and Father Brown had any intention of trying to avoid seeing the Dirus family. As father, mother, and son walked into the study, all three visibly blanched when they saw the two men standing there.

"Father Brown!" Agro blurted. "And… are you Sherlock Holmes?"

"What are you doing here?" Lady Dirus demanded.

"Investigating some very interesting bloodstains," Holmes replied smoothly. "I should like to speak to your housemaid, Agnes."

At this, all three members of the Dirus family swooned. Lady Dirus was the first to recover her composure. She clenched her jaw and pointed at Holmes and Father Brown. "You are not welcome here. Leave this instant or I shall summon the police and have you arrested for trespassing. And you will go to prison, whether you're a famous detective or a priest or not."

When asked about that moment later, Father Brown freely admitted that he had made an enormous leap, and that it would have served him right if he'd fallen flat on his face. Perhaps he was just lucky, and perhaps he had made a brilliant deduction based on meager evidence, but in any case, he came to the correct conclusion. "We'll be happy to leave, if you can produce your land grant to the Castle."

With that statement, Lord Dirus slumped to the floor, all the muscle strength seemed to have dissolved from Lady Dirus's shoulders, and young Agro crossed to the nearest decanter, tossed the stopper over his shoulder, and downed most of the contents with an enormous gulp. "What... what do you mean?" the no longer imperious Lady Dirus quavered.

"I mean, *Mrs.* Dirus," Father Brown put special stress on the title. "That I should like to see the documents that prove your ownership of this building, and your claims to nobility as well."

It is not necessary to describe the next five minutes in detail. Both Lord Dirus and Agro attempted to attack Holmes and Father Brown, but Holmes' knowledge of baritsu helped him to subdue both men. Lady Dirus lunged for Father Brown's throat, but luckily for the priest, the cook heard the commotion and hurried up to the chapel, holding a cast iron frying pan. When the cook saw Lady Dirus attempting to choke Father Brown, the tough but good-natured domestic had realized first, that she didn't care for Lady Dirus, second, that she did like Father Brown, third, that with her cooking skills she could find a better job elsewhere, and fourth, that she was holding a very heavy, blunt object.

One does not need to be a great detective to deduce what happened next.

Later that evening, after all three members of the Dirus family had been arrested, and Holmes and Father Brown were back in London, they told their story to a recently returned Watson.

"But surely an accusation of murder based on such little evidence was rather foolhardy, even for you, Holmes?" Watson remarked.

"I suppose it was, but based on the available clues, it was worth the risk in order to bring the perpetrators to justice. In any event, the nerves of that unholy family were already so badly frayed that it only took a very small tug to lead them to unravel altogether."

"Could the two of you please explain your thought processes from the beginning?"

"Of course, Watson. First of all, there was the issue of the blood on the walls of the former chapel. Let us assume that this is not some supernatural event based on a centuries-old curse– indeed, as Father Brown suspects, the narrative we have been told about the curse of the abbot is very likely highly fictionalized. If so, then why would blood be poured on the walls, blood that was probably that of a sheep, rather than human? The Dirus family would not willingly embrace such a sanguineous form of interior decoration, and it didn't appear to be a practical joke or a threat. If anything, according to Father Brown's narrative, they all seemed airily dismissive of the bloodstains and wanted us to ignore them. This odd behavior indicated that the blood caused no distress for them and did not interest them. Yet why wouldn't they want to make use of such a unique and effective conversation starter? Why did the notoriously irreverent Agro draw attention to the blood and then drop the subject?"

Holmes paused for effect and continued. "I must admit that I was at a loss until I examined the walls and discovered that there were two different patterns to the blood. There was the dribbled blood, and there was another set of stains that resembled a cast-off pattern, perhaps caused by the arterial spray that results when a person sustains a serious wound. In a moment, I realized the true purpose of the dribbled blood. It was meant to cover up blood that fallen on the wall in a violent attack, and from the amount of blood I saw that did not follow the dribbling pattern, the assault was most likely fatal."

"So far, so good," Holmes said after another dramatic pause. "But if there was an attack, there must be a victim. Who could it be? All three members of the Dirus family were accounted for, and they rarely hosted guests. Of course, the possibility of an intruder could not be dismissed, but what of the servants? We made inquiries and learned that at the moment, there were only three servants at the castle. We met the cook, she was unharmed. We heard Lord Dirus calling out to the butler, so we could eliminate him as a potential victim. That left the housemaid, Agnes. She was nowhere to be found, so she was the most likely victim. I formed a theory. The housemaid Agnes had been murdered. Perhaps she was having an affair with the notoriously lecherous Lord Dirus and Lady Dirus had bludgeoned her out of jealousy?"

"Wait a minute," Watson interjected. "How did you deduce that Lady Dirus was the killer? And that the death had been caused by bludgeoning?"

"Father Brown, why don't you expound on that point?" Holmes asked.

"Well, I formed a theory about what happened when I saw Lady Dirus polishing a candelabra with her handkerchief," the priest explained. "That's not the sort of thing that a noblewoman with a very high opinion of her own self-importance does of her own volition. She calls the maid and orders her to do a better job of cleaning. She doesn't lower herself to do a servant's work for her. That put two ideas into my head. First, that there was something on the candelabra that needed to be cleaned up right away and Lady Dirus couldn't wait for someone else to do it, and second, that either the maid wasn't to be trusted with this cleaning job, or more likely, that the maid wasn't around to do it."

"Father Brown and I had independently come to the same conclusions," Holmes continued. "For some reason, Lady Dirus had bludgeoned Agnes the housemaid with a candelabra, and her husband and son had helped her cover up the crime. The precise motive we'll address in a moment. I suspect it was young Agro who came up with the idea to take some sheep's blood– the cook was planning to make some mutton blood pudding that evening, so Agro probably crept downstairs and stole the bottle of sheep's blood from the larder. His mother's attack on poor Agnes led to stains on the wall, so what to do? They didn't have a maid to clean them up anymore. In any case, it's a time-consuming process to scrub blood out of the kind of absorbent stone used to build that part of the castle. With Father Brown and his niece coming soon, there was no time to clean it. Only one thing to do– spill a little sheep's blood to cover it all up. Father Brown just happened to take a sample from the sheep blood part by chance, though he could have easily taken some from the human blood portion, or some of both."

"But what was the motive?" Watson asked. "Are you saying that it wasn't jealousy over Agnes' affair with Lord Dirus?"

"Oh, no," Father Brown explained. "Lady Dirus was quite used to her husband's adultery, and in any case, she was sufficiently dispassionate towards her husband that any feelings of jealousy would have been completely impossible. Indeed, I don't think Agnes had an affair with Lord Dirus at all. No, there had to be another reason, only I never would have thought of it if I hadn't heard Lord Dirus talking about finding a forger to create a sixteenth-century document. I knew the history of how the family gained control of the castle through massacring a monastery, and everybody assumed that Henry VIII had given them the title and property through a royal land grant and decree. But what if for whatever reason, that never happened? If the King never signed an official document, then the Dirus family have no legal right to the castle, and they're not even really titled nobility. They've just occupied the property for centuries and called themselves "Lord" and "Lady," when in fact they're just squatters with pretensions of grandeur. I suppose that it's been a dark family secret generations, and somehow, poor Agnes came across some document or journal or something that revealed the truth while she was cleaning up and peeking through Lord Dirus's papers. And she realized that Lord and Lady Dirus were just "Mr. and Mrs. Dirus," and when for whatever reason she confronted them… Well, you know the rest. Holmes and I caught them returning from burying the body, which they'd hidden somewhere while they were waiting for my niece and I to leave. The police found poor Agnes in the woods after only a few minutes of searching."

After a long period of quiet, Watson asked, "What will happen to the castle? Will it be returned to the Church and become a monastery again?"

"Unlikely," Father Brown sighed. "That would require the British government admitting that most of the Church of England's property and much of the aristocracy's lands came from murder, theft, and centuries of denial. More likely, the powers that be in the government will find some loyal Member of Parliament who they think deserves a promotion, and they'll give him the estate and award him and his descendants some nice, impressive-sounding title."

The three men sat in silence for a moment.

"It seems your niece's engagement is at an end," Holmes remarked to the priest.

"And a good thing, too," Father Brown replied.

The Adventure of the Specious Spouse

"Will your wife be joining you tonight, Mr. Holmes?"

I was standing several feet behind Holmes, so I could not see the expression on his face. I did, however, observe his back stiffening and his hands clenching very slightly at the question posed by the maître d'.

"I am not married, sir. I will be dining with my colleague Dr. Watson tonight."

The maître d's eyebrows knotted. "Are you sure, sir?"

"Young man, I freely admit that I am not so young as I used to be. The Great War has taken its toll on all of us. Yet while the years may have passed, I can assure you that I am not completely senile. I am fully aware that I have never been married."

"I was certain that you were, Mr. Holmes."

"Are you a regular reader of my colleague's accounts of my cases? I am aware that, among the collection of individuals who enjoy his work, there is a subset who are convinced that I have been carrying on a relationship with one Irene Adler, but I can assure you that there is absolutely no truth to that rumor."

"Oh, not Miss Adler, sir, though I must say that I have wondered about her and you. No, I'm referring to Mary Grace Quackenbos Humiston. They call her 'Mrs. Sherlock Holmes,' you know, and seeing as how you've come all the way to New York City, sir, I thought that you were here to spend time with the missus."

Holmes's back stiffened even more. "I have never heard of this Mary Grace Quackenbos Humiston, and therefore there is no relationship between us. Will you show us to our table, please?"

"Of course, sir. Right away. I meant no offense, sir."

With a slight grunt of acknowledgement, Holmes followed the maître d' to a table in the far corner of the restaurant, and I was close behind them. After sending the maître d' on his way with a curt nod, Holmes and I picked up the menus.

"Does anything look particularly appetizing to you, Watson?"

"Aren't we going to discuss what just happened?"

"I fail to see any reason why I should upset myself shortly before eating. We came here to celebrate resolving a particularly sticky diplomatic situation between the United States, Great Britain, and Canada. I will not spoil my dinner by dwelling on a restaurant employee's comments."

I was about to speak, but I decided to hold my tongue. Holmes seemed to be in an uncharacteristically sour temper, and I did not wish to upset him further. Upon completing my second read-through of the menu, a realization struck me, and I was unable to stop myself from blurting out, "This isn't the first time that someone has asked you about being married to that woman, is it?"

Fortunately, Holmes did not appear to be annoyed at me for asking that question. "No, just the first instance of such inquiries being made in your presence, Watson. Over the course of the last two days, I have been asked that question nine times by people from walks of life ranging from shoeshine boys to city councilmen, all of them congratulating me on my marriage to this Mrs. Mary Grace Quackenbos Humiston. Invariably, when I insist that this woman is not my wife, I am met with skepticism. As if I would marry a woman, and then disclaim any connection to her in public."

"Why do you think that people are so adamant that you are indeed married to this lady?"

"I can only suppose that their imaginations have latched onto this pairing. I have often noticed with great bemusement that many individuals become fixated with the romantic lives of people in the public eye, and they develop irrational attachments to the relationships of the famous. Consider how people obsess about the marriage of members of the Royal Family. I dare say that a number of people here in New York rather like the idea of a local woman marrying me. Perhaps they think that I shall leave London and take up residence here."

"There are a great deal of interesting crimes here in New York City."

"Most certainly there are, and I believe that there are several skilled detectives who already call this metropolis home who are more than capable of solving any mysteries that the local criminal classes have to offer."

"I've heard of this Mrs. Humiston, you know. There was a profile of her in a magazine I read a couple of days ago. Do you know anything about her?"

"Other than that a surprising number of people are sorely confused as to her marital status, nothing at all."

"She's a lawyer, I believe, one of the few females to hold such a job, and she makes a career out of helping the poor and downtrodden. There was an Italian woman who was convicted of killing a man, and she was condemned to die. Mrs. Humiston took the case, found a number of problems with this trial, argued it was self-defense, and eventually had the sentence reduced to seven or eight years. Then she exposed a couple of scandals regarding immigrants to the American South — who were being held as slaves in all but name

— and ruffled a lot of feathers trying to drum up popular opinion against the practice. Then there was a young girl who disappeared, and after the police failed to find her, Mrs. Humiston identified a likely culprit, and after some clever strategizing, found the missing girl's body on the suspect's property. That was when they started to call her 'Mrs. Sherlock Holmes.' "

"If the reports that you read are correct, then she sounds like a very impressive woman."

"Yes, I…. Good heavens, Holmes!"

"What is it?"

"There was a picture of Mrs. Humiston in the article I read. I believe that she's here now!" I gestured toward the entryway. A woman in her fifties, with a bun of mostly dark hair covered with a large hat, was walking toward us. She had a rather regal bearing, and her dress was long and black, aside from a couple of thin white stripes on the sleeves. She exchanged a few words with the maître d', and after he pointed at us, she gave him a little nod; though I could not be certain of it, it was very possible that she slipped a little money onto the podium he was standing behind before she walked toward us.

Holmes turned and watched her approach us. He rose to his feet, and for a fleeting second I wondered if he was going to hurry out of the restaurant, but a moment's reflection told me that Holmes would never run away from a woman, at least a lady that did not intend him any physical harm. When Mrs. Humiston arrived at our table, he gave her a little nod of greeting.

"Mrs. Humiston?"

"That is correct."

"Would you care to join us?"

I have no idea how successful I was in masking my surprise when I rose and pulled over a chair from a nearby empty table, but Mrs. Humiston said "hello" to me with evident warmth and graciousness before taking her seat.

"You know who I am then, Mr. Holmes?"

"Watson has just provided me with a brief overview of your career."

"I suppose you know my nickname."

"Unfortunately, yes."

"I dare say you aren't very pleased about it."

"Admittedly, when I first heard the moniker 'Mrs. Sherlock Holmes' I was a trifle peeved. My initial reaction was that someone was building a reputation off of my name and career."

"It was not I who came up with that nickname, Mr. Holmes."

"I was rather certain that was the truth of the matter. And now, you wish for my help on a case?"

After many years of acquaintance with Holmes, I know never to be surprised by any of Holmes's deductions. Mrs. Humiston was not so used to Holmes's powers of observation. For a moment, I was afraid that she might fall back in her chair, but thankfully — even before I could reach to catch her — she regained her balance and gripped the table. "How did you know I needed your assistance, Mr. Holmes?"

"Why does anybody want to speak to me? You clearly have been trying to track me down, seeing as how you found me at this restaurant. I would not be surprised if you had allies or employees trying to find me."

"Mr. Julius Kron is a private detective who has worked with me on many occasions. He and a few assistants have spent the last day trying to track down the two of you. I heard from a mutual acquaintance that you were in town, and I realized that you might be able to help me. As soon as Mr. Kron informed me of your reservation at this restaurant, I decided to seize this opportunity."

"From the agitation in your manner, it seems to be a matter of some urgency."

"It is."

"A death penalty case, with the execution looming?"

Mrs. Humiston blanched and turned to me. "I've read your accounts of Mr. Holmes's cases, but I never really believed that his powers of deduction were that effective."

"Many other people have made similar comments over the decades, Mrs. Humiston," I replied. "I must say, my friend never tires of proving other people wrong."

"What is particularly vexing is the fact that many people seem positively desperate to receive confirmation that my powers of acumen are not as skillful as is commonly publicized. It seems that every week I come across someone who is positively crushed by the fact that I am able to figure out trifling details of their lives and habits." Holmes groaned softly and tented his fingertips. "I have no wish to discuss people's conceptions of me and my observational skills. A person has been condemned to death, correct?"

"Yes."

"And you are convinced that the person facing the gallows is innocent?"

"She's to face the electric chair, not the hangman's rope, but yes, I know in my heart that she had nothing to do with the murder."

"When is she scheduled to die?"

"In less than a week."

"That is a relief."

"I beg your pardon?"

For a brief moment, a flicker of embarrassment passed over Holmes's face. "I expressed myself badly. I feared that your client was to be executed tonight. I did not relish the prospect of a frantic rush to gather up enough evidence to earn a stay of execution at the very last moment."

Mrs. Humiston did not appear completely mollified. "I'm pleased that you won't have to rush your dinner and skip dessert."

Holmes showed no contrition in response to this remark. "Yes, it would be such a shame to travel across the Atlantic Ocean, visit a restaurant that came highly recommended by a longtime acquaintance, and be forced to rapidly consume my meal like a ravenous wolf. And as we're on the topic...." A waiter arrived at our table. "Will you be dining with us as our guest, Mrs. Humiston? You can provide us with the details of the case while we eat."

Mrs. Humiston looked a bit ruffled by the offer. "What? Oh, yes. I've dined here many times. The sole meunière is excellent. I shall have that."

Neither of us followed Mrs. Humiston on her recommendation. I ordered the Lobster Newberg, and Holmes selected the sirloin of beef with mashed potatoes and carrots.

As soon as the waiter had filled our water glasses, Mrs. Humiston took a deep sip and turned back to Holmes. "Have you heard about the Flora Blundell case?"

"I'm afraid I've been too busy resolving a rather delicate matter to follow the local papers."

"It hasn't been in the newspapers for some weeks. Not since poor Flora was convicted. As far as most of New York City is concerned, the whole affair is over. So there's no reason why you would have heard about it."

The waiter arrived with three bowls of consommé and set them before us. Mrs. Humiston scooped up a few drops and set them delicately in her mouth. "As you have probably heard, Mr. Holmes, I am the founder of the People's Law Firm. For over fifteen years, we have provided quality legal representation for the indigent and for immigrants who are struggling to survive in a strange country. Sometimes we provide services completely *pro bono*, and often we charge very modest fees that our clients can easily afford."

"Is that meant to be a subtle way of telling me that I should not expect much in the way of financial remuneration for my troubles?" Holmes asked dryly, but with a twinkle in his eye.

Mrs. Humiston looked taken aback. "If you can help me clear Flora's name, I will gladly pay whatever you ask out of my own pocket."

"I will not commit to anything at present. Please, continue."

"Flora worked as a barmaid at the Yellow Primrose. Despite the rather pretty name, it was a dark, seedy speakeasy in a residential area of the city. The liquor served there was cheap and watered-down, the lighting was almost non-existent, and of course, it's completely illegal under Prohibition. Flora's a nice girl, but it's hard to make a living, and serving at that horrid dive was the only way she could earn enough money to scrape by, you see."

"I would never condemn a young woman for taking a job as a barmaid. It's a perfectly acceptable way to keep body and soul together in London, and just because your government has seen fit to criminalize the sale of alcoholic beverages, I cannot say that I consider her work to be especially criminal."

"That is a welcome viewpoint to hear, Mr. Holmes. At her trial, the prosecutor made it sound like serving up a glass of bathtub gin was evidence of a complete lack of moral fiber, and he even made veiled insinuations that Flora was supplementing her income by performing certain … indecent actions with the male clientele. I can assure you that there was no truth to this whatsoever. It was simply a vile innuendo on the part of the prosecutor, utilized in the hopes of demonizing the defendant and causing the morally outraged men of the jury to vote 'guilty,' despite the fact that there was no solid evidence of her guilt."

"There were no witnesses, then? No direct physical proof that she had committed the crime?"

"None. It happened very late at night, half an hour after closing time at the Yellow Primrose. Flora, the bartender, and another barmaid were washing up the glasses and cleaning up the establishment for the night. The proprietor of the establishment, a Mr. Gideon Dorewell, collected the night's take and brought it downstairs into the basement to lock it away in his safe. This was standard operating procedure. Every night Mr. Dorewell would lock away the profits from the speakeasy, walk a block down the street to his apartment, and upon waking in the mid-afternoon, return to the speakeasy, take the money from the safe, and deposit it — or at least most of it — in the bank a quarter of a mile away. He was in the habit of carrying a revolver with him for protection."

Holmes finished the last of his soup, then stroked the tip of his chin. "But surely, Mr. Dorewell could not have deposited money into the bank every day."

"You are correct, Mr. Holmes. Banks are closed on Sundays, and by the time Mr. Dorewell usually awoke on Saturdays, his bank was shuttered, as it closed early that day. By Sunday night, the safe was filled with a weekend's worth of cash, as the proceeds from Friday, Saturday, and Sunday were in there. Every Monday, Mr. Dorewell would take all that money, stuff it all in a bag he had strapped to his chest, throw on an overcoat, and hurry as fast as he could to the bank, with one hand on the revolver in his pocket. Apparently, he had a much lighter overcoat for summer, though in any event wearing such a garment was bound to attract attention during the dog days."

"But he wasn't killed on the way to the bank."

"No. He was not. When Flora went downstairs to pick up a few more bottles of the establishment's best — to use the word loosely — product, she came downstairs and found Mr. Dorewell lying dead on the floor. He'd been hit over the head with a bottle, and his body was in front of the open safe. The safe was not empty — there was still a large quantity of money in it, although when the bartender examined it, he thought that there was somewhat less than there ought to have been, though he couldn't be sure, as they don't keep very careful records in that business."

The waiter brought a platter of paté, olives, and triangles of toast. Holmes and I both helped ourselves, but Mrs. Humiston left it untouched. After taking what he wanted, Holmes remarked, "It seems to me reasonable to suppose that when the police investigated, they found no one else in the basement, and — as Mr. Dorewell went down there alone, and Flora was the only one to follow him there — they assumed that she murdered him."

"Exactly! Isn't it ridiculous? They believe that she went down there, hit him over the head, and then just ran upstairs screaming, claiming that she found him there, dead."

"It's not a totally irrational supposition. So far as the police could tell, it was just her there. No one else had the opportunity."

"But what could be the motive?" I asked.

Mrs. Humiston groaned. "The police believe that Flora was trying to steal money from the safe. Mr. Dorewell caught her, perhaps he fired her, and in a blind rage she supposedly struck him with the bottle. Then she ran upstairs in a state of shock, not realizing that no one else could be blamed for the crime."

"On the face of it, it sounds reasonable. But did they find any fingerprints on the bottle? Any blood on Flora's clothing? Did she waver in protesting her innocence for even a second?"

"No! Not for one moment!" Mrs. Humiston groaned and picked up an olive. "Mr. Holmes, I tell you that I believe in Flora one hundred per cent. I have dedicated my life to protecting people who cannot help themselves, even when the authorities care little for them. To most of society, women like Flora do not matter. She is not very intelligent, she is nowhere near beautiful, and if we are to be honest, left to her own devices her life would not be an especially distinctive one, though one can hope that she will find happiness in it. Her life will almost certainly be one of poverty and hard work. She's a kind person, and it's possible she could meet a decent man. Perhaps she could find love and have children. Surely that's a pleasant enough future."

"I am told that many people deem a life like the one you describe as a totally acceptable fate."

"But she will have no happy ending in the death house, Mr. Holmes. I just found out about her case a couple of weeks ago, and I've thought of nothing but rescuing her ever since."

"You didn't handle her defense at the trial, then?" I asked.

"No. Her lawyer did his best, I suppose. He tried to argue that Dorewell had made improper advances toward her, and that she'd hit him over the head in order to defend her honor."

I shrugged. "A plea of self-defense sounds like a sensible plan."

"Unfortunately, Flora would have none of it. She insisted on pleading 'not guilty' without any qualifier, and when her lawyer tried to suggest the situation I just described to the jury, she stood up and yelled, 'No, no, no, no! That didn't happen! I never touched him!' She demanded to be put on the stand to tell her story, but the poor girl is very highly strung. When the prosecutor cross-examined her she fell to pieces and started crying. I suppose the jury took that as an admission of guilt."

Our main courses arrived, and as Holmes picked up his fork and knife, he said, "It would help me if I could see the scene of the crime."

"I'm afraid you can't visit the actual Yellow Primrose. It burned to the ground not long after the murder."

"I wondered why you used the past tense when describing it," Holmes commented.

"I can, however, show you these photographs," Mrs. Humiston added. She drew a large envelope from her purse. "These should give you a good idea of what the basement looked like."

Holmes swallowed a bite of beef. "Do you have any pictures of the deceased?"

"Well, yes, but you're eating."

Cutting himself another piece of meat, Holmes replied, "And why should that matter in the slightest?"

Mrs. Humiston opened her mouth to speak, apparently thought better of it, and then handed the envelope to Holmes. After a few moments of rustling around in her purse, she found a second, smaller envelope and passed it to Holmes as well. "I also have a copy of the autopsy report in here."

"I shall need a few minutes to focus, please," Holmes said. He took out the photographs and sorted through them one at a time, continuing to eat his food as he examined the evidence. Mrs. Humiston and I silently ate our dinners as well. By the time Holmes had finished scrutinizing all of the pictures, all of our plates were nearly clean.

"How tall is Flora?" Holmes finally asked.

"A shade over five feet tall, but strongly built."

"Hmm. According to the autopsy report, Mr. Dorewell was five foot nine. His head was totally bald, which makes it easier to see the wounds. The photographs of the body indicate that the deceased was struck directly over the head. The killer must have been significantly taller than Dorewell. At least six foot two, I should say, if not more."

"Perhaps he was kneeling on the ground," I ventured.

"I considered that possibility, but the photographs indicate that the floor of the basement was covered with dust and mud. Dorewell fell on his side when he was killed. I see no stains on the knees of his trousers. Was this point brought up at the trial?"

"It was not," Mrs. Humiston looked hopeful. "This is a start. Perhaps it's enough to ask the Governor for clemency."

"Let's wait for a little while. There is still the question of how the actual killer got in and out of the basement. You never had a chance to examine the Yellow Primrose yourself before it burned?"

"No. I should mention that Mr. Kron has been performing his own investigation into the fire."

"It's arson, then?"

"It's a strong possibility. Two men were seen carrying large metal canisters away from the Yellow Primrose right after the conflagration started. Mr. Kron and I think that if we find the arsonists, it may help lead us to the real killer."

"Take a look at these photographs, Watson." Holmes passed the pictures to me. "Do you see anything of note?"

I did not. There were several shelves throughout the room filled with bottles of various sizes and labels. There were six large barrels on their sides, resting on stands against one wall, and some lanterns were hanging from hooks on the ceiling.

"Unfortunately, the police inadvertently destroyed crucial evidence when they searched the crime scene. They walked around the basement, and in the dim light, they did not see the footprints they were erasing."

"Footprints?"

"In the dust and mud, in front of the barrels, you can just barely see a footprint pointing directly at that barrel on the end."

I looked closely at the barrel. "Nothing sinister about that. Someone walked up to the barrel to pour a pitcher of beer. I didn't know that American speakeasies were smuggling in beer from France. *Bière Échappatoire.*"

"More likely, they've been taking alcohol across the Canadian border. They voted against prohibition there in 1919. Some people have been going there for liquor," Mrs. Humiston explained.

"I have learned French from spending time with my relatives, the Vernets. 'Échappatoire' translates to 'exit' or 'way out.' " Holmes smiled. "I know that many speakeasies make a point of concealing passageways in their establishments in case of a raid. I believe that the barrel is a carefully designed door that leads into a tunnel. I have no idea who committed the murder, nor do I know for certain what the motive was, but that's how the true killer got in and out of the basement."

Before either of us could respond, the waiter approached the table. "Mr. Holmes, will you, your wife, or Dr. Watson care for any dessert?"

"She is *not* my wife!" Holmes replied with such intense firmness that the formerly implacable waiter sidled away so quickly that I was compelled to rise from my chair and follow him in order to request the menu for puddings.

"None for me," Mrs. Humiston told us as she gathered up all the photographs into her purse. "I have to talk to Mr. Kron and get him to look into this."

"They may have burned the Yellow Primrose," Holmes commented, "but I dare say that the end of the tunnel can still be found in the basement of the building next door. "That hasn't been burned, has it?"

"No. It's a private home."

"Then I would not be surprised if a member of that household was responsible for the killing."

Mrs. Humiston agreed, thanked us, and hurried away after a very brief set of goodbyes. As I enjoyed my charlotte russe, I asked Holmes, "Do you think that will be enough to save that poor Flora woman?"

"I hope so. Of course, it never hurts to exercise a little bit of influence wherever possible. My recent investigation has brought me into contact with gentlemen in high places. A word or two to them may lead to helpful results."

*   *   *

The next afternoon, Holmes and I were packing our suitcases, preparing for our voyage back to England. A bellhop knocked at the door, delivering a envelope addressed to Holmes. Tearing it open, Holmes read aloud:

My dear Mr. Holmes:

I cannot possibly express all the gratitude that I feel toward you, but I hope that this letter will serve as a start. You were quite right about the secret tunnel. Mr. Kron was able to enter the house next door to the former Yellow Primrose disguised as a plumber (I won't tell you about the little subterfuge we had to use in order to convince the housekeeper to let him inside). While there, he uncovered the tunnel in the basement. A little more digging revealed that the owner of the house, a greengrocer named Mr. Munderman, enjoys a lifestyle far more luxurious than that of the average shopkeeper. Mr. Kron's informants explained that Mr. Munderman has long been suspected of being a pivotal player in the illegal liquor importing business from Canada to New York City. When Mr. Kron confronted the housekeeper with his discovery, she quickly broke down. Apparently, she'd witnessed Mr. Dorewell visiting the house on numerous occasions, and the night before the murder, Dorewell had an argument with Mr. Munderman and his son. She couldn't hear much distinctly, but she did catch the phrase "skimming off the top." I believe that Dorewell was taking more than his share of the proceeds, and since Mr. Munderman is five foot eight while his son is six foot three, I'm sure that it was the son who committed the actual crime, though it was the father who ordered the arson to prevent anyone from discovering the passageway. I dare say that this was not a premeditated murder. Mr. Munderman's son probably slipped through the secret passageway to confront Dorewell about stealing money, and the two men fought, and Mr. Munderman's son killed him in a fit of rage. Mr. Munderman seems like a sensible businessman, who never would have had his business partner killed next door to his own home. Mr. Kron's investigation indicated that certain precautions had been taken to assure that the fire did not spread to the Munderman residence. The authorities are in the process of gathering evidence, but in the meantime, I have been assured by the governor that dear Flora is in no danger of being executed. Once again, thank you so much, Mr. Holmes.

Sincerely,

Grace Quackenbos Humiston

P.S. Again, I must apologize for people's false belief that we are married. I feel thankful that my husband Howard is more amused by this than annoyed.

"It seems as though this matter has come to a satisfactory conclusion," I informed Holmes. Before he could reply, there was another knock at the door, revealing a different bellhop bringing me the afternoon paper. "Oh, dear," I said as I rifled through the pages.

"What's the matter, Watson?"

"Look at this." I handed him the newspaper, folded back to the society pages. There was an image of Holmes and Mrs. Humiston there, though I had been cropped out of the photograph. The headline read, "Mr. and Mrs. Sherlock Holmes Enjoy Dinner Together."

Holmes threw down the paper with a disgusted groan and once again made it clear to me that my account of this case would be consigned to a battered tin dispatch-box for a very long time. "I trust that you will not release the details of this case to your readers, Watson. I do not wish for false rumors of my marriage to spread across the Atlantic."

The Search for Mycroft's Successor

As much as it pains me to admit it, none of us are immortal. Sooner or later we all must leave this world and face whatever comes next. In the months following the Armistice at the end of the Great War, I found that I was not the only one reflecting on the fact that all of our times must come to an end. While every life has value, some admittedly have a deeper impact than others on the fates of nations. This was the case with Mycroft, Holmes' elder brother.

When a monarch dies, the heir to the throne is always in waiting. As much as Britons may revere their best kings and queens, deep in all of our minds is the unspoken realization that all crowned heads are replaceable, and the line of succession is well-known. But there are other individuals who are genuinely and unquestionably indispensable. One such man is Holmes' brother Mycroft.

Mycroft invited us to his rooms a few months after the signing of the Treaty of Versailles. It was a time when most were relieved, even jubilant, in the knowledge that the long years of war were over, and peace was restored. From the expression on Mycroft's face, he was nowhere near relaxed. His eyes had the fog of a man who had not slept as much as he ought to have, and his clothes appeared rather tight, as if the already corpulent man had turned to his favorite foods in order to assuage the stress that was evident in his demeanor.

Holmes sized up his brother's mental state with a swift up and down glance. "I can see that you have been worrying lately, my dear brother."

"Can you blame me, brother Sherlock?"

"I most certainly cannot. The last four years have been a terrible strain for most people. It must have been exponentially horrible for the man who at times, to all intents and purposes, *is* the British Government."

"The world could have been spared a great many needless deaths and sleepless nights if the Prime Minister had not sidelined me at the worst possible time in 1914," Mycroft groaned. "Those fools informed me that they had no further need of my services, gave me a miniscule pension and a gold watch that loses two minutes every hour, and then, not two weeks after the start of hostilities, called me back to work without so much as a "please." I have spent the last four years trying to clean up their messes and prevent the nation from crumbling, and now that the wretched war has finally ended, those silly diplomats have put together a so-called "peace" treaty that will lead to yet another massive war within a generation. Possibly I may be able to assuage the situation, or maybe delay the horrors for several more years, but I doubt it very much." Mycroft sagged back in his chair, and he looked far older, more exhausted, and weaker than I had ever seen him.

"Cheer up," I informed him. "I'm sure that all will turn out for the best."

I had never seen so much pure contempt in Mycroft's face. "No, Watson, it will *not* be all right! I am not a particularly vain man, but I know for a fact that without me, England will not be able to withstand another terrible war. I am not flattering myself when I assert that my presence is necessary to the nation's survival. And I will not live forever. I have never fussed much over my health, and it is too late to start now. I may have another year or two in me, perhaps another couple of decades if I am extraordinarily lucky, but eventually, I will meet my Maker and there will be no one to take my place. We cannot trust our statesmen to handle the increasingly volatile situation. I need a replacement for myself. I cannot rest until I know that when I finally pass on, the nation will be in sound hands. I am too busy with my work to launch a search of my own. That is why I have summoned you today. Find my successor. Search England for the best and the brightest, and when you believe that you have found as man– a *young* man, mind you, one who will be able to handle this job for decades to come– and convince him to come work for me. We need someone with a mind sufficiently clever and dexterous to handle all of the complexities connected to managing the intricacies of the British government. This is a full-time job, so we need someone willing to devote his entire life to this project, preferably one who is content to forgo the distractions of a wife and children as well so he can focus on his work."

Mycroft shifted his weight in his chair, and took a long sip from a glass of water on the table next to him. "I have never regretted not marrying, at least, not until now. Perhaps I might have had a son who could have taken over this position. Then again, I might have been too overwhelmed by the duties of fatherhood to have saved England from hundreds of near disasters. In any case, dear brother, you know as well as I do that intelligence of the kind that the two of us possess does not necessarily pass from father to son. We have many clever fellows in our family, and one or two might make fine detectives like yourself, but none of them have the brain stamina and calculating abilities to take over my role in the government. In any event, it's likely that I might have sired an utter dunderhead, fit for nothing more cranially strenuous that the easy life of a country squire. And that would have done us no good whatsoever in this situation."

"Have you come across anybody in your work who might be able to take on the duties of your protégé, Mycroft?" Holmes asked.

"None. The British Civil Service is filled with a handful of smart men and a great many workaday pudding-heads. Many are called out of a sincere desire to serve their country, but men of the kind of inspired genius that we need are nonexistent." Mycroft drank more water. "I trust that you will not think me arrogant by using that word to describe the brainpower that is essential for this position, but it is a simple fact that one needs a certain kind of mind to handle the facts, figures, and intricacies of my job. When I created this position for myself, I observed a need and chose to fill it myself. At the time, I did not realize how essential I would become to the wellbeing of England, not did I ever suspect the seeming impossibility of teaching someone else how to perform this job. But it *must* be done, and you, brother, are the only one who has the wherewithal to find a worthy man."

"Or woman," I suggested.

"Don't be ridiculous," Mycroft snapped at me.

"Do you have any suggestions on how to proceed, Mycroft?" Holmes asked.

"Nothing that will significantly improve success. I know of only three young men who *might* have the brains to take on the position, and one is from southern China, another lives in northern India, and the third calls the American Midwest home. But they are all loyal to their current nations, and two of them already have large families. None of them will be persuaded to come to England and serve our interests. That means that you can limit your search to our country. I have started a study of the students and recent graduates of our nation's universities and best schools, and though we have lots of able men…"

"None of them are what we are looking for," Holmes finished.

"Precisely. And you, dear brother, would not find my intellectually stimulating yet physically sedentary job to your tastes. Is there no one of your acquaintance that springs to mind?"

"No specific living person. There was one man who might have managed this epic task, but he chose to devote his incredible abilities to more destructive habits. However…"

"Of course!" A glint flashed in Mycroft's eyes. "I wondered if you would consider that possibility, Sherlock. It is possible that a member of his extended family might be up to the task, if genetics are any guide. Which, as I mentioned earlier, is not always the case."

"But we must be careful. While some of them may have the ability, I doubt that most of them have the character necessary for the job. Indeed, that is the curse of that family. The decent, moral members of that family uniformly have pedestrian, mediocre minds. In contrast, the most brilliant individuals with the moniker in question are dangerous. Upon reflection, I can think of one man from that family, who at thirty-nine is probably not too old for our purposes, who could very likely learn how to take over your job… but he would use it to take over the nation as well. Within ten years, Parliament would be his puppets, and he would be the dictator of England, and possibly of most of Western Europe as well."

"You have maintained your files on that family?"

"Of course. I am forever on the lookout for the possibility that one will follow in their patriarch's infamous footsteps."

"Excuse me, but which family are you talking about?" I asked with a touch of irritation.

Holmes glanced at me with mild surprise. "The Moriarty family, Watson. Who else would we be discussing?"

Holmes went into another room and spent ten minutes making telephone calls. Soon afterwards, the two of us were in a car heading to the West End. "Holmes, are you seriously considering turning over England's security and stability to a Moriarty?"

"I can assure, Watson, that I am not exploring this possibility lightly. No one is more aware than I am of how dangerous a Moriarty can be. I am also aware that while intelligence may be passed on from one generation to the next, there is no scientific proof that criminality is inherited as well. In any case, most of the Moriarty family is composed of harmless blockheads. Colonel James Moriarty was a man of no great ability, but he rose in the ranks thanks to the well-hidden intervention of his brother, the Professor. The Colonel's main claim to fame is an insistence that his brother was completely innocent, and that I am a malicious fool who slandered an innocent man. Their other brother, the stationmaster James–"

"I can't understand why the Moriarty family named all three brothers James."

"It is a family tradition. Most male members of the family go by their middle names. In any case, Stationmaster James is as decent enough man, who has no particular aptitude for anything in particular save for crossword puzzles. Meanwhile, the children of Colonel and Stationmaster have reached adulthood, and their mental abilities are a mixed bag. Both brothers have three children. The Colonel has two daughters, one of whom is an amiable featherbrain, and the other is woman of rare intelligence who is unhappily married to a philanderer. I might consider this woman for the position, were it not for the fact that she has devised no less than four brilliant schemes to murder her husband and put the blame on his latest mistress, and it is only thorough my own fortunate intervention that her plans have never succeeded. The couple has separated many times, yet for reasons I cannot understand, a reconciliation inevitably follows a couple of weeks later."

"And the Colonel's third child is a son?"

"Yes. James Albert Moriarty is an actor, and he is currently taking on a part that is made for him– the role of his uncle, Professor Moriarty in one of those endless revivals of that play by William Gillette very loosely based on my career."

"An actor? Do you really think that he has the ability to replace Mycroft?"

"I grant you that his talents lie in the creative arts, but he is surprisingly talented. His Iago was a minor sensation, and he has risen to fame as a skilled portrayer of villains. I have attended a couple of his performances before the war, and he has a certain amount of charisma, but more important, he has imagination. I believe that he is consistently able to bring a fresh and innovative approach to a well-known character, which shows a certain level of innovation and an ability to take the familiar and make it fresh."

"Do you really think that ability could be applied to handling the affairs of government?"

"It has been my experience, Watson, that creativity is a great asset when it is combined with logic and extensive knowledge. Albert– I shall refer to him by his middle name for the sake of clarity– has never been to university, and he is primarily an autodidact. I know that he studied the history of ancient Rome extensively for his preparation of the role of Brutus in *Julius Caesar*. He served in the military before being wounded and sent home after four months, and he has no known attachments, either romantic or those of ordinary friendship. His fellow actors consider him talented but distant. He is respected as a thespian but not particularly well-liked as a person."

"But can an actor perform Mycroft's duties?"

"From what I've heard, he has taken an active role in the management duties of one performing company, where he managed to clean up their financial situation and eliminated their debt. A stunning achievement, especially for those working in the dramatic arts. Again, I need to view this with some skepticism. There may be something less than honest behind the company's sudden solvency. We shall see."

Moments later, we arrived at a small, shabby-looking theater and walked inside. When we asked to see Albert Moriarty (it should be noted that he performed under a stage name, but for reasons of clarity I have chosen to refer to him by his real moniker), we were told he had not yet arrived, but would in half an hour. Holmes asked to wait in the manager's office, and after slipping the stage manager two one-pound notes, we were allowed inside.

"What are you looking for?" I asked as Holmes started rifling through the papers on a desk.

As he withdrew a ledger from under a stack of assorted playbills and posters, Holmes explained, "Financial records. If this is what I hope to find…" His voice trailed off as he flipped through the pages, running his finger along columns. I could see the calculations flashing in his eyes as he totaled the numbers in his mind.

I said nothing for nearly thirty minutes, until a knock on the door snapped Holmes out of his reflections, and he shoved the ledger back under a pile of paper just as the door opened. The stage manager informed us that the man we were looking for had arrived, and we were led to a dimly lit dressing room.

Albert Moriarty was sprawled out in a chair, with a silver-headed cane across his knees. "Ah! Sherlock Holmes! Have you come to play yourself on the stage? That certainly would be a boon to ticket sales. I wish I'd thought of it earlier."

"That is not why I am here," Holmes said as he lowered himself onto a rickety-looking bench. I did not think that it would support my weight as well, so I leaned against the corner walls.

"A pity. I should have liked to have been paired against you on the stage. And you as well, Dr. Watson," he told me with an expression that I thought was a combination of a leer and a sneer. "Wouldn't it be wonderful to have the three of us on stage together? You as yourselves, and me as my illustrious relative?"

"Illustrious?" I snorted.

Albert shrugged. "I chose my words without much thought. He was a magnificent man, even if he was a criminal. Most of our politicians are like that. Power-hungry, unscrupulous, and caring nothing for other people. Yet because they have managed to persuade people to cast ballots for them, they are respected, while my relative is now one of history's greatest villains. He could have been Prime Minister if he'd set his mind that way. But he wouldn't have been happy pandering to constituents or his party. He'd have much preferred to have been king, but monarchs don't have any real power these days anyway. So maybe it was best that he made his mark on the world in the way he did."

"As a criminal and murderer?" I asked before I could regain control of the tone of my voice.

Luckily, Albert didn't seem offended. "Well, if you're going to be judgmental about it…" He leaned back in his chair and kicked up his legs, resting his feet on the ends of the table.

Holmes stood up with a little groan. "Thank you for seeing us. We'll be leaving now."

"Will you be coming to see the show tonight?"

"No."

"Aren't you going to tell me to break a leg?"

"I think you've had quite enough damage to your legs, haven't you? Good day." Holmes strode out of the dressing-room with impressive speed, and I followed him back to the car.

Holmes was clearly in a sour humor, and I said nothing for several minutes, until the awkwardness overwhelmed my desire to allow him the quiet time he so deeply appreciates. "Well? What was wrong with him?"

"Where to start?"

"How about the ledger? There was clearly something wrong with that."

"Indeed. The totals make it look like the dramatic company's in sound financial health, which is suspicious in itself. In any case, I performed some simple arithmetic, and it seems as if their debts have been paid off with nonexistent funds."

"I don't understand. How is that possible?"

"Simply put, Alfred has created a financial house of cards. It allows for seeming prosperity for a limited period of time, but everything will fall apart eventually, and at that point, the company will be totally bankrupt, and even though Alfred is responsible for the financial malfeasance, he won't be on the hook for the debts himself."

"Are you sure he's behind the... creative accounting?"

"The handwriting on the ledger matches the scribbles on a script in his dressing-room."

"What was that comment you made about his leg?"

"You remember I mentioned he was injured and invalided out of the war?"

"Yes."

"And he carries the cane as an affectation. He doesn't really need it. But when he raised his leg, I saw his trouser leg slide back enough to see the wound caused by the bullet that sent him home from the front."

"I didn't get a close enough look at it to examine it properly."

"That is understandable. Had you been able to apply your trained medical eyes to it, you would have discovered that from the angle of the scarring, his wound was almost certainly self-inflicted. He shot himself with a handgun, just badly enough to be released from his duties."

"What a coward."

"Well, enough young men saw such terrible horrors on the front lines that I cannot judge them too harshly for wanting to escape with their lives. Still, combined with his accounting, it shows a distinct lack of character. Possibly with sufficient guidance and influence he could be molded into what we are looking for, but he's over thirty now and far too old for his character to be reshaped. Had he received proper training at a younger age, he could have replaced Mycroft eventually. As it is now, his moral compass is too shaky for us to trust him with anything. I suppose I should tell the owners of the theater to hire a proper accountant to examine the books to find out just how deep a hole they're currently in, and we'll see what happens. I doubt that Alfred will learn a lesson, though. I saw no signs of conscience or contrition in his face. He is clearly off the list."

"So where are we off to now, Holmes?"

"The Old Bailey, Watson, to speak to James Walter Moriarty. He is the elder son of Stationmaster James. Walter is a barrister of moderate reputation who specializes in criminal cases."

"Are any of his clients connected to his uncle?"

"A few low-level miscreants. Petty thieves and brutal lads who fell into the Professor's webs as youths and grew up to be inept professional criminals who spend their wasted lives drifting in and out of prison. No one of particular interest to me. Walter does, however, defend the occasional client of means, and is able to make a simple living off of these fees."

"Is a mediocre barrister our best hope of finding a successor for Mycroft?"

"I doubt it. Yet Walter intrigues me. According to my records, Walter was a brilliant student and on track to become one of the most celebrated attorneys of his generation. And now he languishes in relative obscurity. I wonder why this is the case."

"Perhaps his excellent grades were the result of cheating, and he was unable to find a similar path to success in the workforce."

"That is suspicious-minded of you, Watson, but what you say is not impossible. The only way to find out for certain what is behind his undistinguished to career is to meet with him."

Soon afterwards, we arrived at the Old Bailey, and were informed that Walter was still in court, but he would be finished for the day soon. Not wishing to wait any longer than necessary, Holmes and I quietly entered the courtroom where the case Walter was defending was being heard, and found seats in the gallery.

We arrived in the middle of Walter's summation to the jury. "–it is clear that the prosecution has failed to prove beyond a reasonable doubt that my client was responsible for the thefts. Their sole witness is an elderly man with a degenerative eye condition. There is no proof that the pound notes in his pockets were not his own, won earlier that evening in a card game. Furthermore–"

At this point, Holmes nudged me, and we both exited the courtroom. "I've seen enough," Holmes told me as soon as the door had closed behind us.

"We were there less than thirty seconds."

"More than enough time for me to determine the reason for Walter's middling career. I could see it in his eyes. He has contracted pupils and a skin pallor... he's a drug addict, Watson."

I nodded. "I observed what you did. He's clearly not a well man. I would say that he has been abusing drugs for years."

"While I am in no position to criticize a man who is addicted to drugs, I can state definitively that such a man should not be considered for a position as important as Mycroft's."

I chose my next words very carefully. "Holmes, are you... absolutely certain that Mycroft's role is absolutely necessary? After all, England survived for centuries without him. Other countries appear to be functioning fine without men like Mycroft behind the scenes." A thought struck me. "At least... I *think* that other countries don't have men like Mycroft performing vital roles out of the sight of the average citizen. I could be wrong."

"I'm afraid you are, Watson. Most of the world's great powers have their own versions of Mycroft, though to the best of my knowledge, most of them are not nearly as skilled as my brother. And it is not an exaggeration to say that Mycroft's temporary sidelining was directly responsible for the Great War. The Boer War only occurred because Mycroft was laid up for three weeks with influenza. If Mycroft dies, and we have no one to replace him, it will lead to disaster on a global scale."

"After all we've endured with the Great War, no one will want another conflict on that magnitude," I assured Holmes.

"That may be at the heart of the problem, Watson. If one side is determined to avoid another war, a belligerent nation may be able to extract concessions up to the point where either the other country will fall, or will be forced to fight. Either possibility is unacceptable."

"Then do all of our hopes rely on Stationmaster James' younger son?"

"Unless you can think of an alternative, you are correct. He is known as J.J."

"J.J." I mulled over this for a moment. "No, his parents couldn't possibly have named him–"

"They did. James James."

"Why?"

"The Moriarty family is an odd one, full of eccentricities and inside jokes, as well as copious amounts of brilliance and twisted psyches. It's quite possible that J.J.'s father considered this a great joke. It's also within the bounds of probability that it was some sort of sadistic plan to make sure the boy would be mocked by his schoolfellows. I cannot tell at present. I can say that J.J. has taken it upon himself to follow in the footsteps of his uncle, the Colonel, and become the protector of his family name."

"How so?"

"You are not the only one to take an interest in writing about my cases, Watson. Shortly before the war, J.J. wrote a lengthy book in defense of his uncle, arguing that dear old Uncle James was nothing more than a misunderstood, slandered academic who was framed by a cocaine-addled, overrated, incompetent consulting detective."

"But surely he must have realized that you weren't trying to slander the Professor."

"Oh, J.J.'s book posited that I was sincere enough in my convictions. His thesis is that Colonel Sebastian Moran was the real mastermind of the criminal gang, and the Professor was nothing more than a sacrificial lamb- an innocent man plucked from obscurity to serve as a dupe. J.J. reached out to several publishers, but none would touch it. One of them informed me of the manuscript, and after reading it, I realized that J.J. had a brilliant and creative mind, even if his conclusions were utter tommyrot. I confronted him shortly before the war began and tried to persuade him that he was mistaken, but he did not take kindly to my arguments, and became quite enraged by what I had to say. He has a terrible temper, which is why I put him at the bottom of the list. Still, it's possible that the years have mellowed him."

"Where is he now?"

"He was a medic during the war. According to my informant that I telephoned earlier, he is currently at the Dunstable Hospital. Perhaps he has become a doctor, or at least an orderly. We shall see."

Half an hour later we arrived at the Dunstable Hospital, a grim and unsettling place on the outskirts of London, surrounded by massive walls. After some cajoling, Holmes was allowed to speak to the head nurse.

"Why do you want to see Mr. Moriarty?" she asked.

"I wish to interview him about a job," Holmes replied.

"He will not be able to accept any position you offer."

"Is he under contract at this hospital?"

"You misunderstand me. He is a patient here."

A sudden flash of realization passed over my face. "This hospital... it is an asylum."

"Yes. Mr. Moriarty had a breakdown three years into the war. The doctors have done their best, but they believe that he is incurable..."

This news left Holmes looking desolate. He said nothing as we rode back to our hotel, and he refused to join me for dinner. He locked himself in his room, and I heard no more from him until after breakfast the following morning, when he emerged looking disheveled and unslept, but triumphant.

"I may have a solution to our problem, Watson," he said as he buttered a piece of cold toast that had been brought to his room hours earlier. "It is unwieldy, but it could serve our purposes adequately."

"What is it?"

"I need a few more minutes to refine my ideas. In half an hour we have a meeting with Mycroft and a representative from the government, a Mr. Chumbley. Apparently he is well-connected and has the ear of the Prime Minister. You will learn all when we meet with them."

Thirty minutes later, we were gathered in Mycroft's rooms, as the young, lean, dour-looking Mr. Chumbley glared at us. "Why did you wish to speak to me?"

"You are aware of how indispensable my brother is to the workings of the British government. In matters of foreign policy, spycraft, economics, domestic affairs, and other issues, he is absolutely vital. When he dies, which will hopefully not be for many more years, England will be crippled. If a replacement for my brother exists, I do not know of him. Then I realized, if no one man can replace Mycroft, perhaps several can. Consider this. A specialist or team of experts, maybe two or three, each handling one aspect of what Mycroft does. I have broken Mycroft's duties down into seven fields. I have adjusted the wording for reasons that will become evident once you read the first letter of each topic." Holmes withdrew a piece of paper from his pocket and set it on the table in front of Mr. Chumbley. It read:

MILITARY STRATEGY

YEOMANRY

COMMERCE AND CURRENCY

ROYAL ISSUES

OMBUDSMAN

FOREIGN AFFAIRS

TRADECRAFT

"Think of it," Holmes explained. "The brightest minds in their fields, all contributing to do the work that Mycroft does now. A secret team of the cleverest men in the country, all working in their respective topics for the good of the nation. It would..." Holmes' voice trailed off as he caught Mycroft's eye.

"Not a bad idea, brother," Mycroft sighed. "But I came up with something very similar months ago. Only without the silly acrostic."

"And I rejected it then and will again," Mr. Chumbley replied. "We already have quite enough supposed geniuses on the government payroll. There is no need to hire more."

"But who will replace–"

"People higher up than me put a great deal of faith in your brother. I do not share this high opinion. When he retires or dies, or once his patrons in the upper echelons of the British government are no longer there to protect him, the work he does will cease."

"But Mycroft is–"

"He's a relic! A superannuated fat fossil who has no place in the modern world. He should have died of a heart attack years ago. We don't need him!"

"Mr. Chumbley and I have a history," Mycroft growled. "I proved a few years ago that his wife was leaking secrets to a paramour in the German government."

"It's a lie!"

"It's the truth. Your wife is a traitor and an adulteress and you are a fool for shielding her. But as you see, dear brother, Mr. Chumbley resents me, and due to his parentage, he is extremely well-connected and has been placed in a position of power he has not earned and does not deserve."

Chumbley rose. "Insult me all you want. My friends in the government agree with me. You are no longer necessary. The world is too complex for the British government to rely upon the caprices of an old-fashioned man like yourself. Our current crop of politicians, diplomats, and civil service employees can handle the workings of the country perfectly well without one enormous crank telling us what we can and cannot do. We forced you into retirement once, Mycroft. I will do what I can to make sure you are put out to pasture again and stay there. Good day to you all." With that, Chumbley flounced out and left the room.

After a few moments I spoke. "Well. What do we do now?"

"Sit back and watch the world burn," Mycroft seethed. "I've made too many enemies, especially amongst the younger generation. They don't like me and they don't want me in a position of power."

"But does that mean that they'd be willing to harm the nation to spite you?"

"They genuinely believe that I'm no longer necessary," Mycroft sighed. "In any event, they're jealous of the power I hold and they want it for themselves."

"What will this mean for the future of the nation?" I wondered.

Holmes pressed his hand against his forehead. "I'm very much afraid that it means that the future of Europe is not as bright as we may have hoped. Without someone performing Mycroft's duties at Mycroft's level of competence, I believe that another Great War is inevitable…"

I felt utterly despondent. "So there's nothing we can do?"

Mycroft shrugged. "Sherlock and I will continue to look for a solution, but if the fools in the government continue to resist, they may cause the annihilation of another generation."

Holmes nodded. "For now, unfortunately, you must view this case as one of my failures."

As I write these words, I hope that someday I will be able to pen a conclusion to this case that proves that Holmes' statement was wrong. I have never before wished so desperately that one of our investigations will have a sequel.

The Outline of Mystery

(AUTHOR'S NOTE: The claims of the lawsuit at the center of this story really were alleged. The other crime that takes place in this story is completely fictional, and though most of the characters in this story are based on real-life people, the purely made-up creations will be identified at the end of the tale.)

Sherlock Holmes was happily analyzing a sample of honey. His bees had produced an abundant amount that year, but recently he had noticed that a heretofore absent shade of red had entered the honey after straining, and he was determined to seek out the cause. Could it be due to some new species of flower, not native to the Sussex Downs, that one of his neighbors had planted? Or could there be some sort of contamination affecting the honey? There was no discernable change to the taste or consistency, and Holmes found himself enjoying his chemical analysis. It was therefore quite vexing to him when his research was interrupted with a loud series of knocks at his door.

Not being in the mood to interact with anybody, Holmes decided that the best course of action was to ignore the knocking, but the pounding continued, and his best attempts to keep his attention focused on the honey were permanently thwarted by the sound of a woman's voice calling out, "Mr. Holmes! Mr. Holmes! Please! I know you're in there! I must speak to you!"

Holmes considered his options, and decided that a direct approach was best. He turned off the flame, jotted down a quick note, and crossed over to the door, opening it as the knocking was growing faster. The woman on the other side of the door was in the process of rapping her fist against the door again, and had Holmes not taken a quick step backwards he might have been struck in the chest.

"Mr. Holmes?" The woman was in her mid-sixties, with neatly arranged grey hair and wearing inexpensive but well cared-for garments. "My name is Florence Deeks. I must speak to you immediately!"

"Miss Deeks, I can tell that you are in a state of some agitation, but I must inform you that I am long retired from the business of private detection. I enjoy a quiet life and regrettably, at my age– I am nearly eighty– I cannot investigate as I did in my younger days."

"Please, Mr. Holmes! I have nowhere else to turn to. The courts have failed me. The government thinks I'm a hysterical old fool, the newspapers refuse to hear what I have to say, and now, even members of my own family have turned against me. I have nowhere else to go, and now I'm afraid that I will be arrested for murder! They've taken everything from me– my book, my reputation, and nearly all of my money. If you don't help me, I'll be thrown into jail and possibly hanged. I have nowhere else to turn. I have lost every scrap of faith I once had in our legal system, Mr. Holmes. If you shut the door on me, I shall sit down on your doorstep and I will not leave until the police come to take me away for a crime I did not commit. You are my only chance at justice. Please, sir, you must listen to me!"

Irritation was Holmes' primary emotion at that moment, but despite himself he also felt a genuine sense of sympathy towards Miss Deeks. Whether he wanted to or not, it was likely that he would be drawn into whatever situation she was entangled in, and he decided that despite his personal inclinations, he might as well grant her the opportunity to speak her piece.

"Miss Deeks, I shall make you a deal. I will give you five minutes of my valuable time for you to explain yourself. When that time has passed– and I will cut you off mid-sentence if I have to– I will tell you whether or not I am interested in hearing more. If I do not wish to hear any more of your story, I will tell you as much and you will be on your way. Do I have your word that you will follow the terms of this agreement?"

"Yes, Mr. Holmes, of course."

Holmes sighed and stepped away from the door, gesturing towards a pair of armchairs as he did so. Miss Deeks hung her coat upon a free hook, and as she was sitting down, Holmes commented, "I suppose at this point you are wondering if you would have been better off staying in Ontario."

"How did you know I was Canadian, Mr. Holmes?"

"Your accent, of course. I can also tell that you have been living in England for quite some time, judging from the type and amount of coal dust that has worked its way into your coat. But you don't live alone– you share lodgings with another woman– your sister, perhaps?"

"Yes, but–"

"Multiple hairs from a woman on your clothing, not yours. A sister seemed like your most likely flatmate."

"Extraordinary. You're just as I imagined from Dr. Watson's stories. When does my five minutes begin?"

"Right now."

"Very well." Miss Deeks cleared her throat. "I was born in Ontario in 1864. From my earliest youth, I have believed strongly that women can make a great contribution to the world's knowledge. I spent most of my third decade studying all over Europe, and I was finally able to enroll at the University of Toronto upon my return. After completing my education, I started teaching at Presbyterian Ladies' College."

"Miss Deeks, perhaps you should minimize your biographical details and focus at the crime you may be accused of committing."

"I'm getting there, Mr. Holmes, but if you're to understand, you must hear the story from the beginning. I've always been fascinated by history. Two decades ago I wrote a little article on the Women's Art Association of Canada, and through my work there and elsewhere, I got the idea to create a history of the world with special emphasis on the role that women have played in civilization since the beginning of recorded time. That's how I spent my war years, Mr. Holmes. I passed countless hours in the city's libraries, taking notes and honing my skills as a researcher. Then I finally got to work writing my book, and I finished it around the February before the war ended– 1918. I called it *The Web of the World's Romance*. The first book of its kind– a feminist history of the world."

Holmes believed that he was keeping his face impassive, but Miss Deeks seemed to detect something in his eyes. "Oh, I can see that such a book has no interest to you, Mr. Holmes. It didn't interest many publishers either. I met with editors, I sent them copies of my manuscript, and none of them believed that there was any market for *The Web*. In August of 1918, I sent a copy of my manuscript to the Macmillan Company, thinking they might be willing to publish it. They held onto the manuscript for nearly nine months. My hopes were very high, Mr. Holmes. Finally, they returned it to me, saying that they did not believe that my book could find an audience. I was very upset, and I didn't even unwrap the package containing the returned manuscript."

After glancing at the wall clock, Holmes sighed, saying, "Miss Deeks, you have two minutes remaining."

"Very well, Mr. Holmes. Have you read H.G. Wells' book *The Outline of History?*"

"I have not. I have heard of the volume, though."

"Very well. I first learned of Mr. Wells' *Outline* when I read a review of it, and I was thunderstruck. It sounded very much like my *Web*, in terms of scope and in other ways, so at my first opportunity I marched down to the department store and bought a copy. When I started reading it, I was stunned. My surprise turned to horror, and then to anger. Mr. Holmes, *The Outline* is based upon my *Web*. The general structure of the book, the events covered… it's all taken from my work!"

Holmes leaned forward. "Are you accusing Mr. Wells of plagiarism?"

"Yes! Yes, I am! Oh, he didn't copy my *Web* word for word, but he took what I said and rephrased it in his own style. I was so upset that I rushed back to the department store and demanded my money back for the book. This was a mistake, and I regretted it soon afterwards, so I had to go and buy another copy. But then I finally found the package containing the manuscript I'd sent to Macmillan and unwrapped it, and I was stunned. I expected the manuscript to possibly have a crease here and there, but the papers in that parcel were a mess. They were dog-eared, covered with stains, and heavily battered. It looked as if someone had been poring through it over and over again, not just for a cursory read-through, but to mine it for every scrap of information it contained. I compared my manuscript for *The Web* to Wells' *Outline*. It was amazing! The general narrative matched as if it were a stencil. So many of Wells' sentences were basically mine with a little bit of rewording. Oh, it made me furious! But the worst part was what Mr. Wells left out of his *Outline*! He deleted almost every reference I made to women's roles in history! He replaced them with his own musings on science and his denigration of religion and his predictions for the future of society."

Holmes stirred. "Miss Deeks, as you were both writing a history of the world, it's not surprising that you would both cover the same events."

"Yes, Mr. Holmes, that's true. But the point is that Mr. Wells also *overlooked the events that I ignored in my book*. Furthermore, I realized that I'd made a number of factual errors. Mr. Holmes, those exact factual errors are in *The Outline* as well!" Miss Deeks glanced at the clock. "My time is up. May I please continue?"

It would have been very easy for Holmes to have said "no," but the familiar stirrings of interest were arising, and despite himself he found himself wanting to hear more. "Five more minutes. The terms of the original deal will apply at the end of them."

"Thank you. I wasn't sure what to do, Mr. Holmes. I consulted with historians at universities, and they told me that I had a case for plagiarism. I kept up my comparison, finding every point of similarity, every match that was too close to be a coincidence. It was astounding, Mr. Holmes! It's like Mr. Wells couldn't be bothered to outline his own *Outline* and built upon my work instead. I spent several years showing the manuscript to respected historians, and they were amazed by the similarities. No publisher wanted to touch my book, largely because of Mr. Wells' book essentially having filled the market for a world history at this time. His *Outline* has become a massive bestseller, Mr. Holmes. He's made an absolute fortune from it!"

"And you think that you deserve a share of those profits, as you contend that he based his book on your scholarship without permission?"

"Yes, Mr. Holmes, I do. I am morally certain that the publishing company Macmillan sent my manuscript for *The Web* to Wells, and he used it as the basis of his own work. He claims to have written that massive two-volume work in only a year and a half. I don't believe that he could have done that level of research on his own, having done it myself. He had help, and he and the publishing house were so brazen that they thought that either I'd never learn about it, or that no one would believe me." Her lip trembled. "And hardly anybody outside of my own family has for twelve years now. A few years ago, right before the statute of limitations for filing a lawsuit passed, I sued Mr. Wells and Macmillan for plagiarizing my work and demanded credit and compensation."

"How much did you ask for, Miss Deeks?"

"Half a million Canadian dollars. Justice isn't cheap, Mr. Holmes. I am a woman of very limited means. Fortunately, I had a very generous and wealthy brother who thought it was his duty to support me in my litigation. Unfortunately, he passed away not long ago, and without his financial support I have been forced to deliver my appeals myself, without hired counsel."

"Then you have already received court judgments?"

"Yes. I filed in Ontario in 1928, but the judge, Justice– or rather, I should call him Mr. *Injustice* Raney– pooh-poohed all my claims without properly considering the evidence. He simply took the publishers and Mr. Wells' word, blithely declaring that they were honorable men and we could accept their word as gospel. I appealed, and to a man, the judges on the appellate panel upheld the previous unjust verdict. Everybody expected me to simply give up, but I remembered that several years ago, when the Canadian courts declared that women could not serve as senators because they were not legally considered persons under the law, that some determined women travelled across the Atlantic and filed suit in England, asking London's Privy Council to review the case. In that instance, Mr. Holmes, the Privy Council wisely threw out the previous verdict. I thought they might show similar good sense if I came to them. Unfortunately, with my brother gone and his widow and sons receiving all of his substantial wealth, I was left with just the little annuity he provided for me in his will. I have two sisters, Mr. Holmes. We got the use of a house for our lifetimes and six hundred dollars a year each. That's enough if you live very frugally. But in order to pursue my case, my sister Mabel and I had to move to London. We have found a very inexpensive hotel, and we make do on small rations. As I cannot afford a lawyer, I have put my own case forward in court. Unfortunately, just a couple of days ago–November 3rd, the judges ruled against me. They said that my evidence was not convincing, but I can't see how they can say that with a straight face!"

Holmes said nothing for a few moments, but once he realized that Miss Deeks needed a few moments to catch her breath, he remarked, "Then it seems that your legal battle is at an end, though it is not the conclusion that you would have hoped for, unfortunately."

"At an end? Hardly! I can assure you, Mr. Holmes, I have plenty of fight in me yet. I still have one more option available to me."

"But what can you do with the Privy Council ruling against you?"

"I can send a petition for assistance directly to the King. If he fulfills his duties as a monarch, he will see that one of his loyal subjects has been cruelly mistreated by the courts that are bound to administer his laws."

Holmes took a few moments to consider his reaction to his guest. There was something admirable in Miss Deeks' tenacity, though upon further reflection, he was uncertain as to whether this focus and drive was propelled by a thirst for justice or an unhealthy obsession. This woman was convinced that one of the most prominent authors in the world had utilized her work to propel the project that had made his fortune. It was small wonder that the judiciary had refused to consider that possibility. Holmes knew from experience that the courts were unwilling to question the word or the reputation of supposedly respectable men without adamantine proof of guilt.

"Are you asking me to find further proof of plagiarism, Miss Deeks?"

"What?" She looked rather stunned by this question. "No. I have no need of that. I believe that I have proven my case, and anybody who reads my report with an open mind can see at once that I am the victim of a particularly bold intellectual property theft." She reached into her bag and withdrew a thick sheaf of papers. "There's a copy of my report," she declared generously as she forced it into Holmes' reluctant hands. "You can read that at your leisure."

After a grunt that Miss Deeks chose to interpret as a "thank you," Holmes asked, "If you feel that you've made your own case plain, then I repeat, why did you come to me?"

"Because I'm afraid that I might be arrested for a murder I didn't commit!"

Holmes blinked. "Continue, please."

"Yesterday, a young woman came to my hotel room and told me that she believed that she had evidence that could prove that the publishers sent my manuscript to England, with the express intention of Mr. Wells reading it and building upon it for his own work. She claimed she used to work for the company in a secretarial capacity, and that she had a couple of memoranda that would prove my contentions beyond a shadow of a doubt."

"Did she ask for money, Miss Deeks?"

"Well, yes. She said that she had been fired for asking too many questions, and without a decent letter of reference she couldn't find another job."

"How much did she want? A hundred pounds? Two hundred?"

"Two hundred and fifty if you must know, Mr. Holmes."

"I must say, Miss Deeks, that is a considerable sum."

"My nephews would be happy to pay it if it meant that I could be vindicated."

"I see. And what is the name of this young woman?"

"Jane Jones. And before you say a word, Mr. Holmes, I am aware that it was a pseudonym. She was deathly afraid of repercussions."

"Very well. Describe Miss Jones, please."

"Young, I'd say no more than twenty-two. Reddish-gold hair, bobbed. Plenty of freckles, about five foot four."

"How are you supposed to get in touch with her?"

"I can't get in touch with her, Mr. Holmes. Not anymore. She's dead!"

The flames of interest were starting to burn much brighter in Holmes' mind. "Was this a homicide?"

"Yes! She told me to meet her at her friend's flat– really just a tiny room barely bigger than a closet in a rather seedy boarding house. Naturally I was suspicious. I do not claim to be an expert in crime and preventing oneself from being targeted by criminals. If I were, I would not have had to file my lawsuit. I was told to come alone, but I asked my sister Mabel to disguise herself and follow behind me. My sister was at the end of the corridor when I knocked on Miss Jones' door. There was no reply, but as the door wasn't locked, I pushed it open and saw Miss Jones lying on the floor with a bloodstain on her chest. I didn't even enter the room, and I saw no weapon. But then this woman– I never met her before and I don't know her name, came rushing out from behind the corner and started screaming, "What have you done! You've killed Jane!" I tried to tell her that she was utterly mistaken, but she kept howling, and I was afraid that I might be arrested, and that would completely destroy any chance of having my petition heard by the king. My sister grabbed my arm, and we made our escape. Luckily, that screaming woman didn't follow us."

"Very fortunate," Holmes murmured.

"Mr. Holmes, you look as if you've gotten an idea."

"Merely the germ of one, Miss Deeks."

"Would you care to share it?"

"No. It is dangerous to speculate upon insufficient evidence, and I shall need further information before venturing to express an opinion."

Pure joy seemed to radiate across Miss Deeks' face. "Then you will investigate?"

"The fate of Miss Jones, yes."

Miss Deeks observed that Holmes was not committing himself to looking into the plagiarism case and decided not to press her luck. "Thank you, Mr. Holmes! Thank you!"

"Please allow me twenty minutes to make some preparations. We will travel to London on the next available train."

As Miss Deeks sat quietly in Holmes' parlor, she heard him placing a telephone call, though she could not understand the words being said. Holmes eventually emerged wearing a suit styled for the city rather than the countryside, and carried a satchel.

The pair said little on the train. Every now and then Miss Deeks attempted to start a conversation, but all of her attempts produced minimal responses. When they finally disembarked at the station in London, a uniformed policeman walked straight up to them.

"Mr. Holmes, he's going to arrest me!" Miss Deeks shuddered.

"I very much doubt that. This is a friend of mine." As Holmes shook hands with the constable, he said, "Thank you for meeting us, Nestor."

"My pleasure, Holmes. It's good to have you back. Is there any chance of your resuming a permanent residence in London again?"

"None at all. I am quite content in my retirement."

"A great pity, sir. We really could use your help more often."

"You both flatter me and denigrate your colleagues. Am I correct in assuming that there is currently no warrant out for Miss Deeks?"

"No, sir. She's not wanted for murder."

"I'm not?" Miss Deeks' relief was obvious. "You know I didn't commit the crime?"

"Actually, ma'am, we're not sure there is a crime." As they talked, the three of them made their way out of the station. "No dead woman matching the description your provided has been found in the last twenty-four hours, Mr. Holmes. I examined the location you sent me to and found no corpse."

"And there was nothing of interest?"

"There was one thing, sir. I explored the alley behind the boarding house and found this." Nestor pulled a paper bag out from under his jacket. "As you'll soon see, there was a reason why I didn't consider it proper evidence."

As Holmes unwrapped the parcel and revealed the contents, Miss Deeks gasped. "That's the shirt Miss Jones was wearing!"

"And was the stain in this position?" Holmes turned the garment around to reveal a bright red oval.

"Yes! Is that her blood?"

"Almost certainly not. You will observe the intense crimson color, and the stained fabric is still quite soft and flexible. If this were actual blood, it would likely have darkened into a shade of brown, and what is more, the tainted cloth would have stiffened. Holmes held the stain to his nose and sniffed. "Vinegar and other chemicals. This is ink."

"Then Miss Jones isn't really dead?"

"I highly doubt it. She was feigning death, waiting for you to arrive. The woman who started screaming and accusing you of the murder was almost certainly an accomplice."

"But why would someone do that to me?"

"I can think of multiple reasons. One might be blackmail. You have very little money of your own, it is true, but you do have exceedingly wealthy nephews who inherited a fortune from your brother. If you absolutely needed the funds, you could almost certainly rely on them for a certain level of financial support. Someone could conceivably make a considerable profit from placing you in a position where you'd gladly pay to avoid arrest."

"You don't look convinced, Mr. Holmes."

"That's because it's too risky. It would take a while to get the money, and how much could really be expected? Of course, in my time I have known confidence tricksters to go to astounding lengths to cheat gullible people out of a few shillings, but I am particularly struck by the fact that the screaming, accusing woman didn't follow you out the door to stop you, nor was your flight impeded by another member of the conspiracy." Holmes shook his head. "That leads to an alternative explanation. The situation was meant to get you to flee. The goal of this whole rigmarole was to get you to flee England at once and return to Canada in order to avoid arrest and public censure. By doing so, this entire lawsuit would be permanently put to rest."

"But who would be behind it?" Miss Deeks demanded. "Mr. Wells? The publisher?"

"Unknown at present. It will require more information, and I hope to get it from an interview I have in just under an hour."

"Who are you meeting, Mr. Holmes?"

"H.G. Wells, of course. By a lucky coincidence, he's giving a lecture at a museum tonight, and some colleagues of mine were able to help me make an appointment with him."

"I'd like to come with you," Miss Deeks sighed, "but I don't think that Mr. Wells would take too kindly to my presence."

"Meaning no offense, I completely agree. I suggest that you return to your hotel and assure your sister that you are all right. In the meantime, I've arranged for someone I know to wait outside your room as your bodyguard. If my theory is correct, someone tried to drive you out of England, and it's possible that they may be impatient to get results. If so, then there's a slight but very real chance that you might be in danger, so a protector's presence will minimize that risk."

Holmes had feared that Miss Deeks would resent the presence of a man watching over them, but to his relief, she quickly acquiesced. After she left with Nestor as her escort, Holmes made his way to the British Museum, where he was led to a small room down the corridor from the hall where Wells would deliver a speech in a short while.

Wells professed himself delighted to meet Holmes, and the first few minutes of their conversation was devoted to Wells asking questions about some of Holmes' scientific discoveries, as well as Holmes' thoughts on various international questions. Holmes was pleased to talk about his forensic experiments, but was largely uninterested in politics. After he sensed that Wells was properly relaxed in the conversation, Holmes explained the reason for the meeting. Taking great care not to say anything that might potentially antagonize Wells, Holmes explained the situation of Miss Deeks and the faked murder, and deftly tried to convey that he did not suspect Wells of having anything to do with it while carefully not actually committing himself to a position on the matter.

Holmes had presented the situation adroitly, and Wells did not appear the least bit antagonized. "So, you think some unscrupulous criminals are trying to profit from this ridiculous lawsuit?" Wells asked.

"That certainly is possible," Holmes replied blandly.

"Hmm, it makes sense to me. Why would just one deluded old woman try to pick my pocket? Why wouldn't others try their luck as well?" Wells shook his head. "Just as I think that this whole situation is finally put to bed, that woman keeps finding another way to prolong the inconvenience."

"I can see how this whole situation can be distressing for you."

"I'm not worried about it. I know there's nothing to her claims and I've always been quite confident that the courts will see the situation clearly. I've never had the slightest doubt about that. Still, the legal fees are an annoyance. Goodness knows I can afford them, especially after my royalties from *The Outline*, but still, I hate to see my bank account drained unnecessarily. I've instructed my attorneys to pursue recoupment of costs, you know. They're considering a forced bankruptcy, or finding a way to break the annuity her brother left her in order to take the costs from the principal. The fees are running up to three or four thousand pounds by now."

"Surely that would ruin Miss Deeks," Holmes noted.

Wells shrugged. "Her brother was a millionaire. Her relatives will look after her. Anyway, what sort of precedent would that set if I just let the matter lie? Every Tom, Dick, and Harry would scribble together a manuscript based on my latest book and claim I'd taken their idea. The only way to vindicate myself and save myself future headaches is to make it clear to the world that false allegations will only impoverish you."

"Do you bear Miss Deeks much ill will?"

"Not at all," Wells waved his hand and laughed. "I feel rather sorry for her, as a matter of fact. Elderly woman, repressed– never married. Never got a chance to explore the womanly aspects of her character, I suspect. Not a bad woman, just a deluded one. A little…" Wells placed a finger to his temple and started tracing circles on the side of his head. "She's not a well woman, you know. Clearly delusional. Fancies herself a great writer and historian. I actually think she really believes that she wrote my book. I don't know if she found my book and wrote a manuscript based on it, or if she actually tried to write a history of the world and produced that laughable result, but it's all the ravings of a ridiculous old woman. Her relatives really ought to have taken her aside long ago and made it clear that she can't just sling false allegations like that, but as I said, I think she really believes them now. It's sad, really. She's sinking into her dotage, looking back at a life full of missed opportunities, and she's desperate to grab a little glory in the twilight of her years. Unfortunately, she just happened to fixate on me. But I can't really be angry at her. It's pity I feel."

Holmes carefully asked a few more questions, but Wells was unable to provide him with any more useful information. When Wells announced his need to end the interview and begin preparations for his talk, the two men shook hands and Holmes took his leave.

The next item on Holmes' agenda was to speak to someone familiar with Wells who might be able to provide some information as to whether the author or a colleague of his might have been involved in the faked murder. One of Holmes' many sources who kept a close eye on the comings and goings of London's citizenry had suggested a pair of prominent authors who were currently sharing a meal at a local pub. A quick journey a mile and a half east, and Holmes found himself at a brightly lit and pleasant establishment. Sitting in the corner were an enormous man with a great cape and pince-nez, and a much smaller man seated next to him. Both men had platters of bacon and eggs in front of them, with bread and cheese on a board between them, and tankards of beer as well.

The larger man saw Holmes approaching and immediately rose. "Sherlock Holmes! How wonderful to see you again!"

Holmes gripped the hand of G.K. Chesterton, and then similarly greeted Hilaire Belloc. "The pleasure's all mine. It's been a year since we last met, hasn't it? When our mutual friend, Father Brown and I were wrapping up the case of the Blood of Hailes."

"I believe so, yes." Chesterton pushed the board of bread and cheese to Holmes and indicated that he should help himself. "Of course, I completely understand why this story can't be revealed to the general public for quite some time, given the nature of the scandal you unearthed, but the manuscript will remain in my lawyer's strongbox for at least ninety years."

"Thank you for your understanding, Chesterton. If it were up to me, the world would know exactly what happened, but a great many innocent people might be harmed by the release of the details of that case. I thank you for your discretion as Father Brown's literary agent."

Belloc took a sip from his tankard. "So Holmes, what are you doing back in London? A case of some kind?"

"Yes. It involves a mutual acquaintance of ours. H.G. Wells."

Belloc's eyebrows arched. "Please, tell us more."

Holmes summarized the story of Miss Deeks' visit and the mysterious death that was very likely a hoax. By the end of it, Chesterton appeared thoughtful and Belloc looked triumphant.

"I heard rumors about the lawsuit against Wells, but the newspapers have been suspiciously reticent in providing details."

"You appear to take pleasure in hearing the details of Miss Deeks' argument, Belloc."

"It's not pleasure so much as vindication, and I can only hope that Miss Deeks is able to discredit Wells' *Outline* even further than I have."

"You have issues with the book?" Holmes wondered.

"I most certainly do. It's an impressive tome until Wells starts covering the history of humanity, which means that it all falls apart at about page seven. It's a monolithic mishmash of false assumptions, stretched-out half-truths, and outright bigotry. It's not a proper exploration of the history of the world, it's a chopped-up, twisted, and distorted vision of Wells trying to remake several millennia in his own image."

Chesterton chuckled. "I believe that Wells once compared debating with Belloc to arguing with a hailstorm."

"If only I were an actual hailstorm, perhaps I could knock some sense into him. The entire book is a malicious sneer against religion in general, particularly Christianity. The life of Christ is barely given any attention. Ancient Greco-Persian battles receive more ink and paper that Jesus. Wells has the very grievous fault of being ignorant that he is ignorant. He has the strange cocksuredness of the man who knows only the old conventional textbook of his schooldays and mistakes it for universal knowledge."

"Try to not to sugarcoat your thoughts," Chesterton murmured with a small smile.

"You and I have a very different approach to intellectual battle with our opponents," Belloc said with an indignant sniff. "You've managed to maintain your friendship with Wells despite your differences. He and I will remain at loggerheads until one of us dies. Our literary rejoinders reflect our contrasting styles."

"Literary rejoinders? I was not aware that you'd written books in response to Wells' *Outline*," Holmes remarked.

"Oh, yes. Chesterton produced a wonderful volume titled *The Everlasting Man*," Belloc explained, "which put a proper focus on the benefits and cultural impact that Christ has had on the last nineteen hundred years. And our mutual friend was very polite in his introduction. What was that you said, Gilbert?"

"I may not be quoting myself word for word, but I believe I wrote, *"As I have more than once differed from Mr. H. G. Wells in his view of history, it is the more right that I should here congratulate him on the courage and constructive imagination which carried through his vast and varied and intensely interesting work; but still more on having asserted the reasonable right of the amateur to do what he can with the facts which the specialists provide."* Wells was much like a writer who didn't care for the protagonist of his book–which is why he marginalized Jesus so much in it."

"Very civilized. Would you like to hear what I wrote in my articles, Holmes?"

"I would. Even if I didn't, I don't believe I'd be able to stop you."

"You would not. I wrote two dozen articles ripping his specious arguments and misplaced assertions to shreds. I put them together into a combined volume titled *A Companion to Mr. Wells' "Outline of History."* Wells didn't like that one bit. He wrote several articles in reply, but couldn't find anybody to print them until he put them together into a book titled *Mr. Belloc Objects to "The Outline of History."* He said my "apparent arrogance is largely the protection of a fundamentally fearful man," and that I am "the sort of man who talks loud and fast for fear of hearing the other side.""

"How did you reply to that, Belloc?"

Belloc took another sip of beer. "I wrote one more book critiquing his poor arguments and titled it *Mr. Belloc Still Objects*."

"You had so much to criticize that you were able to fill two books?" Holmes asked.

"Well, the second book is rather short. You know, Wells' work is full of silly mistakes. On one page, he said that early humans had no knowledge of arrow-firing bows, only to show reproductions of cave paintings with the figures holding archery weapons later. When Wells wrote his response to me, he opened his volume by declaring that he was "the least controversial of men." Perhaps he was sincere, and perhaps his tongue was firmly affixed to his cheek."

Holmes hesitated before asking his next questions. "You two are acquainted with Wells. I can assure you that your opinions will not go no further than this table. Do you give any credence to the allegations of plagiarism, and do you think that Wells could have had anything to do with this attempt to frighten Miss Deeks out of England?"

Chesterton stroked his chin. "As for the question of whether he would fake a murder to drive Miss Deeks away, I would say not. Wells is a confident man, and I'm quite certain he has complete faith in the courts to rule in his favor, especially seeing as how everything has gone completely his way so far. He has triumphed multiple times with the use of lawyers, he has no need to devise dramatic scenes in order to end the litigation. In any event, from what you've told us, Wells actually wants to initiate further legal proceedings in order to recoup his costs. If he wanted Miss Deeks out of his life, he could just forget the money and not jump through the additional hoops of forced bankruptcy. I believe he could afford the loss."

"And what about the allegations of plagiarism?"

Chesterton hesitated. "I will not say anything potentially defamatory against a man I consider a friend. I will, however, say that I do *not* believe that Miss Deeks is a hysterical woman and that I think that attempts to paint her as such are unfair. There is one more rumor I've heard… I'm not sure if you're aware of this, but I've heard through some colleagues that there was a minor scandal some years back regarding the Canadian branch of the publishing house in question. It was a case very much like Miss Deeks'. A woman wrote a monograph on some aspect of astronomy, I don't remember which. She submitted it to the publishing house, which rejected it after a substantial period of time. Then, the publishers soon produced another work on astronomy, and the woman started alleging that her manuscript had been plundered and repurposed."

Holmes' eyes widened. "The same editors? Essentially the same allegations?"

"Quite a coincidence, isn't it?" Belloc noted. "An unknown writer produces an educational text. The publishers already have a much more prominent author at work on a similar subject, but they realize that the production of their preferred author's work could be substantially sped up using this obscure writer's manuscript as a template. A few changes, deletions, expansions, and a reworking by a much more gifted prose stylist, and they could have a bestseller on their hands."

"Indeed. I now would like your thoughts on those same questions, Belloc."

"I think I answered the first one with my recent comments. Wells paints himself as a fearless advocate of women's emancipation, but is he really? His wife– his *second* wife, Catherine, their relationship was the cause of his divorce from his first wife. And poor departed Catherine. Do you know what he called her? Jane! He gave her that name because it represents the epitome of domesticity and loyalty to him. He refused to call her by her true name, and for all their marriage he forced her to play the role he demanded of her. He took away her true name, the name she loved, and forced her to play the role of the uncomplaining, efficient house-manager whose only whim was to support his careers and desires." Belloc took a deep breath. "And there was no shortage of women during his marriage to Catherine. The most famous name is probably that birth control woman, Margaret Sanger. It's been my experience that the men who are the most outspoken champions of women's equality are often the men who treat women most cruelly."

"Be careful of wandering into the realms of gossip," Chesterton warned.

"Then let's return to the realms of literary criticism. The first books that pop into the average person on the street's mind when they think of Wells are his science fiction novels. In truth, he's hardly penned anything in that genre since around the turn of the century. Most of his fiction has been realistic domestic fare, featuring a brilliant, misunderstood man who can only find happiness and fulfillment through his extramarital affairs, and he's continually thwarted by the oppressive demands of society, though he is often buttressed by an understanding wife, who sympathizes with him even if she cannot satisfy him. This is a recurring theme of many of Wells' novels over the last few decades. Are the protagonists of these novels all self-portraits? The critics can debate this for years."

After a moment's pause, Belloc added. "There's one more point. Earlier in his career, Wells was accused of plagiarizing another author's work. I believe that case was settled somehow."

Holmes mulled over all of this for a few moments until the silence was broken by Chesterton.

"Have you spoken to Miss Mabel Deeks?" Chesterton asked. "Speaking of women, I would say that if something's been going on, she'd be a sharp observer. Perhaps she noted something that Miss Florence missed."

"That is an excellent point. I should speak to her immediately."

Holmes was true to his word, and soon afterwards, he was speaking to the Deeks sisters in their hotel room. "Miss Mabel, have you noticed anything unusual lately?"

"I'm not sure what you mean, Mr. Holmes. Everything's a bit unusual. London life is rather different from living in Ontario in many ways."

"Have you noticed anything that might potentially be connected to a criminal action?"

"If I had, I would have reported it, Mr. Holmes," Mabel Deeks replied virtuously.

"My sister is an observant and intelligent woman," Florence noted. "If she'd seen something amiss, we'd know."

"Sometimes, the most important details are the ones that we don't attach much significance at the time," Holmes explained.

"Well, I've been having restless nights, and I've been hearing all sorts of odd noises around bedtime, but that's probably due to the brandy."

"What brandy?"

"My sister and I are not habitual imbibers, Mr. Holmes, but since we moved to this hotel, we've found it necessary to take a little nip of brandy every night before we retire," Florence Deeks explained. "The building is not well-insulated, and taken strictly for medicinal purposes, a bit of spirits helps keep out the cold during the chilly nights."

"But I don't respond well to it," Mabel Deeks mourned. "It makes me come out in gooseflesh all over. It affects my sleep, and I keep hearing noises that are probably just my imagination. Last week, around midnight, I heard some clomping noises and thought there was a horse galloping down the hall. I hurried out and didn't even think to put on my dressing-gown. I saw a man rushing out the door at the end of the corridor, and I saw something slip out of his pocket and roll away into that corner under the table there, but before I could call him back, it was too late. He was gone. And I've seen– or thought I've seen– people coming in and out of that room across from ours at all hours of the night. Many's the time I've looked out when I've heard a noise at one or two in the morning and seen somebody with the face of a ghost there."

"Why haven't I seen those people?" Florence Deeks demanded.

"You've been sleeping sounder than I have."

"Did you check under that table for the dropped item?" Holmes asked.

"No, sir. It slipped my mind, and anyway, at my age, my knees aren't what they used to be."

Holmes had a quick word with Nestor, who was still standing guard outside. A moment later he returned with a small phial in one hand. "It must've rolled right behind the leg of the table," Nestor explained.

Holmes took it from him, uncorked the top, and sniffed it. "Cocaine," he pronounced.

"Are you sure, Mr. Holmes?" Florence Deeks wondered.

"Believe me, I know. A rather weak one, I believe. No more than a four percent solution." Holmes replaced the phial's stopper and handed it back to Nestor. "The room directly across from yours, you said, Miss Mabel?"

"Yes, that's right."

"I see. We shall have to find different accommodations for you tonight. I believe that the police will need this room for an investigation."

That night, a team of Scotland Yard officers waited inside the Deeks sisters' hotel room, and after a brief period of observation, noticed several figures entering and leaving the room across the hall. When stopped and searched on their way out of the hotel, they were all carrying phials containing solutions of cocaine.

The next day, Holmes explained the entire situation to the Deeks sisters. "You mean we've been living across the hall from drug-sellers?" an indignant Florence asked.

"It appears so, yes. We'll need you to make some identifications…"

An hour later, Florence identified two women who had been arrested in connection with the case as Jane Jones and the woman who had accused her of the murder.

"None of this had anything whatsoever to do with the lawsuit," Holmes explained, "aside from the fact that your participation in the litigation meant that you had to take up residence at this hotel. The gang moved their distribution centers about frequently, but this was a particularly convenient location for them. Most hotel staff and residents studiously ignore the goings-on of the residents, but when Miss Mabel's nocturnal observations became more frequent, the gang decided that to avoid suspicion, they needed to get rid of her."

"But they didn't try to kill me!"

"No. A murder would have only drawn attention to this location, and the best course of action was to drive you and your sister from the hotel. They did a little background research on you, learned about the lawsuit, and decided that if they could lure Miss Florence somewhere and frighten her with being accused of murder, you'd take the next ship back to Canada. They reasoned that you were low on funds, and hoped you were sufficiently demoralized to give up the lawsuit as a bad job. They thought that your experiences would crush any faith you had in the British justice system, making you all the more willing to flee."

"They didn't know me well at all," Florence Deeks sniffed. "So this whole affair was all about Mabel? She was the dangerous witness they wanted out the country, and they had no interest whatsoever in the lawsuit?"

"Precisely."

"Thank you, Mr. Holmes." Florence Deeks sighed. "I regret that I lack the funds to recompense you for your assistance, but perhaps if I speak to my nephews—"

"There will be no fee," Holmes assured her.

"I see. Well, if anybody can find evidence of plagiarism that will convince the King, it's you, but I cannot ask you to continue working for me for free. My sense of honor will not allow me to accept any more charity from a man who has already been very generous to me." Florence Deeks spoke with firm finality.

"What do you intend to do now, Miss Deeks?"

"What I have been doing for the last several years, Mr. Holmes. I will see this through to the end, and I will appeal directly to the King, and hope that our monarch, in his wisdom, will see fit to reopen the case and encourage to look at the evidence with fresh and unprejudiced eyes. I will not deny that the odds are against me, but a high chance of failure is not reason to refrain from continuing in a righteous cause."

"And no matter what happens, Florence will have me right by her side," Mabel Deeks added. "We've been investigating this together for over a decade. There's nothing in the world that can convince us to give this up now. No matter what happens, we'll keep telling the world what we know is the truth."

"I see." Holmes rose to his feet. "Then as my role in this case appears to be completed, I shall return home to my bees. My very best wishes to both of you!"

(Author's note: Other than Holmes, the only fictional characters in this story are Nestor, Jane Jones, and the other unnamed characters involved in the drug gang. All of the other characters and events are real, and are portrayed as true to life as possible.

Florence Deeks' appeal to the King was rejected, and with all of her options exhausted, and their finances strained to the breaking point, Florence and Mabel returned to Canada. Florence outlived Wells by thirteen years and died in 1959 at the age of ninety-four. She continued writing, including another work of history centered on the achievements of women, but none of her work was ever published, and her papers were archived in Canada.

They remained there until the historian A.B. (Alexander Brian) McKillop researched and wrote his book The Spinster and the Prophet: Florence Deeks, H.G. Wells, and the Mystery of the Purloined Past, published in 2002. This book was a central source for the background research for this story, and many of the words spoken by Wells, Chesterton, and Belloc are the authors' own words, taken from their writings, Wikipedia articles, and essays by Dale Ahlquist, Karl Keating, and Joseph Pearce. I first learned about this case by reading Robert Evans' 2009 Cracked article "5 Great Men Who Built Their Careers on Plagiarism."

McKillop's work is sympathetic to Deeks, though his research did not produce a "smoking gun" of plagiarism. The many similarities between the works are undeniable, but that is not conclusive evidence of Wells' guilt. There is one possibility that has not been looked into to the best of my knowledge– forensic analysis. If the original manuscript of Deeks' <u>Web</u> is safely housed in the archives, there is an outside chance that century-old fingerprints, preserved in ink or grease, might remain on the manuscript. The best place to look would be the dog-eared corners of the papers. Of course, handling by archivists and researchers may have obliterated some evidence, and the detection of fingerprints (or even DNA from traces of sweat or perhaps a licked fingertip) is worthless without fingerprint records or DNA indisputable from Wells to compare against carefully. To the best of my knowledge, there are currently no plans to analyze the manuscript for such evidence, but if by some remote chance an inky partial fingerprint was found on the underside of a dog-eared corner and it could be matched, it might disprove Wells' assertions that he never saw Florence Deeks' manuscript. An absence of forensic evidence would certainly be a point in Wells' favor, but it would not disprove Deeks' claims. Barring a long-hidden written confession by one of the parties involved in the case, it's unlikely that this historical mystery will ever be solved to everybody's satisfaction. This remains a highly controversial topic, *with supporters of both Wells and Deeks taking strong stances on opposite sides of the debate.)*

Lightning Source UK Ltd.
Milton Keynes UK
UKHW020259280722
406468UK00001B/7/J

9 781804 240564